FALLING OUT OF TIME

THE SEQUEL TO *RUNNING OUT OF TIME*

ALSO BY MARGARET PETERSON HADDIX

THE SCHOOL FOR WHATNOTS

REMARKABLES

THE GREYSTONE SECRETS SERIES
THE STRANGERS
THE DECEIVERS
THE MESSENGERS

**THE MYSTERIES OF TRASH &
TREASURE SERIES**
THE SECRET LETTERS

CHILDREN OF EXILE SERIES
CHILDREN OF EXILE
CHILDREN OF REFUGE
CHILDREN OF JUBILEE

UNDER THEIR SKIN SERIES
UNDER THEIR SKIN
IN OVER THEIR HEADS

THE MISSING SERIES
FOUND
SENT
SABOTAGED
TORN
CAUGHT
RISKED
REVEALED
REDEEMED

THE SHADOW CHILDREN SERIES
AMONG THE HIDDEN
AMONG THE IMPOSTORS
AMONG THE BETRAYED
AMONG THE BARONS
AMONG THE BRAVE
AMONG THE ENEMY
AMONG THE FREE

THE PALACE CHRONICLES
JUST ELLA
PALACE OF MIRRORS
PALACE OF LIES

THE GIRL WITH 500
MIDDLE NAMES

BECAUSE OF ANYA

SAY WHAT?

DEXTER THE TOUGH

RUNNING OUT OF TIME

FULL RIDE

GAME CHANGER

THE ALWAYS WAR

CLAIM TO FAME

UPRISING

DOUBLE IDENTITY

THE HOUSE ON THE GULF

ESCAPE FROM MEMORY

TAKEOFFS AND LANDINGS

TURNABOUT

LEAVING FISHERS

DON'T YOU DARE READ THIS,
MRS. DUNPHREY

THE SUMMER OF BROKEN THING

THE 39 CLUES BOOK TEN:
INTO THE GAUNTLET

MARGARET PETERSON HADDIX

FALLING OUT OF TIME

THE SEQUEL TO *RUNNING OUT OF TIME*

KATHERINE TEGEN BOOKS
An Imprint of HarperCollins Publishers

Katherine Tegen Books is an imprint of HarperCollins Publishers.

Falling Out of Time
Copyright © 2023 by Margaret Peterson Haddix
All rights reserved. Printed in the United States of America.
No part of this book may be used or reproduced in any manner whatsoever
without written permission except in the case of brief quotations embodied in
critical articles and reviews. For information address HarperCollins
Children's Books, a division of HarperCollins Publishers, 195 Broadway,
New York, NY 10007.
www.harpercollinschildrens.com

ISBN 978-0-06-325161-8

Typography by Molly Fehr
23 24 25 26 27 LBC 5 4 3 2 1

First Edition

For all the kids who asked,
"What happened next?"

1

Zola's entire room began to glow—the sign that it was ready.

"Tahiti," Zola mumbled from her cozy nest of blankets and pillows. Even though she'd been sound asleep a moment earlier, she bolted upright, her eyes open wide. When she was little, she'd been convinced that if she sat up fast enough, she'd catch the Picture Wall opposite her bed in its exact moment of change. She'd believed she might see pixies or elves scattering sand right up to the foot of her bed; she might see the ocean rolling in from the other side of the globe to lap gently at her toes.

But Zola was twelve now, and sitting up quickly was only a habit. A silly one. She knew that the Picture Wall was only an illusion. She knew that the sensation of sand squishing between her toes and being washed away by sun-warmed water and gentle beach breezes was just as unreal. She'd even done a report at school once about the technology that made it all happen. She supposed it truly was amazing, that the Picture Wall worked so seamlessly with the tiny electrodes embedded in her comforter, to make her feel as though she were waking up in a tropical paradise.

But it was hard to stay amazed by something that happened every morning.

Zola slumped back against the throne of pillows behind her. For a moment, she regarded the glorious sunrise-over-water that the Picture Wall was showing her. It was so beautiful, the first rays of light reaching the peaks of the waves. Her Picture Wall request the day before had been beautiful, too: she'd watched the sun rising over the Alps. That one had included the sensation that she was drinking hot chocolate (which she knew was only from the odor of cocoa being piped into her room—but sometimes it was nice to have taste buds that were easily tricked). The day before that, she'd awakened in the midst of sequoia trees in California. Before that, she'd been on a savanna watching elephants meander by. And before that . . . she didn't quite remember. Who cared? It had all been beautiful.

Zola was supposed to lie in bed and watch the entire sunrise—that was supposed to grant her a peaceful waking, a peaceful day, a happy life. But somehow Zola didn't have the patience for the Picture Wall's whole glorious cycle of scenes today.

"You know what, Sirilexagoogle?" she said aloud, addressing the artificial intelligence that governed her room's scenes and sensations—as well as pretty much everything else around her. "Just make my wall normal again."

"By 'normal,' do you mean 'typical'?" Sirilex's disembodied voice echoed around her. "By my calculations, the scene you request most often *is* a Pacific beach. But would you prefer one in Hawaii instead? Jeju Island? Bora-Bora? The Philippines?"

"I mean, just make the wall look like it really looks," Zola said through gritted teeth. "Without any scene at all. Like nowhere."

Sirilex made a sound that would have been a harrumph, if it had been human.

"Your house is a place, too," the AI corrected in its usual know-it-all tone. "Even a bare wall is—"

"Just do it," Zola said. "Please!"

Sirilex obeyed. The wall across from Zola's bed instantly went blank. Without the imaginary sand, sun, water, and palm trees, Zola could see how empty her room really was. A plain desk stood against the wall to the left, unadorned for once by any Picture Wall–style transformation of its own. To the right was the floor-to-ceiling Insta-Closet where Zola could trade in her clothes any time she wanted.

And beside the Insta-Closet was the door out into the rest of the house . . . a door that opened even as Zola glanced at it.

Right on cue, Zola thought.

"Good morning, you lucky girl, you!" Zola's mom exclaimed as she stepped into the room—her usual greeting. "What glorious scene shall we enjoy together today? Er—"

Zola saw the confusion spread over her mother's face. Mom's usual cheery grin slipped, and she pressed her hand to her mouth. But when Mom dropped her hand again, her smile was back. It just seemed more fake than usual.

Mom sank down gently onto the side of Zola's bed, perching on the very edge as if she wasn't sure if Zola wanted her there or not.

"Is there anything you'd like to talk about?" Mom asked, her voice unimaginably soft and kind. "Anything you'd like to share?"

Oh no! Zola thought. *What have I done?*

When Zola was younger, she'd loved the way Mom could seem to understand Zola's every emotion, Zola's every mood. She'd loved the way Mom lifted one eyebrow as she gazed at her, the way Mom's blue eyes glowed with sympathy, the way Mom always wanted to help.

More and more often lately, though, Zola just wanted some privacy.

Was it weird that I had Sirilex shut down the Picture Wall? she wondered. *Why did I do that?*

For an instant, Zola considered lying, and claiming the Picture Wall had broken somehow. But technology didn't break. Not anymore. Perfect Tech had been around since at least the early 2100s—almost a full century.

And anyhow, even if Mom couldn't see through such a lie, Sirilex would tattle.

The various mood sensors and monitors in her room were probably already measuring tiny changes in her expression, her temperature, her body language. She was probably only moments away from being sent to counseling that would simultaneously assure her that everything she felt and did was completely normal for someone her age—but also that she needed hours with the digital therapist to get through it.

That had happened before.

"I . . . I just wanted to see the regular wall," Zola stammered. "I wanted to remind myself . . . what's really there."

Mom froze, her eyebrow still cocked, her sympathetic gaze almost painfully intense. For a second, Zola felt like she had after shutting down the Picture Wall—as if she was seeing Mom's real face for once, not the cheerful mask she always wore.

Then Mom laughed and reached out to ruffle Zola's hair.

"Poor kid," she said. "Forced to wake up in paradise every day. A paradise you get to *choose*."

"Yeah, but then I have to get up and go to school," Zola groused half-heartedly.

"You like school," Mom said. "You *are* lucky."

It felt like Mom was groping her way back to their usual

5

script, a typical morning conversation.

That was fine with Zola. She really didn't want some long, drawn-out interrogation about what was going on inside Zola's head—or why she'd had such a strange impulse this morning, to want to see a blank wall.

"I know, I know," Zola said quickly. "I'm so much luckier than you were as a kid." Mom still looked a little shaken, so Zola joked, "Didn't you have to walk ten miles through blizzards to get to school? And it was uphill in both directions?"

Mom didn't laugh the way Zola expected.

"Where'd you hear that line?" Mom asked, her voice gone stiff. When Zola glanced over at her, Mom's artificially wrinkle-less face was completely taut. If Zola hadn't known better, she would have said Mom looked scared. Terrified, even.

But that wasn't possible. It was 2193, and fear—like unreliable technology—was a thing of the past.

"Relax, Mom." Zola rolled her eyes as she scrambled out of bed. "I'm not accusing you of being a hundred years old. Or would it be two hundred? I heard that saying in school. In one of the history VRs. It's something parents used to say to kids. I know that even when you were a kid, school was always virtual, too. You didn't have to walk anywhere, except for exercise."

"Right," Mom said, settling back more comfortably against the multiple pillows of Zola's bed.

"Anyway, if I was *truly* lucky, my Insta-Closet really would work instantly," Zola muttered, tapping impatiently on the screen on the closet's door. She'd actually ordered an outfit the night before. But she always thought of last-minute changes. The screen showed a countdown clock, and Zola groaned. "Five minutes is way too long to have to wait for new clothes."

"Recycled," Mom corrected. "The Insta-Closet *recycles* clothes."

Zola didn't bother rolling her eyes again. It was so annoying how Mom always did that, constantly reminding Zola how wonderful the technology in their home was, how lucky they were to be living in 2193. But at least it was normal for Mom to be this annoying.

Zola knew from the history VRs at school how it used to be for kids. A hundred years ago—or, well, two hundred years ago, anyway—kids getting ready for school in the morning didn't have to deal with parents lolling around in their kids' rooms, expecting to have "meaningful conversations." Back then, the parents were also rushing around getting ready for work, fixing breakfast, taking care of younger kids (because people used to have bigger families). Parents back then had sometimes ignored their kids completely.

Right now, that sounded wonderful to Zola.

But Zola was, as Mom constantly reminded her, "the sun, the moon, and the stars" to her mother. Zola's full name—Zola Luna Stellae Keyser—was supposed to reflect that. "Luna" did mean "moon," and "Stellae" did mean "stars," but "Zola" actually meant "earth," not "sun."

"You might as well have named me 'dirt'!" Zola had complained when she found out, during a school project about self-identity. "Why didn't you and Dad just ask Sirilexagoogle before you put it on the birth certificate?"

"We were young and in love and so excited about our new baby—we didn't want to spare even a moment for research like that," Mom had said.

Zola could have continued the argument—because, how was it "research" to ask Sirilex a question? Everybody did that all the time. But the sad, dreamy look in Mom's eye stopped her. Dad had died when Zola was only two days old.

Now Zola truly was all Mom had.

Zola really should be nicer and not so determined to argue with her mother all the time.

The Insta-Closet gave a cheerful "Ding!" and spoke in its usual snobby-sounding voice. "The outfit you requested has now been prepared. It's ready for your donning."

"Sirilex," Zola said. "Reprogram the Insta-Closet voice. I want something slangier from now on. More fun."

"Your desire has been noted and that wish shall be granted," Sirilex responded instantly.

"Change yours, too!" Zola commanded.

"Sure thing, kiddo!"

Zola heard Mom sigh, but Zola tuned that out. The door of the Insta-Closet automatically clicked open. When Zola was little, she had asked Mom once, "What would happen if I was inside the Insta-Closet when it was making my clothes?"

Disappointingly, Mom had said only, "That's not possible. There are all sorts of safeguards to prevent that." But as a small child, Zola had been a little obsessed. She'd had nightmares about being knit into her own clothes. She'd had nightmares about things climbing out of the Insta-Closet in the middle of the night. Things that weren't clothes.

But, even as a small child, Zola had known better than to ask Mom or Sirilex about that. They just would have sent her to more long, boring sessions with the kindergarten transition counselor.

Zola gave a sigh of her own and stepped into the Insta-Closet, pulling the door shut behind her. Instantly, she felt better. As much as she'd feared the Insta-Closet when she was little, she loved it now. It was soundproof—Mom couldn't keep yammering at her while she was getting dressed. And it was completely private—besides the bathroom, this was the only place Zola ever entered where there weren't security or mood sensor cameras silently recording every moment of her life.

Automatically, as she always did, Zola stuck out her tongue at the mirrored wall facing her.

Mirror, mirror, on the wall . . . , she thought, a line from an old fairy tale where kids took turns asking, "Who's the bravest of them all?" "Who's the kindest of them all?" "Who's the hardest-working of them all?" etc. It was a dull, dull story, and illogical, too. Because a mirror couldn't tell you any of that. A mirror could tell you that you had straight, light brown hair like your mom's and that when you looked at a mirror, you preferred to make silly faces. And of course, until Zola had reprogrammed it to stay silent, this mirror had always said encouraging slogans every morning like, "You look ready for a great day!" and "I can tell just by looking that you are a wonderful person!"

Why would anyone need to hear that every morning? Why would anyone trust a talking mirror?

Zola rolled her eyes at the mirror and turned to take today's newly refabricated outfit from the hanger beside her. She'd just detached the swingy purple top from the hanger when something fell to the floor.

That was odd, because Zola hadn't asked for any belts or beads or bows or other accessories. The clothing she'd requested shouldn't have come with any tiny, fussy parts that could fall off.

She bent down. The thing on the floor was a scrap of paper. Paper! Who even used that anymore except in obscure retro artwork?

The paper was folded over twice. Zola's experience with paper was almost all virtual—she'd had that one art history class about origami, which had given the illusion that they were working with real paper. Maybe that was why it felt instinctive to scoop up the paper and take it by its corners and pull them open, flattening the paper onto the palm of her hand.

Now Zola could see writing, actual *hand*writing that must have been done with an actual old-fashioned pencil or pen. And she could make out words in one large scrawl:

If you want to see things as they really are, come find me. And <u>HELP</u> us!

2

Zola blinked, not believing her own eyes. But this wasn't like some dream or VR game, where things appeared and disappeared at will. The paper stayed in her hand; the words "And <u>HELP</u> us!" kept staring up at her, silently begging. Now she also noticed another line, much smaller, at the bottom of the page:

But don't let anyone see this note.

What?

For a moment, Zola felt a jolt of something like hope. Or excitement. Someone needed her help! She could make a difference! This wasn't like being asked to be brave or heroic in some stupid history VR where the right choices were always so obvious, and already accomplished, anyway. (Oppose the Nazis, speak out against racism, stop the Spanish Inquisition . . . duh.)

Then Zola's brain kicked in. Of course this note couldn't be *real*.

Zola slammed her shoulder against the door of the Insta-Closet, bursting back out into her bedroom. She clutched the paper note in her hand and held it high over her head.

"Mom, this isn't fair!" she complained. "If school's going to spring surprise 'moral dilemma' homework assignments on me even when I'm getting dressed in the morning—that's *wrong*. We studied this in school. People have a right to their own leisure time outside of work or school, and—"

Mom scrambled up from Zola's bed as quickly as if the bed had burst into flames. Mom was middle-aged and (Zola had always thought) a little stodgy; Zola had never seen her move so fast.

And Mom was *laughing*.

"There's some issue with the Insta-Closet, and you think it's a moral dilemma test from school?" Mom asked, sounding all jolly and amused. "Don't tell me you're starting that kind of teenaged drama already!"

"Mom, you know I'm not a teenager yet!" Zola protested. "And this isn't drama! Don't . . ." She had all sorts of indignant responses on the tip of her tongue: "Don't assume I'm overreacting when you don't even know what I'm talking about! Don't belittle me and my experiences! Don't laugh at me!"

But it suddenly struck Zola that Mom's laughter and words

and tone didn't match the way she was sprinting across the room. The way Mom was running—Mom! Who never ran anywhere!—you'd think Zola herself had just burst into flames, and Mom was desperate to tackle her and roll her on the floor and put the fire out, to save Zola's life.

And it wasn't *Mom* who usually accused her of drama. It was Sirilex.

Mom reached Zola's side and grabbed first for Zola's hand—the hand that clutched the paper. Mom's hand covered Zola's. Then Mom yanked Zola's arm down and drew her close.

"I *do* remember what it felt like to be a teenager—and preteen—and so filled with big emotions," Mom said, patting Zola's back. "Does somebody just need a hug?"

No, now I just want to punch something, Zola thought.

She would have jerked away, but Mom was tugging her back into the Insta-Closet. Zola had been ordering her own clothes and dressing herself alone in the Insta-Closet since she was four. Now that Zola was twelve and just as tall as Mom, there really wasn't room for both of them in the small cubicle. Not comfortably, anyway.

But Mom started pulling the door shut.

"Oh, you say the problem was behind the door?" Mom asked loudly, even though Zola had said no such thing. "It was probably just your imagination, but we'll check it out. . . ."

The door latched behind them. Mom let go of Zola's shoulders.

"Quick," Mom said, in a pinched, urgent tone that contained none of the humor of only a moment earlier. Mom's face was completely solemn now, her dark blue eyes boring into Zola's hazel ones. It was as if Mom had completely taken off her mask. Or discarded an avatar. "We only have a few seconds. Tell me what happened. Did you see someone? Did someone talk to you? Or—"

"Nobody else would be in *my* Insta-Closet!" Zola protested automatically. Because that was ludicrous. The privacy of an Insta-Closet was almost sacred. But she looked down at the note crumpled in her hand. The way Mom was reacting, did that mean the plea might be real? And serious?

But that would also mean that I shouldn't tell anyone about it, Zola thought. *Not even Mom!*

Mom was already looking toward Zola's hand. Zola turned her hand over so the note was hidden again.

"Just a note then, huh?" Mom said. "That's right—don't show it to me. It's better that way, especially if they resort to lie detector tests. But I need to deliver a message." She tilted her head back, as if she were no longer addressing Zola. Even though Zola was the only other person in the Insta-Closet. "Leave my daughter alone, do you hear? You know I'm sympathetic to your cause. You know *I* want to help you. But children are off-limits. She's too young for this! All right?"

"Mom, who are you talking to?" Zola asked. "What's going on? And what do you mean, 'lie detector tests'?"

Mom gazed at her with what appeared to be real sympathy.

Zola couldn't remember the last time Mom's face had seemed so sad and soft and . . . unguarded. Was it the unguarded part that Zola had missed?

"I'm so sorry, Zola, but there's no time to explain," Mom said. Her voice was achingly gentle now. "To avoid setting off any alarms, we have to get out of here. Once we're back in your bedroom, you need to follow my lead. We have to be careful. I know you weren't overreacting, and I wish I could tell you everything, but it's not safe. Please, please, please, don't make a scene. People's lives might depend on it."

"'People's lives might depend on it'?" Zola echoed numbly. "And you're accusing *me* of being a drama queen?"

"People's lives might depend on it" could have been a line from a history VR. It was 2193 now. People were safe. They were *always* safe. Danger, like fear, was a thing of the past.

But Mom didn't answer. She was already unlatching the Insta-Closet door, swinging it open.

"That's it," Mom said, the jolliness back in her voice. Except, now Zola could hear how fake that jolliness was. "Mystery solved. One little scrap from one of my most recent art experiments shows up in your Insta-Closet, and you start acting like it's the crime of the century!"

Mom was an artist, and she did occasionally use old-fashioned materials, like actual paint. So that kind of made sense. But the look she shot Zola was desperate. Her eyes seemed to be begging Zola to play along.

Then Mom stepped out of the Insta-Closet, and there was nothing in her expression but amusement.

Zola gulped.

"Ha ha, silly me," she said, her voice a little too shaky. She clutched the edge of the Insta-Closet doorway to steady herself. "But I don't think it was that weird not to want some scrap of . . . of your artwork ending up in my recycled clothes."

"Oh, the things a kid has to worry about in the twenty-second century," Mom mocked even as she fixed Zola with a warm gaze. The mockery was fake, but the approval and relief in Mom's eyes were real. Weren't they?

"Now, hurry and get dressed, or you'll be late to school," Mom said.

"Yeah, yeah, always with the nagging," Zola griped, hoping she sounded good-natured enough for all the mood sensors in the room. Or, if the mood sensors picked up on her tension, she hoped it would seem like she and Mom were just recovering from a typical mother-daughter spat.

"Surely all my nagging is the reason you've turned out to be such a great kid," Mom replied.

Normally that would have annoyed Zola beyond belief. But now Zola felt like she'd been handed an Insta-Translator. This was how Mom was saying thank you. And announcing that Zola really was a great kid for obeying.

Maybe everything Mom said had always been in code?

Zola pulled the door of the Insta-Closet shut again,

enclosing herself inside, away from Mom.

"Okay, that was weird," she told her own image in the mirror.

In the reflection, her hazel eyes were wide with amazement—and maybe shock, too. Her cheeks were flushed.

Was someone watching her? Or listening for an answer?

Around her, the Insta-Closet looked like it always did: every wall made of sleek, polished blond wood that joined with the ceiling and the floor at perfect right angles. The closet held one hook for new outfits and one shelf off to the side for her to deposit the clothes she wanted to return.

But the possibility of someone watching meant that she was careful pulling the swingy purple top over her head; she waited until it had settled into place on her shoulders before she shrugged out of her pajama top and dropped it to the floor. And she hunched over as she traded her pajama bottoms for the more snazzily patterned daytime leggings.

Mom didn't act like someone was watching, she reminded herself. *She acted like someone could hear.*

She looked at herself in the mirror again. The mirror gleamed extra-bright, like it always did when Zola finished dressing. Zola knew that meant sensors had been tripped the moment her pajamas hit the floor. The idea was that she would want to admire herself in her brand-new (er, newly recycled) clothes. But Zola didn't spare a second glance at how the clothes fit. She kept her gaze trained on her own face. Maybe she'd been too harsh about the whole "Mirror, mirror, on the wall" story. Maybe you really could tell by looking at someone if they were ready to be brave, if they were ready to be kind.

Or, at least, maybe you could tell that when you were looking at your own reflection.

"No matter what my mom says, I'm not too young," Zola announced. Her voice didn't even quiver. "I do want to find you. I do want to help. But how?"

3

Nobody answered.

Zola stood waiting, long enough to feel ridiculous. What was she expecting? Another note to flutter down? A booming voice to call out, "Great! Thanks! Here's what you have to do . . ."?

Even if somebody heard me, why would they believe me instead of Mom?

The door of the Insta-Closet rattled.

"So, yeah. Your mom's out there freaking out, worrying that she's going to have to send you off to school without breakfast," a voice swelled around Zola. "Go on. Ya gotta get some eats!"

Zola jolted. This wasn't the usual Insta-Closet voice. Or the mirror voice. Or—

Oh, right, Zola remembered. *I told Sirilex, like, just five minutes ago I wanted the Insta-Closet voice to be slangier and more fun. That's all I'm hearing.*

She was so used to digital voices. How was she supposed to know when someone real started talking to her?

The gleaming mirror before her dimmed. Zola knew it had just timed out for a typical "admire yourself" session for a twelve-year-old girl. But it felt like a sign that whoever might have been listening earlier was gone.

"I'll be back later," Zola vowed. She wasn't sure if she was making that promise to herself or the mystery listener. "I'll figure this out. I'm not giving up."

She was still clutching the odd paper note. She tucked it into her pocket (Zola *always* asked the Insta-Closet for clothing with pockets) and opened the door. Mom was right there, relief painted across her face.

Zola paid no attention to what she ordered for breakfast when the two of them stepped into the kitchen. She listened only half-heartedly as Mom yammered on as usual about how wonderful it was that ovens and refrigerators now functioned like the best 3D printers ever, able to create even the most gourmet meal in seconds, blah, blah, blah....

"Mom!" Zola wanted to shout. "How can you act like today's the same as every other day? How can you pretend everything's normal when I could whip out this weird note at any moment and start asking questions? In front of the security cameras and everything?"

But the look in Mom's eye was more intense than usual. That—and the memory of Mom saying, so grimly, "People's lives might depend on it"—kept Zola from doing anything but brushing her fingers against the note inside her pocket.

"If you want to see things as they really are . . . ," she thought.

She glanced around the kitchen. It looked as it always did, with its usual spotless counters and cabinets that were only there for show. Everything they ate came out of the Insta-Oven or the Insta-Fridge, two stainless steel boxes that slid out like drawers from beneath the counters. The wall beside the table also held a drawer, so Mom and Zola could just shove their dishes into the combination Robo-Washer/ Robo-Recycler/Robo-Composter as soon as they were done eating. Or, if they forgot that step, Sirilex would turn on the table's self-clearing mode, and slide the dishes away anyway.

Above the table, the kitchen's Picture Wall showed a boring garden scene, something Mom must have chosen. Zola leaned in, ready to look closely even at that scene. But she knew her instinct was ridiculous. It wasn't like the Picture Wall showed their backyard as it truly was.

Or does it? Zola wondered suddenly.

She couldn't actually remember the last time she'd stepped foot in their backyard. There'd been no reason to.

"—ready for school?" Mom was asking.

"Uh . . . yeah. I think I'll walk today," Zola said, trying once again to make her voice sound normal.

"Of course you'll walk!" Sirilex interrupted. "Centuries of research about what's best for kids shows that exercise before school is essential to—"

"I mean, outdoors," Zola said. "For real."

Mom frowned and gave a little shake of her head. Was that supposed to be some secret code? Some other clue about the note Zola had found in her Insta-Closet?

But Mom quickly shifted into laughter.

"My little daydreamer," Mom said fondly, patting Zola's arm. "Didn't you hear Sirilex just give the weather report?"

"I can repeat it," Sirilex said, with its usual exaggerated patience. "You know I monitor all possible factors that might affect a pleasant stroll, any time of day. The temperature outside is still a few degrees below the optimal sixty degrees Fahrenheit, fifteen point five Celsius. That alone could make this a treadmill day. But there's also a twenty-three point eight five three percent chance of a thunderstorm starting in the next fifteen minutes. That's too high. Sorry."

Sirilex didn't sound sorry at all.

"You're so lucky, Zola!" Mom exclaimed. "It's not just that you don't have to walk to school through blizzards or even rain—or dust storms, desert heat, or swampy humidity. You don't have to go outside if the weather is anything *but* ideal!"

Laying it on a little thick there, Mom, Zola thought. *As usual.*

Mom walked over to the treadmill in their living room

and picked up Zola's VR goggles.

"You know school's a virtual-reality experience whether you're there in person or joining from home," Mom said, handing Zola the goggles. "You know that's one of the best things about education in the twenty-second century—consistency!"

"Yeah, yeah," Zola mumbled, which was the reply she would have given regardless. But secretly she wondered, *Did Mom—or Sirilex—see the "Come find me" part of the note I found in the Insta-Closet? Did they know I was planning to look outside?*

Not that she could have looked anywhere without all the sensors and security cameras seeing her. Not that she could have been even a second late to school without Sirilex intervening.

Zola slid the VR goggles back and forth in her hands. History VRs had taught her that way back at the beginning of the twenty-first century, people had used something called Google Glass—spectacles that linked them to a primitive digital world called "the internet." And then shortly after that, twenty-first-century kids often played games using VR goggles that were just huge brownish boxes covering their eyes. In the history VRs, the kids in those goggles looked like they'd turned into Cyclops creatures; they always looked so funny jerking around and waving their arms at nothing.

Zola's VR goggles were much more sophisticated than that. Oh, sure, they looked simple. They had a small, sleek black band at the front to cover her eyes without hiding them, and a wide black strap at the back to slip over her head in a way that never became painful even when she wore them for a long day of school and then homework or playtime afterward. But she knew the goggles contained just as much advanced technology as the Picture Walls or the Insta-Oven or Insta-Fridge.

She'd heard someone in a history VR describe them as "the most elegant-looking swim goggles ever," and she guessed that was true—not that she'd ever been swimming for real.

That was because everybody used the VR goggles for everything outside their homes, and a lot of the time inside their homes, too. The VR goggles meant that everyone could have full, rich, exciting lives without encountering the slightest risk of danger, ever.

So how could anyone ever be lost? Zola wondered, remembering the plaintive "Come find me" of the mysterious note in her Insta-Closet.

How could anyone ever need her help for real?

4

"*Zola?" Mom said softly, bringing* Zola out of her reverie. "Have a great day at school!"

She gave Zola a quick hug that also served to steer Zola onto the treadmill. Before letting go, Mom locked eyes in a way that felt more like a warning.

"Oh, right," Zola said, stumbling to catch up. "Have a great day at work. Um . . . doing art with old-fashioned paper!"

She thought Mom should be happy she'd remembered to throw that in. But Mom only watched warily as Zola pulled on the goggles, letting the earbuds on the strap slide into place.

"Route?" Sirilex asked, the voice now coming directly into her ears. All other sounds in the room—including whatever Mom might say—were blocked by the noise-canceling portion of the earbuds. The sight of Mom turning toward her art studio at the back of the house was quickly replaced by a spinning globe, giving Zola a choice of destinations anywhere on the planet.

"Want to get a jump on your homework by doing more of your history VR sessions now?" Sirilex suggested. "Want to finish the one where you're a spy in 1944 Paris, carrying messages for the underground resistance?"

Tantalizingly, Sirilex called up an image of Paris, the Eiffel Tower in the background. Now Zola could see nothing else. It did feel like she was really there. There was even the smell of cooked cabbage hovering in the air—wartime food. A route across the cobblestones glowed ahead of Zola, pointing to a door. When Zola tilted her head ever so slightly, she saw the words "Helpful Clue Source located inside" appear on the door.

Yesterday, Zola had had so much fun working on this particular homework assignment. But today, after receiving a real note, a real plea for help, this VR just felt fake. (The note in Zola's closet had been real, hadn't it? *Wasn't* the plea genuine?)

"The streets of my own town," Zola said stubbornly. "The scene I would really see, this very morning, if I took a walk here. If it was warm enough. And not stormy."

Sirilex might decide she was being sulky—even recalcitrant. But Zola didn't care.

"Are you sure you don't want a more educational site?"

Sirilex was just a computerized voice, but it could still be annoying.

"I'm sure."

The treadmill lurched into motion. Zola stepped forward. And if she didn't take this kind of walk all the time—if she had been, say, one of those kids from long ago who really did have to walk uphill through blizzards to get an education—she probably would have found it amazing how the VR goggles delivered such an authentic experience. The door of her own house appeared before her and she turned the doorknob. And it really did feel like she was touching a solid, real, *actual* doorknob. Outside (or, what appeared to be outside), the early-morning sunlight truly did feel warm on her cheeks. She even had the sensation that the sleeves of her swingy purple top fluttered against her arms because of the gentle breeze.

It had been a long time since Zola had picked her own town as the background scene for her morning walk. Sirilex was right to doubt her choice—her most common request was some faraway location: Shanghai, perhaps, or Cape Town or London or Mumbai. For a while, she'd even been on a kick of wanting a different city every day. At age nine or ten, she'd thought it would be possible to see every single centimeter of the planet; that had been her biggest goal.

Then she'd made the mistake of telling her fourth-grade teacher about her plans, and he'd turned it into a math and geography problem. He said that would help her learn exactly how big the planet was and how long it would take to see everything . . . and that took all the fun out of it.

Now she looked around with extra attention. The whole scene had the same sparkly, shiny glow the VR goggles always gave her morning walks. Flowers bloomed along the sidewalk, and they could have been the flowers in one of those antique Disney movies Mom had shown her once; Zola wouldn't have been all that surprised to see the daisies and pansies with eyes and smiling mouths that called out to the bees gently buzzing nearby. The house where Mom and Zola lived looked fresh-scrubbed and cheerful in the streaming sunlight, and so did all their neighbors' houses. Everyone's solar panels glinted and glistened. Zola exited the neighborhood—that is, the VR goggles made her feel as though she was exiting her neighborhood—and now she could peer to the left and to the right, and see charming little shops around her. When Zola was younger, she had convinced Mom to while away hours in those shops, looking at colorful, clever toys created with designs from all around the world, or paintings done by the best artists of every country, all of them ready for purchase (or downloading, anyway) to adorn the walls of anyone's house. But now Zola knew all of the shops' wares were just as easy to see with a simple question to Sirilexagoogle; there was no reason to actually walk into the shops. Zola wondered sometimes if the shops still existed or if they were just remnants of the past, left in the VR walks for nostalgia's sake.

Zola didn't know anyone else who wondered things like that.

Zola knew from history classes that most people had once lived in large cities, with millions of people clustered in small apartments in places like Tokyo or Delhi or New York City or Rio de Janeiro. Back in the past, people had to live as close as possible to their jobs. But jobs were almost all virtual now, so people were spread out more evenly across the globe, often in smaller, more intimate communities. People could live in Outer Mongolia or Timbuktu—or some small town in Indiana—and have just as much access to good jobs and fancy restaurants and cultural treasures as anywhere else.

Zola and her mom happened to live in small-town Indiana.

So everybody Zola passed waved or nodded or gently bowed at her—the storekeepers propping open their doors, and the parents or Robo-Nannies chasing after small preschoolers pointing excitedly at the store windows, and the other walkers or runners getting their morning exercise, too. Zola gave the same waves and nods and bows in return.

What would happen if I stopped? Zola wondered. *What would happen if I grabbed one of the adults by the arm and asked, "Have you ever seen a mysterious note show up in your Insta-Closet? Can you think of anyone who might need my help? Can you tell me what's going on?"*

But Zola was forgetting that she was seeing her own town only in VR; she wasn't *really* surrounded by anyone. For all she knew, everyone she saw was "strolling" through the town by VR, too. She saw only their avatars; they saw only hers.

And asking questions wouldn't give her answers. It would only tip off the security cameras in her own living room that *Zola* had gotten a mysterious note, that *Zola* thought she was supposed to help someone.

Anyhow, why would any of their neighbors be willing to answer questions that Zola's own mother didn't want her to ask?

The blocks of quaint little shops ended. Zola turned to the right, and joined a crowd of kids filing into the town's school building. A *virtual* crowd. Even if it hadn't been too "cold" for kids to walk to school for real, a large portion of Zola's school would have been present only as avatars regardless. Young children went to school with others in their neighborhood. But after kindergarten, kids were grouped with other kids from anywhere else in the world whose learning patterns fit theirs most closely. So Zola's "class" included kids who were actually in Texas and Maine and Sierra Leone and India and Romania. Her best friends were from Egypt and Sri Lanka and Bolivia. Zola stepped into the "class" just as the bell rang, so she only had time to wave at Amir and Eromi and Beatriz.

"Nice shirt," Beatriz—or, rather, Beatriz's avatar— whispered. "Did you dress up for Visitors' Day?"

"No, I just . . . wait—it's really Visitors' Day? Again?" Zola groaned.

Teachers always had the idea that kids needed a mix of familiar and unfamiliar in school. So while Zola had had the same classmates for years, at least once a week they also had Visitors' Day. Kids from all over the world, with all sorts of different learning patterns, were randomly assigned to join Zola's class. Zola would have loved that if they could have all sat down and had ordinary conversations or maybe played some sort of game together. She would have loved *really* getting to know so many different kids. But the conversations were always so stilted. The Visitors asked questions like, "How well do you think you are learning?" "What do you like about school?" "What is your home life like?"

How was anybody supposed to answer questions like that?

And because the Visitors were guests, Zola could never ask all the nosy questions she wondered about. "Do you really look like the faky, flickering VR avatar the school has assigned you?" "Is *your* regular classroom anything like mine?" "Where do you live? Earth? Mars? Some other planet? In another solar system?"

Back in fourth grade, Zola had *tried* asking some of those questions, but every conversation with the Visitors was on a time delay, so the teachers always blocked her feed. (Or whoever controlled it—maybe it was all done by AI. Zola didn't even know who to blame.)

So even though she was twelve and entirely too old to continue believing in anything supernatural, Zola had started thinking of the Visitors as something like ghosts. They flickered; their Insta-Translators didn't work instantaneously—it really did feel like they were visiting from another realm.

The Visitors were already starting to flock in through the back door of the classroom: kids of various races, their clothing representing a range of nationalities and religions. That, of course, wasn't any different from Zola's regular class.

Zola knew the barrage of Visitor questions would start soon. Quickly, she leaned toward Beatriz again.

"When you picked out your clothes with your Insta-Closet this morning . . . ," she began, "did you notice—"

Just in time, Zola stopped herself. It *seemed* like she and Beatriz were just having a private conversation, two schoolgirls whispering together before the start of their school day. Most of the time, Zola completely forgot that the two of them weren't actually right there in a real classroom together, side by side, settling in on matching ergonomic exercise balls. But Beatriz was actually thousands of miles away. And their conversations only took place because of VR, Insta-Translator services, and probably loads of other technological assists that Zola didn't even know about.

And all those things could be monitored.

Zola remembered again what Mom had said in Zola's Insta-Closet: "Please, please, please don't make a scene. People's lives might depend on it."

The way Mom had acted, even Zola whispering to Beatriz could endanger someone.

". . . did you notice that the Insta-Closet took longer than usual?" Zola finished, trying to make it seem like she was just another impatient kid, annoyed at having to wait a few extra seconds to get dressed in the morning.

That actually *had* been her greatest concern before finding the note in her Insta-Closet.

Beatriz laughed.

"You always want everything to hurry up, don't you?" she teased. "My mama's always telling me, 'Do you realize that skirt you're wearing would have taken your ancestors a whole year to weave? Do you realize that blanket over your shoulder would have been your great-great-grandmother's most valued possession—and you're just going to throw it back in the Insta-Closet recycler tonight and get one with a different pattern tomorrow?'"

Zola was pretty sure that Beatriz was actually speaking Spanish—or maybe Quechua or one of the other indigenous languages of Bolivia—and "blanket over your shoulder" was probably a bland translation.

It made her a little sad suddenly, not to know exactly what Beatriz was saying. Maybe it would be fun to learn Spanish or Quechua, instead of always hearing the translation.

But at least she'd avoided giving away anything about her strange morning.

The school day dragged on. Zola paid only enough attention to avoid being scolded. She kept trying to make plans: *After school I'll confront Mom, and . . .* No, that wouldn't work. *Maybe I should have checked out the Insta-Oven and the Insta-Fridge to see if they contained notes, too. Or . . .* Again and again, she ran into her same old worries about the security cameras, the mood sensors.

So after school, when Zola finally pulled her VR goggles from her face and set them down on one of the living room tables, she was stunned to find Mom standing right there beside her, tapping her foot impatiently.

"*What* did you eat for lunch that you got all over that shirt?" Mom asked.

Automatically, Zola looked down. There was nothing on her purple shirt.

And yet, Mom scrubbed a finger against the fabric covering Zola's belly button as if she was trying to wipe away some disgraceful stain.

"Quick," Mom said. "Go throw this shirt in your Insta-Closet and put on . . . I don't know . . . you've got a pair of pajamas ready, don't you?"

What was wrong with Mom? She knew the routine—she'd *taught* it to Zola. Pajamas were recycled every morning into a pair for the next night, so of course there would be something ready and waiting whenever Zola took off her school clothes. But . . . it was truly odd for Mom to act like Zola should change instantly after leaving school.

Or to act as though she had a stain on her shirt when she didn't.

Ooooh, Zola thought. *She's making an excuse to get me to look in the Insta-Closet again.*

"That must be chocolate pudding," Zola said. "Oops. I'll be right back."

She practically ran into her room, and over to the Insta-Closet. The door was slightly ajar. She whipped it open, stepped through, and closed the door behind her. The light around the full-length mirror came on automatically, illuminating the lightweight cotton pajamas folded neatly on the shelf off to the side. Zola lifted the T-shirt-style top, which was such a bright hot pink it practically vibrated.

And then Zola dropped the shirt.

Something had been hidden beneath the shirt.

It was rectangular, with a stiff-looking cover—was it some kind of box? Or, no—the cover stretched across both the top and the bottom of the thing, and along one of the longer sides. And there were pages of soft-looking paper in between the top and bottom covers.

This was a book. Not an eeb—the term everyone used for books printed electronically, available only in digital form. This was a book as the term had originally been used: an old-fashioned, printed-completely-on-paper book.

Zola had seen such a thing in history VRs before. But this book was real.

Zola leaned closer. Now she could make out words on the cover, the letters hard to puzzle out since they were in an odd, old-fashioned script superimposed over a picture of strange old log cabins clustered together against a backdrop of heavy woods.

The words on the cover of this book said:

All My Questions Answered

That was exactly what Zola wanted, wasn't it?

Then Zola noticed another, smaller line of type beneath the first set of words:

The Jessie Keyser Story

5

Keyser? Zola thought. Like my name? Like Mom's?

Maybe this was some kind of family heirloom.

Why had Zola never seen it before? Or at least an image of it?

Maybe the better question was about why Mom was showing it to her now. Or why Mom had hidden it in her Insta-Closet, instead of handing it to her directly. Or . . .

Hesitantly, Zola lifted the book from the shelf. It felt surprisingly heavy in her hands, as if it weren't just a contraption of paper and cardboard—it almost seemed as though the words themselves had weight.

Zola knew from the history VRs how to operate a book. She lifted the top cover.

The first page that appeared was a dark forest green but completely wordless. Zola touched the page to get it to turn, but nothing happened.

Oh, that's right—it requires manual operation every step of the way. . . .

Zola had to physically lift the page—gently enough not to tear it—and physically lay it back down again on the book's front cover.

The second page repeated the title from the cover, but there were extra words now after "The Jessie Keyser Story." They said, "How One Girl Escaped from Clifton Village and Rescued Her Family and Friends."

Escaped? Zola thought. *Rescued?*

Her heart beat faster.

Zola touched the words "Clifton Village," because she'd never heard of such a place, and she needed to have it explained. But nothing happened.

Oh, right. Old-fashioned book. No instant definitions . . .

Automatically, she started to shove open the door of her Insta-Closet so she could call out to Sirilex, "What's Clifton Village?"

Just in time, she reconsidered.

If Mom didn't want me seeing this book in front of the security cameras and mood sensors, do I dare ask questions about it?

Zola reached up to shut the Insta-Closet door again. She'd just have to stay curious. But she heard Mom's voice disturbingly close: "Sirilex, can you tell me why it's taking Zola so long to change clothes? Oh, never mind. I remember. She's hit that age, hasn't she? It wouldn't be unusual for a twelve-year-old to spend half an hour in an Insta-Closet, staring at herself in the mirror, would it? I know, I know, I need to stop thinking of her as a little girl. Just for reference, what's the longest a normal twelve-year-old ever spent in an Insta-Closet, deciding between outfits, figuring out her own personal look?"

Sirilex answered Mom instantly: "We have no statistics on the longest time. But an hour and a half certainly would not be abnormal."

Mom asked that question for *me, not* about *me,* Zola thought. *She's trying to tell me I have an hour and a half to read this book.*

Zola pulled the Insta-Closet door shut again, lowered herself to the floor of the Insta-Closet with the old-fashioned book braced against her knees, and turned another page.

It took five more page turns to get to something labeled "Foreword," but that page also rewarded Zola with thick chunks of type:

> *Everyone who lived through 1996 remembers the media sensation caused by Jessie Keyser's revelations about the seemingly innocent Indiana tourist site that was a cover for a diabolical scientific experiment— or perhaps we should say, "diabolical anti-scientific experiment." Jessie Keyser will go down in history for her extraordinary courage. First, she rescued herself.*

And then, armed with only the knowledge a typical child would have had in 1840, she managed to outsmart the evildoers who would have been perfectly content to sacrifice Jessie's life—and the lives of many other children just like her—on the altar of their false "scientific" theories.

The particulars of Jessie Keyser's story are a mix of nineteenth-century pluck and twentieth-century evil. But you can be certain: Jessie Keyser is a heroine for the ages. Oh, who needs the dated, gendered language? Jessie Keyser is a hero for all time!

Zola had to pause at that. It sounded like Jessie Keyser, whoever she was, had been incredibly famous some two hundred years ago. Two hundred years wasn't *that* long ago, when Zola considered that her history teachers seemed to think it necessary for her and her classmates to learn about ancient Greece and prehistoric Mesopotamia. Given Jessie's last name—and the fact that this book had shown up in Zola's Insta-Closet—Zola and this long-ago girl must be connected. For all Zola knew, she might even be a direct ancestor.

So why hadn't Zola heard of her before?

It was so frustrating not to be able to just ask, "Sirilex, how am I related to Jessie Keyser from 1996 Indiana?" and have an answer instantly.

How did people bear not knowing things immediately

back in the old days before Sirilex? How did they avoid dying of curiosity?

Zola went back to the book.

Gradually—waaaay slower than she had patience for—Zola began assembling details in her head. Jessie Keyser had been thirteen years old in 1996. Her parents had five other kids besides Jessie. Jessie was the second oldest, and the bravest and boldest. (The author hinted that it was unusual in 1996 for a girl to be considered braver and bolder than her brothers—was 1996 prehistoric, after all?) Jessie's family was unusual in many ways for 1996, because of how and where they lived. The author helpfully gave examples of typical 1996 technology: cars, airplanes, cameras, TVs, refrigerators, freezers, something called a "desktop" computer. But Jessie and her siblings and friends had been kept unaware that any of those things existed. That's because their parents had chosen to raise them in a historic preserve designed to look and seem exactly like a typical Indiana frontier village from the early 1800s.

Why would anybody do that? Zola wondered.

Off the top of her head, she could think of many unbearable things about early 1800s North America: Slavery. The Trail of Tears. The fact that women and certain people of color were not allowed to vote.

My history teachers would be so proud of me for remembering all that, Zola thought.

But slavery hadn't been allowed in Indiana in the 1800s. Zola couldn't remember the exact route of the Trail of Tears, but it hadn't been near Indiana, either.

And how much did females' lives change between the 1800s and the 1990s? Zola wondered.

She wasn't sure. Maybe Zola just didn't know enough about either era. It was all so long ago.

The book said Jessie's parents—her dad, anyway—thought some things were better in the early 1800s than the 1990s. He liked the idea of roughing it in the wilderness. He liked working with his hands, which was much more important in the 1800s than the 1990s. He liked the sense of community possible in the distant past, with everyone knowing their neighbors and taking care of one another.

And, the book said, originally Jessie's parents (along with all the other adults in Clifton Village) were promised that they'd secretly have access to "modern" medicine. And all the kids, when they reached the age of thirteen, were supposed to be told the truth about what year it really was, and they would have the right to decide for themselves where *they* wanted to live.

But how would anyone who only knew 1800s life feel comfortable in 1996? Zola wondered.

She tried to imagine someone showing up and telling her, "Hey, guess what? It's not really 2193! It's almost two hundred years later!"

Her imagination failed. How was it even possible to think of centuries more of technological advances?

She felt a little sorry for Jessie Keyser. And maybe even sorrier for her less brave, less bold brothers and sisters.

If I were in Jessie's shoes—er, old-fashioned boots—would I be brave enough to risk my life to rescue other kids? Zola wondered. *Or would I be more like the sisters and brothers?*

She reached the section of the book where Jessie's mother went rogue and pulled Jessie aside to tell her the shocking news about what century it actually was. But that was only the first part of the secrets Jessie's mother whispered to her. Jessie's mother, who was a nurse, said lots of kids in their village had a disease called diphtheria. And the evil men who ran Clifton Village weren't allowing them to have 1990s medicine. Jessie's mother was afraid children would *die*. So she sent Jessie out into the "modern" 1990s world to get help.

Why didn't they just ask Sirilex for help? Zola wondered. Then she remembered: Sirilexagoogle hadn't existed in the early 1800s. For all Zola knew, it might not have even existed in the 1990s.

So weird, Zola thought.

Even in the history VRs she saw in school, she and her classmates always had what they jokingly called "Schoolilex" to answer any of their questions along the way. But in olden times, sometimes people lived their entire lives without *ever* knowing the most basic facts. Or they believed things that were completely untrue.

Her heart pounding as if Jessie's fear were her own, Zola went back to reading. Jessie had bravely strolled out of her tiny 1800s village, only barely comprehending that she should avoid being seen by the security cameras all around her. Oh, wait. She *was* seen. But—

Zola turned the page, and the story didn't continue on the next page. Instead, there were pictures. Or, to be more accurate, it was like someone had crammed a whole sheaf of pictures on glossy white paper into the binding of the book, between the clumps of rougher, tan, word-covered pages. Zola held the book sideways: it looked like there would be two more sections of pictures coming in the pages ahead. She was torn. Should she look at all the pictures at once, or continue reading?

The first photo was of a primitive log structure labeled "The Keyser Cabin," superimposed on a map of the entire Clifton Village. Zola shivered spotting the cluster of greenery labeled "Haunted Trees," but she didn't have the patience to look for other locations already mentioned in the book: the schoolhouse, the store, the smithy, the King of the Mountain rock. . . . She decided to keep reading, and then come back and study all the photos.

But Zola's fingers were clumsy with the unaccustomed sensation of paper. She tried to flip past the pictures to resume the story, but she only managed to turn to the next spread of pictures. And . . .

These were photos of Jessie Keyser.

On the left side of the book, a shadowy Jessie stood in her 1800s clothes. She wore a long, light blue cotton dress with a rough-spun, scratchy-looking apron tied around it. The boots on her feet were fastened with what must have been homemade buttons; on her head, she wore a calico sunbonnet that tilted back so far that it was a wonder it didn't fall off completely. It looked like Jessie was too eager to see everything around her to care about protecting her skin from the sun. Her greenish-brown eyes snapped with lively curiosity; the edges of her mouth curled up as though she was on the verge of a giggle. Even the two long brown braids that snaked out from beneath the sunbonnet seemed to have a personality of their own. Escaping tendrils of hair vined across Jessie's shoulders as if even her hair objected to being confined; even her hair was ready to explore.

On the right side of the book was a second version of Jessie labeled "School photo, fall 1996." This was clearly the same girl, but the sunbonnet had vanished. The braids were replaced by a waterfall of freed, wavy curls, and the T-shirt beneath the curls was a lime-green color that even Zola could tell couldn't have been produced in the 1800s. In this picture, Jessie's eyes were still lively and curious, but they were sadder somehow, less trusting. The corners of her mouth still curled up into a grin, but it seemed more cautious now, less happy-go-lucky—more an expression of hope than certainty.

Maybe she didn't manage to rescue everyone? Zola thought.

*Maybe some kids did die, no matter how much Jessie and her
mom risked to try to save them?*

Zola put her fingers over the first picture, trying to block
out the period details—the tight braids, the sunbonnet, the
dress's prim collar—to see if she could compare the two versions of Jessie without getting distracted. It would have been
easy to do that if this book were an eeb. She could have cop-
ied the two pictures, edited each one to show only the face,
and made a direct comparison.

As it was, putting Zola's fingers along the sides of Jessie's
face made it look like the girl's old-fashioned braids and sunbonnet were replaced with long, straight, pale hair. Just that
one change made Zola gasp, and almost drop the book. Her
hands trembling, she lifted the book so she could see the face
of 1840s-style Jessie flipped around, reflected in the mirror
alongside Zola's own.

Zola no longer cared about the differences between the
two views of Jessie Keyser. All she could think about now
were similarities.

Mirror-image Jessie Keyser looked *so* much like mirror-
image Zola.

6

Jessie Keyser has to have been related to me, Zola thought. *Closely related.*

But how closely related could two girls be when they lived two hundred years apart?

Zola had studied genetics at school. She knew about DNA and chromosome pairs. She'd drawn charts showing inherited traits with pea plants. She'd even filmed videos for a class project showing how certain recessive traits resurfaced or hid, generation after generation.

But how likely was it that Zola and Jessie would have the same straight nose, the same dancing hazel eyes, the same wide mouth?

You didn't even see it yourself until you made it look like Jessie had straight hair like yours—maybe you're just imagining it, Zola chided herself. *Because you* want *to be like someone as brave as Jessie.*

She nudged the door of the Insta-Closet open a crack. How could she get help from Sirilex without giving anything away?

Oh, yeah . . .

"Sirilex, can you call up an ancestry chart for my genealogy, going back ten generations?" she asked.

Ten generations were enough that no one would know what she was really looking for, right?

"Sure thing," Sirilex responded.

Across the room, Zola saw a spinning circle appear on the computer screen hovering above her desk. But then the circle froze.

"Oops— sorry," Sirilex said, without a tinge of even artificial regret. "That file of information is labeled as something a parent would want to tell a child. So I can't spill the beans. It has to be your mom having this talk with you. Not that I'm saying there are any beans in your ancestry. Just human 'beans.' Ha. Ha."

"Seriously?" Zola groaned.

It was an all-purpose grumble, bemoaning both Mom's secrecy and Sirilex's stupid joke.

Zola started to shove the Insta-Closet completely open, to take her complaint directly to Mom. But then she reconsidered. *What if the Insta-Closet recycles this book as soon as I step away?* So instead, she stuffed the book under her shirt, and held it flat against her stomach by crossing her arms. It wasn't unusual for her to stalk over to Mom in a crossed-arm, irritated huff, so this wouldn't set off any alarms.

Well, except that Mom will probably do her usual "Zola, you need to speak respectfully to grown-ups. Especially your own mother" talk, Zola thought.

She flung the Insta-Closet door the rest of the way open and was just starting to dash across her room when she heard Mom's voice out in the living room.

"No, I didn't call for any Technologists," she was saying.

"Your Sirilex must have done it for you," an unfamiliar male voice responded. "You know they're trained to troubleshoot even tiny problems in the home, ones that humans might overlook." Zola could hear the teasing in the man's voice. "Or the ones people put off dealing with until a water pipe bursts or an Insta-Oven burns out. You know it's because of Sirilex that those things never happen anymore."

"That's why Tedeo and I were dispatched to deal with that faulty Insta-Closet you and your daughter were complaining about this morning," an equally unfamiliar female voice agreed.

"I think Sirilex misinterpreted our concerns," Mom replied. She sounded perfectly polite, but Zola knew that tone.

Mom'll get rid of those Technologists, and then she'll scold Sirilex, and then I'll get her to tell Sirilex to tell me everything I want to know . . . and then I can get back to reading Jessie Keyser's story, Zola thought.

But the next thing she heard was the sound of boots

stomping on the floor mat in their entryway.

"Let me . . . go warn my daughter before anyone enters her bedroom," Mom said faintly. What had the Technologists done besides stomping their boots? Mom's voice had changed completely, from sounding totally in charge to practically begging.

Because she's protecting me, Zola thought. *And protecting this book I'm hiding.*

And maybe she was even protecting the mysterious person who'd left the note that morning asking for help?

Zola stumbled out of her bedroom.

"Mom, who are you talking to?" she asked, trying to sound as innocent as possible. Or maybe as ignorant as possible.

"Oh, Zola," Mom said too brightly, too cheerfully. "You can tell these two Technologists. There's nothing wrong with your Insta-Closet, right? It was just a false alarm this morning."

"Oh, come on." The male Technologist—Tedeo?—grinned at her, his eyes twinkling from behind his VR goggles. "You can't tell me a kid wouldn't want the latest model Insta-Closet, no matter what." He winked and then waggled his eyebrows at her, really pouring on the charm. He'd offset the blandness of his Technologist white coat with a row of jeweled piercings in each ear and along his jawline. It was a cool effect against his shaved head and brown skin. "I'm told these new Insta-Closets deliver clothes practically in the blink of an eye!"

Mom was also waggling her eyebrows at Zola, but more subtly. And more anxiously. All this nonverbal communication made Zola's head hurt. What would happen if Zola just said out loud, "Mom, don't worry. They won't find the book. I made sure of it"?

But I don't know if more notes might appear in my Insta-Closet, that they could find, she told herself. *I don't actually know anything about what's going on.*

Zola went over and gave her mother an awkward one-armed hug, just close enough to let Mom feel the edge of the old-fashioned book hidden under Zola's shirt. The tension in Mom's spine eased instantly.

"Oh, Mom, really?" Zola exclaimed, faking glee. "You ordered a new Insta-Closet for me? That's awesome!"

It felt like they were all acting in a play. But how could Zola play her role when she had no script—and no idea what was at stake?

She pulled slightly away from Mom.

"I know you'd promised to think about getting me a new Insta-Closet if I kept doing well in school this year, but . . . you decided to order it early?" Zola asked, making herself beam at Mom.

I'm going to hate myself forever if I just gave Mom an out, and I didn't have to, Zola thought ruefully.

The female Technologist—an Asian woman wearing a lot of makeup and bedazzled goggles—hoisted an ungainly box onto one shoulder and began striding toward Zola's room.

"Clearly *someone* has confidence in you," she told Zola.

Mom opened her mouth—and immediately shut it. She just stood there looking stymied and miserable.

And scared.

And that made it so Zola couldn't ask any of the questions crowding her mind.

Who has confidence in me besides Mom? What's really going on here?

And how does any of it connect to that long-ago girl, Jessie Keyser?

7

Zola woke in the night and couldn't go back to sleep. At first she tossed and turned, but then Sirilex whispered to her, "It appears you are having trouble sleeping. Do you need warm milk? Soothing music? A warmer or cooler temperature in your bedroom?"

It was all Zola could do not to shout back, "I need answers!"

"I just . . . want to think about what to wear tomorrow," Zola mumbled, slipping out of bed.

"Ah yes, you have started into the preteen increased-interest-in-your-appearance," Sirilex whispered back, in a reassuring tone. "Rest assured, this is perfectly normal."

Seeing a note in my Insta-Closet isn't normal, Zola thought. *Having Mom hide a book there—a real, old-fashioned book! Not even an eeb!—that's not normal, either.*

And she had no desire to rest. Every nerve ending in her

body felt jangly; every muscle screamed out that it needed to move.

She tiptoed over to her Insta-Closet—her *new* Insta-Closet.

The Technologists had indeed replaced her Insta-Closet, though it was hard to tell that now, in the sparse moonlight trickling into Zola's room. The new Insta-Closet was just a dim, hulking shape against the wall that Zola's room shared with Mom's. It was a bit wider than Zola's previous Insta-Closet—that was the only difference visible in the dark.

"Sirilex, night-light brightness, please," Zola whispered.

"Introducing any light will make you more alert," Sirilex argued. "And that will make it harder for you to—"

"Forget the 'please,'" Zola muttered. "Just turn on the light."

Sirilex could be sassy, too: the room suddenly glowed as if lit by a noonday sun.

Now the rich sheen of the wooden Insta-Closet was apparent. Its square corners seemed razor-cut precise.

But even out of the shadows, it looked mysterious.

"So now you have a teen girl's Insta-Closet, not a child's version," the female Technologist had said that afternoon.

That had been right before the male Technologist warned, "But it will take several hours for the adhesives to settle and all the setup troubleshooting programs to run. So don't even touch it until after midnight."

Mom, of course, had had to ruin everything by adding,

"Zola will *not* still be awake at midnight. So I'll just make sure she doesn't use it until tomorrow morning."

Zola glanced at the digital clock embedded in her bedroom wall.

It was 12:01.

Joke's on you, Mom, Zola thought.

She reached for the Insta-Closet door and pulled it open.

Zola was already stepping inside when she realized she'd messed up: she'd left the book about Jessie Keyser back in her bed, hidden under the covers. She'd carried it around under her shirt all evening; she'd kept it with her when Mom tucked her into bed. But it had slipped out with all her tossing and turning.

In the old days, how did people keep track of actual, physical things like books all the time? Zola wondered. Eebs were so much easier, when you could call them up whenever, wherever, just by asking Sirilex.

It should have been a simple matter to tiptoe back to bed, hide under the covers long enough to secretly retrieve the book, and then pretend another bout of restlessness before returning to the Insta-Closet. But Zola was rattled by her own forgetfulness, and by all the strangeness of the day. She glanced around the interior of the new Insta-Closet, to make sure it really would be a safe place to read a secret book. She pulled the door completely shut and trailed her fingers along the doorframe, noticing that the wood inside the Insta-Closet was just as highly polished as outside. As far as she could tell, the only difference between this Insta-Closet and her old one was the width, and a few extra shelves and hooks. Otherwise the whole closet was empty, because she hadn't asked for anything yet. Still, she patted a shelf where her folded-over, new clothes would appear the next time she requested them. She tested the sturdiness of the hooks that would hold hanging clothes—they were probably strong enough to bear Zola's full weight, if she ever wanted to try to climb to the ceiling, as she had done in her old Insta-Closet when she was eight.

And then Zola reached out to touch her own face in the mirror. The mirror was so clean and unsmudged that she could almost believe that she wasn't seeing her own reflection, but another girl in another Insta-Closet—maybe the mysterious Jessie Keyser, somehow magically transported from the past. Zola's eyes held the same eager curiosity as the 1800s version of Jessie; her cheeks were just as flushed with excitement. If Zola could stare past the hot-pink sleep shirt and her own tousled, not-so-straight-anymore hair, she did look like the ancient Jessie Keyser.

"Mirror, mirror, on the wall . . . ," Zola murmured. But she was thinking now of another story she sort of remembered Mom telling when she was really little. In that tale, the mirror wasn't a mirror, exactly, but more of a magical object. Like a wishing well, maybe. Or a wishing pebble. Or was Zola getting thoroughly confused? Why would Mom have ever told her such a story?

There was no point to stories like that when Zola had Sir-ilexagoogle and an Insta-Closet that could deliver practically anything Zola wanted, anytime.

Except the explanations about Jessie Keyser.

Or answers about the note Zola had found in her clothes that morning.

Zola's finger brushed the reflected image of her own face, leaving fingerprints behind. And then the fingerprints smeared—not because Zola moved her hand, but because the mirror started sliding down beneath her touch.

Zola jerked her hand back. But the mirror kept moving: down, down, down . . .

And then a gaping hole appeared in the wall, an opening that took up the entire space where the mirror had been.

And Zola could no longer see her own face, but . . .

Beyond.

8

Zola gasped. And then, quickly, before the mirror could reappear and trap her in place again, she shoved her head through the opening.

The bright light from inside the Insta-Closet spilled out through the opening that had replaced her mirror. She was looking out onto a narrow wooden platform, which stood atop a flight of stairs.

Zola couldn't see to the bottom of the stairs. But she could see across the platform to a blank wall. Zola imagined maps rotating in her mind, remembering the blueprint she'd drawn of her own house for a school project last year.

This platform shouldn't exist, she thought. *There are no stairs in our house.*

She *knew* she lived in a one-story house. She *knew* it didn't have a basement. Or an attic, either, for that matter. Their house was just a kitchen, a living room, Mom's art studio, and the two bedrooms, with bathrooms attached. Zola remembered how painstakingly she'd drawn the layout of her room and her mother's room behind it during her school project: Mom's Insta-Closet and Zola's Insta-Closet should have stood back-to-back. During Zola's presentation to the whole class, she'd talked about how the power source for both Insta-Closets was so energy-efficient, it was no thicker than a sheet of paper.

Ha ha, paper, Zola thought, feeling a distinct sense of unease. *Whose idea was it that I made that comparison?*

Had it been Mom's—or Sirilex's? Had she read it somewhere?

Before she lost her nerve, Zola stepped through the hole in her Insta-Closet wall and out onto the platform, which was just wide enough for her to fit comfortably. The platform, she noticed, was not anchored to Zola's wall or Mom's. It seemed to sway, ever so slightly.

It's 2193, Zola told herself firmly. *There's no danger anymore. There's no reason for fear.*

The mirror-back behind her rose again, leaving her in near darkness. In a panic, Zola grasped for the top edge of the mirror.

It slid down easily again as soon as Zola touched it.

For a moment, Zola did nothing but stand on the platform, practically panting to make up for the air that had vanished from her lungs.

Oh, I guess this is what fear's like, Zola thought. *Real fear. Fear for my own fate, not just imagined fear from reading an eeb or participating in a history VR . . .*

The mirror slid back up again, plunging Zola into near darkness once more.

Almost without thinking, Zola reached out again. But this time, she grasped for the wall on her left, instead of her right—she was grabbing for the back of *Mom's* Insta-Closet. A mirror-shaped oval started to slide down there, too. Zola opened her mouth, ready to cry out, "Mom! Mom! Why didn't you tell me our Insta-Closets are connected? Why didn't you tell me our house had secret stairs in the middle? Where do the stairs go?"

But Mom's Insta-Closet, like Zola's, was soundproof. To get Mom's attention, Zola would have to rush through the Insta-Closet and out into Mom's bedroom. She'd have to scream and wake Mom up.

That would set off all sorts of mood sensors. That would alert every single security camera. Mom would still be groggily sitting up while Sirilex launched into soothing platitudes. Zola could just imagine what Sirilex would say: "Zola, did you have a nightmare? Zola, your mother needs her sleep, too. Your imagination is impressive, but you need to save your made-up stories for the morning, when you're both awake."

Zola froze with her mouth half-open.

Sirilex knew everything. Sirilex was always accurate. So why was she so sure that Sirilex would pooh-pooh something Zola was seeing with her own eyes—something Zola knew for a fact was true?

Why did Mom so clearly not *want to acknowledge the paper note or the book when the Technologists were around, or when we were in the parts of the house that the security cameras could see?*

If Zola wanted Mom's help, she'd have to wait until morning when Mom stepped into her Insta-Closet for the usual reason—to change her clothes.

Zola was *not* going to wait six or seven hours for an explanation.

She turned away from Mom's Insta-Closet without even looking into it.

"I can . . . I can find answers on my own," she whispered, though she couldn't have said who she was talking to. "I can believe what my own eyes tell me." She swallowed hard, and added, "I can be brave like Jessie Keyser."

She was being ridiculous. Jessie Keyser had *needed* bravery, because evil men in her village didn't care if innocent children lived or died. Zola didn't have those worries. She lived in a luckier time; fear and danger—and the need for bravery—were all things of the past.

Still, Zola took a hesitant step forward, onto the first stair down from the narrow platform. Behind her, the mirror/wall of Mom's Insta-Closet closed automatically. Zola blinked, letting her eyes adjust. Even without the bright lights of either Insta-Closet, she could see a little. Now she noticed a single metal rod that served as the only railing for the stairway. Zola clutched that and gingerly climbed farther down.

After ten steps, there was another, smaller platform. After ten more, Zola's bare toes touched a solid, rocky floor.

Zola's brain was at war with itself: *What was I thinking? Why didn't I order a pair of shoes from the Insta-Closet before I started climbing down? I should go back and put shoes on— and more sensible clothes, too—and* then *go exploring.*

But she also told herself, *What if this is my only chance to explore? How could I go back now?*

She kept inching forward.

Now that she'd reached the bottom of the stairs, she noticed a stirring in the air. It didn't feel as though she was in a basement; it felt like she'd reached a tunnel or a cave. In the dim light, she could see walls of rock or crumbling concrete to her left and right, and only open air in front of and behind her.

"Sirilex, in a cave, if there's a breeze, which direction do you follow to reach the exit?" she called out softly.

Sirilex didn't answer.

Okay, makes sense, Zola told herself. *If Sirilex can't hear me inside the Insta-Closet, why would I think Sirilex could hear me in this weird space beneath the Insta-Closets?*

Anyhow, she didn't want Sirilex to know where she was. She should be glad that Sirilex didn't answer.

But it was creepy that *no one* answered. Even in the Insta-Closet, there was the Insta-Closet voice.

Had Zola ever before in her life been in a place where no one could hear her—indeed, where no one even knew where she was?

Zola felt itchy and panicky and weird. And not knowing which direction to go made her stomach churn. She could have easily thrown up. She could have easily burst into tears.

Jessie Keyser didn't have a Sirilex to help her when she left Clifton Village, Zola told herself. *Jessie Keyser didn't panic or vomit or cry.*

So Zola didn't, either. Instead, she gritted her teeth and started walking toward the source of the breeze.

When she'd taken about twenty steps, she reached another set of stairs. Twenty more, and a third stairway appeared.

Oooh, Zola thought, trying to picture the world above-ground, and how it lined up with the tunnel. *Those stairs could be below our neighbors' Insta-Closets.*

She didn't test her theory by climbing any stairs. She didn't know any neighbors well enough to think that they might welcome Zola popping out of one of their Insta-Closets in the middle of the night.

Now, if Beatriz or Amir or Eromi lived right next door, that would be a different story, she told herself.

If only her friends from school *did* live right next door, instead of in Bolivia, Egypt, and Sri Lanka! Zola had a moment of imagining the four of them in this tunnel together. If Zola had her friends with her, she wouldn't tiptoe so fearfully. She wouldn't constantly second-guess herself. She wouldn't have to constantly stifle the voice in her own head that kept whispering, *This is all wrong! And dangerous! Turn around now, before something awful happens! Go ask Mom or Sirilex all your questions—that's how to find out everything! Not by risking your life going off into the unknown!*

Zola kept walking, even though she was alone. For a while, she kept count of every single stairway she passed—because how else would she find her way back to her own house? Then, when she reached stairway number thirty-two—and was wondering if she'd maybe skipped counting one, or counted the same one twice—she realized that the stairways were labeled. The sign on stairway number thirty-two (or thirty-one or thirty-three) said, "Elise Choi." The next stairway was labeled "Cash, Nevin, Marisol, and Porter Rodriquez."

So the stairway by my own Insta-Closet was probably labeled, too, Zola realized. *I won't have any problem finding my way back.*

Was it maybe getting a little lighter in the tunnel? Zola could see spots where the tunnel forked off. If every Insta-Closet in town had a stairway beneath it, it made sense that there would be cross streets in this tunnel; it made sense that the tunnel would have a similar grid system to the town above.

But why would every Insta-Closet in town have a stairway

beneath it? Zola wondered. *Why does this tunnel exist? Why didn't anyone ever tell me it's here?*

It was maddening to have so many questions and no answers. It was maddening not to have Sirilex to explain everything.

Zola kept walking anyway.

She was right about the light intensifying. With every step she took, the glow ahead of her grew a little brighter. She could see now how rickety all the stairways were, how shabby and run-down the tunnel was. It was possible the walls had once been painted or wallpapered, and the floor had once been tiled. But that could have been eons ago; the tunnel seemed to have mostly returned to its natural state of rock and dirt. She'd already come so far—she had to have passed fifty or sixty stairways by now.

This tunnel had to be leading *somewhere.*

As the light ahead grew even brighter, Zola started running, her feet slapping carelessly against the uneven tunnel floor.

And then, just as she rounded a corner, Zola tripped.

9

Zola landed hard on her knees. The palms of her hands skidded across the cracked tunnel floor. She'd definitely stubbed the big toe on her right foot. She winced in pain, waiting for Sirilex to assure her, "Don't worry! I've alerted your mom—she's on her way with antibacterial wipes and bandages!" Or "Your teacher's on the way." Or . . . *some* adult authority figure.

But no one spoke. No one came.

Zola had to examine her knees and hands and feet all by herself. The big toe was bleeding, ever so slightly. She'd scraped her knees and the palms of her hands, but the throbbing went away quickly.

Zola looked up, and realized that falling down might have saved her.

It saved her from being seen.

Ahead of her, the tunnel ended. And outside the tunnel . . .

It took Zola a long moment to get her eyes to make sense of what she was seeing. That was fire, wasn't it? A real, live, actual fire, with flames snapping at the night sky, and clouds of filthy, polluting smoke escaping into the air? Zola had to search her memories of all sorts of history VRs to come up with a name for the type of fire before her.

Bonfire, she thought. *That's a bonfire.*

Dark shapes moved around the bonfire—were they people? People were throwing logs and strips of what looked like unfurled rubber tires onto the fire. Other people were holding sticks over the flames. Were they actually cooking like that? One of the dark shapes/people pulled a stick back from the fire, yanked something off the end, and appeared to put that thing into her mouth. Or his mouth. Or . . .

Or, no, that's impossible, Zola thought. *People don't build fires anymore. No human has used anything but an Insta-Oven for cooking since . . . since . . .*

She couldn't come up with an actual year, but she knew it'd been decades and decades and decades. Probably more than a hundred years.

An unfamiliar, acrid, ashy smell reached Zola's nose, and she jerked back and turned her head. This all felt much too real. She reached up to yank off her VR goggles—apparently, she'd accidentally put them on before stepping into her Insta-Closet. Apparently they'd been set to "appalling scenes from the past, with nasty sense-a-round smells included."

But there were no VR goggles on Zola's face. What she was seeing—and smelling—*was* real.

Unless . . . is this just all a nightmare? Did I fall asleep again, after all, and I don't even remember it?

"Sirilex, wake me up," Zola whispered. "Wake me up *now*."

No one answered.

With a normal nightmare, as soon as Zola realized she was only dreaming, she became aware of the pillow against her face, of the soft sheets cradling her body. She could rouse herself enough to turn over and sink back into a deeper, better sleep, with happier dreams.

But here, now, she could still feel the hard, *real* floor of the tunnel beneath her. She could still feel her knees throbbing from hitting that floor. She could feel the real ache of her stubbed toe. She could touch a finger of her right hand against the palm of her left, and feel the tender ridges of scraped skin.

She could hear the crackling of the horrifying, polluting, dangerous fire.

She could smell it.

Every sensation around her was so much more intense than even the scariest VR that Zola felt like she had fallen out of time when she tripped. It was as if she'd dropped straight from her safe, secure, easy twenty-second-century life to some terrifying bygone era.

Maybe this *is a moral dilemma test,* Zola thought. *Maybe once kids reach the spring of their sixth-grade year, schools stop using VR for this kind of thing, because it's too obvious. They came up with simulations that look even more authentic.*

Maybe what Zola needed to do was to rush out of the tunnel and yell, "This is wrong! We all need to work together to protect the air that we breathe! Put out that fire!" And then Mom and her teacher and—who knows—maybe even the principal of her school or the mayor of the town would appear and congratulate her for passing the test.

Zola decided not to do that. Not until she could figure out how anyone could create such a real-seeming simulation without VR goggles or a Picture Wall.

She did inch forward, angling for a better view. The mouth of the tunnel appeared to be surrounded by bushes. She could at least crawl out and hide behind one of the bushes. Then she could see more.

Without letting anyone see you, her brain reminded her.

Her body definitely thought she should be on high alert. She could practically feel the adrenaline coursing through her veins. The muscles in her legs felt taut, as if primed for some fight-or-flight response.

Huh, Zola thought. *What they taught us in science class was true, after all.*

She imagined telling Mom and her teacher—and Beatriz, Amir, and Eromi, if it didn't ruin some test for them— about how aware she was of her body's response, even as her brain assured her she couldn't be witnessing anything but a simulation. She could even ask, "Is it because my body still has inherited memories of my ancestors being terrified of fire?"

That would earn her a star for the day.

Zola reached the back of the nearest leafy bush and cautiously stood up. Now she was no longer looking up toward the bonfire, but more on the same level. The flames were perhaps the length of a tennis court away from her. If she used her hand and a clump of leaves to block her view of the bright fire and the sparks in the rising smoke, she could also see what lay on the other side: low-slung, primitive buildings. Were they houses? Stores? Either way, the wood-framed structures were so ramshackle, it seemed like a strong wind could have blown them down. Or like they might just fall down on their own, even without a breeze. They also seemed deserted, except for a man who sat by a rickety table in front of one of the buildings. By squinting, Zola could just barely make out words on a sign propped against the table: "Pop $1/ Can."

Zola didn't know what "pop" was, but the "can" part stunned her. She knew that, ages ago—centuries? Decades?—people had bought and sold food in disposable containers. But of course that wasteful habit ended long before the twenty-second century.

Maybe this is just . . . a history museum? Zola wondered, remembering the setup her maybe-ancient-ancestor Jessie

Keyser's family had gotten involved with, back in the 1990s.

But, no, if there'd been a history museum like that so near to Zola's own house, Zola's own town, she would have known about it.

And, anyhow, no one in 2193 would allow even a history museum to do something as unhealthy and dangerous as burn a bonfire for *real*.

Zola was back to being mystified.

While she watched, three or four small people—children, maybe?—came rushing out of the darkness near the man and his table.

One of the children grabbed a can from the table.

"No!" the man roared, as he jumped to his feet. "Dirty, rotten, thieving . . . you have to pay!"

"You can't make me!" The boy—or girl?—snarled back. "And I'm no more a thief than you are!"

The child—Zola decided it was definitely a girl—clicked something on the can. And then she threw back her head, lifted the can high in the air, and poured some sort of glistening liquid directly into her open mouth.

"Why, you little—" the man screamed.

The other kids fell on the girl, crying, "My turn!" "No, mine!" Were they punching her? Trying to steal the can she'd stolen? Dark liquid sloshed onto the ground, wasted. The man waded into the ruckus and snatched the can himself. It must have been empty by now—he crumpled it in his hand and threw it at the children.

"I'll beat you up!" he yelled. "I'll teach you what happens when you steal from me!"

But the kids were already rolling to their feet, already scrambling away. Someone screamed, "Can't catch us now!" Someone else hollered, "We're not afraid of you!"

Kids weren't supposed to say things like that. They weren't supposed to steal, either.

But adults weren't supposed to throw things. Or threaten to beat up anyone, especially not kids.

Zola started to step out from behind her bush. If this was a moral dilemma test and she had any hope of passing, it was definitely time to speak up. Past time.

But what am I supposed to say when everyone's *doing something wrong?* she wondered. *How can I make any of this right?*

"Fool! Stay hidden!" someone hissed.

It wasn't someone down by the fire. It wasn't anyone near the screaming man or the running kids.

It was someone in the bush.

Right beside her.

10

Zola whipped her head to the side. After staring toward the brightness of the fire, her eyes took a moment to adjust.

Another kid was huddled beside her, cowering behind the bush. Whoever he was, he seemed more prepared—and more *talented*—at hiding than Zola was. He hadn't been there a moment ago, but Zola hadn't heard so much as a cracking twig to announce his approach. His dark brown shirt and pants served as better camouflage against the hillside than her hot-pink T-shirt and baggy white sleep shorts. And his clothes covered his arms and legs completely; even his raggedly cut dark hair was long enough to hide a good portion of the pale skin of his face. Zola's own bare arms and legs might as well be glowing in the dark. She sniffed, getting a whiff of the peaches-and-cream organic soap she'd used to scrub her face before bedtime. Compared with this boy, she wasn't even good at hiding her own *smell*.

The boy scowled at her.

"I just took a bath," he said. "Don't you go acting like I stink."

"I wasn't—" Zola began. But she didn't care about smells right now. "Who *are* you? Where did you come from? What *is* this place? What's going on?"

She gestured weakly toward the bonfire, the falling-down houses, the screaming man who was settling back into his chair by the table full of old-fashioned beverage cans.

The boy put his finger against his chin, as if he needed to deliberate on which of Zola's questions to answer. Or whether he wanted to answer them at all.

"You can call me Puck," he said.

"Puck?" Zola said. "Like, from Shakespeare?"

"Who's Shakespeare?" Puck said. "Never heard of him. No, it's 'Puck' like 'hockey puck.' Because that's how the big kids used me when I was little." He stood a little taller, though that brought him only to the level of Zola's chin. "Littler, I mean."

Did Zola owe it to this boy to tell him who Shakespeare was? In spite of the height difference, he looked about the same age as her. How could he not have learned about Shakespeare in school?

"Do you . . . do you *live* here?" Zola asked, because it kind of made sense. People who didn't know fire was dangerous and stealing was wrong probably wouldn't know about Shakespeare, either.

Not that it made sense that *any* place existed where people didn't know those things. Not in 2193.

"Do *you* live here?" the boy parroted back to her.

"*No.*" Zola recoiled. Tears pricked at her eyes—a delayed reaction to all the horrible things she'd seen. Or the start of an adrenaline crash, dating back to her fall in the tunnel. Either way, it made her snarly. "Who would want to live *here*?"

She immediately regretted her own words. But, strangely, the boy grinned.

"That's kind of the point, isn't it?" he asked.

He might as well be speaking in riddles.

Don't cry, don't cry, don't cry . . . , Zola thought. She longed to whirl around, run back through the tunnel, and not stop until she was back in her own bed, safe and sound.

But she longed even more for answers.

The boy's grin faded.

"Sorry," he said, as if Zola had failed even at hiding her own emotions. Somehow he must have noticed that she was on the verge of tears. "That wasn't fair. I know so much more than you do. It's hard to talk to someone who doesn't know anything."

How was Zola supposed to take that from a boy who didn't even know about Shakespeare?

"You've never met me before!" she protested. "How do you know what I do or don't know?"

Puck had the nerve to roll his eyes at her.

"You're Zola Keyser," he said. "Your favorite colors are hot pink and purple and lime green. You've eaten toast with acai-berry jam for breakfast the past seven mornings. You think oatmeal is slimy."

"Who doesn't think oatmeal is slimy?" Zola muttered. But her neck prickled with alarm. She glanced back at the tunnel—an easy escape, a direct route home. Still, she wasn't about to run away without speaking up for herself first. "What'd you do—hack into my Insta-Closet *and* our kitchen accounts? That's private information. You probably think you're so smart, but you're in trouble now. What you just said was like a confession. I'm sure there's a security camera somewhere around here that recorded it. I'm going to tell my mom and Sirilex, and they'll report you. You'll be arrested. Or maybe I'll just scream for help, and—"

"No! Please, no!" Puck's voice was still hushed, but it sounded as raw as a scream.

Then Puck grabbed Zola's arm.

Zola looked down at his fingers circling her biceps. This kind of thing had never happened before. So much of school was VR, with Zola and her friends there only digitally—Zola had to think back years to remember another kid touching her skin for real. Or . . . anyone but Mom doing that.

And, really, except for the barely there Visitors who showed up virtually at school, Zola had never even *encountered* a stranger before, let alone had one of them grab her arm.

Puck was looking at his hand on her arm, too. His eyes widened in horror, and he quickly let go and drew his hand back.

"I'm sorry," he said. "I'm so sorry. I'm doing this all wrong. It's just, I can't believe, after all this time . . . this is not the way I meant to ask for help. But can't you tell what a desperate situation we're in? Can't you see how urgently we need—"

"It was you," Zola gasped. "You wrote the note. The one in my Insta-Closet. Somehow. Are you in trouble? Do you have some problem you don't know how to solve?" She gazed out at the horrifying, smoky bonfire; at the man who'd threatened to beat up little kids. "Of course you do. This whole place is an unsolvable problem."

"Not unsolvable," Puck said. His voice was gentle now. He peered directly into Zola's eyes. "But, yes, I'm in trouble. I'm in *danger*." His voice dropped almost achingly low. It seemed like he was the one on the verge of tears now. "But, Zola? So are you. And you don't even know it."

11

"*It's the year 2193,*" *Zola* said automatically. "*Nobody's* ever in danger anymore."

Puck dropped his face into his hands.

"Not . . . really even sure where to start," he muttered.

He was so little and forlorn. Reflexively, Zola reached out her hand to pat him comfortingly on the back. It's what she would have done with Beatriz, Amir, or Eromi. But she'd forgotten again that she wasn't in a VR. This would be touching Puck *for real.*

Zola let her hand drop to her side.

Puck was already lifting his head.

"Did you get the book?" he asked. "Did you read it?"

"You . . . you . . . you're the one who left the book about Jessie Keyser?" Zola stammered. "I thought my mother did that! I thought . . ."

"Let's just say it was teamwork," Puck said. The corners of his mouth dipped down a little grimly. "It *is* your mom's book." He gestured at the crowd around the flames. "Books here would get thrown onto the fire."

Zola had seen book burnings in history VRs, and they were horrifying. But Puck didn't seem to be talking about censorship.

"For warmth," he added. "Or just as kindling. But, anyhow—"

"No, no, you have to explain," Zola pleaded. "How do you know my mother? Why did she tell *you* about that book before she told me? And . . . were you in my Insta-Closet? My private, soundproof Insta-Closet, where even Sirilex doesn't have access?"

Puck made a rude sound that might have been a snort.

"Just because your Sirilex doesn't *answer* in your Insta-Closet, that doesn't necessarily mean that someone isn't *listening*," he muttered.

Zola lifted her hands to her face as if they were blinders. She'd seen those in history VRs involving horses, and she could use any help she could get. Her mind was acting like a runaway horse right now.

"How could my mom have owned that book?" she asked. "*I* never saw it before today. We've lived in that house my whole life. I know every inch of it. Where would she have kept a book?"

"When was the last time you were in your mother's Insta-Closet?" Puck asked.

"Oh, that's not right, to go into someone else's Insta-Closet," Zola explained. "I guess you don't know the rules, but . . . oh."

Suddenly Zola regretted not peeking into Mom's Insta-Closet when she'd had the chance. She'd stood right there on the newly discovered platform between Mom's Insta-Closet and her own—she could have looked behind Mom's Insta-Closet mirror before climbing down the stairs.

But Mom's so boring! Mom wouldn't have had anything in her Insta-Closet except . . .

Except more books? More answers?

Or more mysteries?

Maybe Mom wasn't so boring.

"So you moved that book from Mom's Insta-Closet to mine," Zola said, trying to focus. "Because Mom asked you to? Somehow she knew . . ." Zola glanced back over her shoulder. The mouth of the tunnel behind her looked dark and forbidding, as if that was a route to danger, not safety. "She knew you had access to our Insta-Closets?"

It creeped her out, that anyone from this horrible place with its fire and falling-down buildings—and thieves— could have sneaked into her Insta-Closet. The door between her bedroom and the Insta-Closet was biometrically locked to anyone without her fingerprints, but still.

Puck shook his head as if disappointed in Zola's reasoning skills.

"Your mother moved the book between the Insta-Closets herself," he said. "But she had to make sure I knew so I didn't, uh, 'recycle' it."

"People don't do the recycling in an Insta-Closet," Zola corrected him. "It's automatic. Without any human involvement at all. Except for at the beginning, when I tell the Insta-Closet what I want to wear next."

Now Puck really did snort. He didn't even try to hide it.

"Insta-Closets don't work the way you think," he said. "*Nothing* in your life works the way you've been told."

"How do you know?" Zola challenged. "How can you be so sure that you know everything and I don't know anything?"

"You don't even know what year it is!" Puck spat back at her.

"But that's the easiest thing of all." Zola shook her head in disbelief. "You might as well be saying we're not in Indiana, or not even on planet Earth, or—" The bonfire off in the distance swung into her field of vision again. She was upwind from the smoke and the sparks, but just the sight of the fire was enough to light an ember of doubt in her mind. "Or . . . what are you saying? How could it be anything *but* 2193?"

She remembered what she'd read in the strange, old-fashioned book about Jessie Keyser, the long-ago girl who might be related to Zola. Jessie had thought she was living in the 1800s, but it was really the 1990s.

Zola shook her head again, even harder.

"I'm not some modern-day Jessie Keyser!" she protested. "It *couldn't* be a hundred and fifty or two hundred years later than I think!"

"Oh, you're right about that," Puck said, with a harsh laugh. "I agree, your town isn't a historical preserve."

"Glad we've established that," Zola muttered.

But Puck wasn't done talking. He peered at Zola again with his unnervingly direct gaze.

"But you—you and me both, actually—we *are* like Jessie," he said. "Just kind of in the opposite direction." He smiled in a way that wasn't happy at all. His face looked grimmer than ever.

"Because," he finished, "we're both in a Futureville."

12

"*Futureville?*" *Zola scoffed. She waved* her hand at the horrifying scene before her: the fire and the crowd and the falling-down buildings. "You honestly think anyone would believe *this* is the future of the human race? When we have Insta-Closets and Insta-Ovens and VR and zero-emissions energy and—"

"Except, we don't," Puck said quietly, in a way that silenced Zola.

But that only lasted a moment.

"Oh, I see," she muttered. "Someone . . . I don't know who . . . someone is being really mean, and not letting your town have the technology you need. This is how things 'really are' for you. *That's* why you wanted help. You are so right. Nobody should have to live like this. Who do I tell? What can I do to—"

"Oh, brother," Puck said. He rolled his eyes as much as Zola always did when she was talking to Mom. "Weren't you listening? I said we're *both* living in Futurevilles. My town is fake—maybe you'd want to call it a *future* preserve. But so is yours. We're the two potential futures. Your town is supposed to show what happens if everyone works together and uses technology wisely and takes care of all its citizens. My town is . . . everything going wrong."

"Oh," Zola said. "So all this is just . . . acting?"

"Are you acting when you lie in bed and tell the Insta-Closet you want an orange dress that feels soft, not scratchy, and has pockets big enough to put your hands in?" Puck asked. "Or when you're sitting at your breakfast table, and you say you want a carob-chip waffle with just enough almond syrup to fill the indentations, but not overflow?"

It was freaky how he was repeating orders she'd made practically word for word.

Zola decided to pretend she didn't notice.

"Of course I'm not acting when I say those things!" she protested. "I'm just . . . living my life. Starting my day the way everyone does in the twenty-second century."

Too late, she remembered the scene in front of her—Puck's town. It was pretty clear he wouldn't have an Insta-Closet. The way his "Futureville" looked, she wasn't even sure it had electricity.

"How could it *not* be the twenty-second century?" Zola

asked. "I've had an Insta-Closet my whole life. I've had—"

"You've had people lying to you your entire life," Puck said. "And an army of people like me filling your Insta-Closet and your Insta-Oven and your Insta-Fridge whenever you or your mom so much as snaps your fingers. You've always had people making it *look* like everything in your life is possible."

Silently, Zola stared at Puck. She peered out at the bonfire. She glanced back over her shoulder at the tunnel that ran beneath her entire town—a tunnel she'd never known existed before this night.

"Maybe by the twenty-second century, we'll have all the technology for Insta-Closets and Insta- everything else," Puck said, as if trying to comfort her. "Maybe you'll live long enough to see that, for real. But nobody has exactly that technology *now*."

If Zola hadn't read the book about Jessie Keyser—or started reading it, anyway—she would have kept arguing with Puck.

Or maybe she would have still kept arguing if she weren't right this minute breathing in the damaging, polluting smell of smoke from a bonfire that she *knew* broke about a dozen environmental laws—laws that she'd always been told had been in effect worldwide for the past century.

But now she only swallowed hard and asked him in a small voice, "So what year are you saying it is for real?"

"2023," Puck whispered.

Zola gasped.

"But that's . . . but that's . . ."

"Yes," Puck said. "Exactly."

13

When was the first time Zola had heard about the 2020s?

Zola could remember being three or four, and standing in her yard after a giant snowfall. She'd insisted on going outside to "Tee da tow! Mommy! I have to tee da tow!" So they'd ordered a snowsuit for her and a snowsuit for her mother from their Insta-Closets and ventured out into the cold. But it hadn't been enough for Zola just to see (or "tee") the powdery snow; she'd also wanted to touch it. And then, because it was so amazingly white and unbelievably cold, she'd felt like the snow was just begging to be tasted. She'd scooped up a big handful of the snow and taken a huge bite—she'd had it in her mind that it would taste like whipped cream or powdered sugar or, at the very least, vanilla frozen yogurt.

Mom had immediately grabbed Zola's hand. It'd felt, for a split second, as if Mom was afraid Zola had eaten poison. But then Mom laughed. A little too hard, it seemed to Zola.

"Oh, Zola, don't look so worried!" Mom's face stretched into a too-wide smile. "Eat as much snow as you want! It's perfectly safe! Now, anyway."

And that was the first time Zola could remember hearing the story about how humanity was in such dire straits in the early part of the twenty-first century. Pollution and waste were terrible then; climate change caused tornados and hurricanes and melting glaciers and all sorts of other disasters. And people were mean to each other—they had wars, and people starved to death, and, well, there was no reason to tell Zola *everything* that had gone wrong.

Because . . . the 2020s were also when everything started to get better. Scientists from all over the world worked together and figured out answers. Recycling stopped being something that people kind of sort of sometimes did, and became the solution to all the waste that humans produced. People figured out natural, pollution-less sources of energy, and the air got cleaner, and the water got cleaner, and . . .

And that particular day when Zola was three or four, all she cared about was being allowed to eat snow.

But after that, Zola heard the story all the time. Every adult she'd ever met—teachers, neighbors, shopkeepers, random other parents watching their own kids on the playground—all of them were constantly dropping "Do you know how much the world changed after the first twenty-five or thirty years of the twenty-first century? Do you know how much you owe your ancestors from that era?" into every conversation.

If a kid kicked a soccer ball, the adult would talk about how the ball was made from recycled materials through a process discovered in the 2020s. If a kid picked their nose, the adult would talk about how lucky they were that medical practices improved in the 2020s, and germs were all but conquered. And if a kid cried, the adult talked about how it was a really good thing humanity came to understand the psychology of childhood in—you guessed it—the 2020s.

Now, standing with Puck and hearing *his* outrageous story, Zola started to say, "At least things were starting to get better in 2023."

But Puck was right in the middle of saying, "I know. The 2020s are when everything completely fell apart. Or, at least, that's what they teach us in *my* Futureville."

Zola couldn't help herself: she let out a bitter laugh.

"So whose story is true about the 2020s?" she asked. "Yours or mine?"

"I know how we could find out," Puck said.

His steady gaze was unnerving now. The bonfire off in the distance was starting to die down—fires did that, Zola guessed—and so Puck's face was becoming more and more shadowed. Along with his dark clothes and shaggy dark hair, the growing shadows made it look like he was fading away, blending in even more with the branches and the dark rock behind him. Zola could almost believe he might disappear completely. She could almost believe that all she had to do was trudge back through the tunnel, and in the morning she'd wake up and say, "Wow, *that* was a weird dream!" and she could go on with her life as usual.

But Puck kept looking at her. It felt like he *saw* her. Maybe he even saw what she was thinking.

Zola laughed again, but this time it came out as awkward and uncomfortable.

"You're not suggesting binging on history VRs, are you?" she asked.

"It's not history," Puck said. "It's *now*. And we have to get out of here and—"

"Warn people?" Zola asked. She waved her hand to indicate the "bad" Futureville where Puck claimed to live. (Though, how could anybody *actually* live there?) "Wouldn't it be enough just to let people come and see this place? See what they'll want to avoid in their own futures?"

"People already see this place," Puck said, wincing. "They watch all the time. Just as there are people watching your town all the time."

Zola gulped. It was one thing to think of Sirilex listening and watching all the time, but—people? Strangers?

She'd been angry enough about Puck knowing what she ate for breakfast.

"So that's the danger you're saying we're in?" Zola asked. "The danger of having our privacy violated?"

"No," Puck said. "It's so much worse than that. They're

ramping up everything. They're trying to—"

Puck froze. And then Zola heard what he must have been listening for: a twig snapped somewhere on the hillside behind them. And then another. And another.

Someone was getting close.

"Run!" Puck whispered urgently into Zola's ear. "Don't let anyone see you! Go home as fast as you can! I'll—I'll—"

He shoved her away without even finishing the sentence.

Zola ran.

14

At first, Zola was just trying to get away. She fled blindly back into the tunnel, her bare feet flying across the hard floor. It was a good thing she had a straight shot back to the stairs under her own house, because she wouldn't have been able to count steps, plan turns, or remember any directions at all.

When her lungs began to burn, she started gulping in air—loudly.

What if someone hears me? Zola thought. *What if I'm giving myself away, and I'm caught because of that?*

She stopped and bent forward, her hands on her knees. She forced herself to take slower, deeper, *quieter* breaths.

She couldn't hear anyone following her.

All this talk of danger . . . I don't even know what Puck was so afraid of!

Of course, it made sense that he was afraid, if he lived in a place with fire and pollution and people stealing and shouting and threatening to beat each other up.

But that's not my *life,* Zola thought. *Just because Puck has reasons to be afraid, that doesn't mean I should be scared, too!*

Then Zola remembered how strangely her mother had acted, how fearfully Mom had responded just because Zola found a scrap of paper in her Insta-Closet.

It was possible that Puck was right about both of them being in danger.

But surely his danger's worse. I could see so many things wrong in his town. And he asked *me for help.*

Maybe . . . maybe Zola was being cowardly for running away? Maybe she should have stayed right by his side, so they could face the danger together?

But he told me to run.

As much as it hurt to admit it, Puck did seem to know more about what was really going on in his "Futureville"—or maybe *both* Futurevilles—than Zola did.

Zola turned toward her own home again, and kept going. But she tiptoe-ran this time; she went slowly enough that her breathing never turned ragged and loud again.

After a while, she started squinting at the names on each set of stairs she passed. When she got to the one for their next-door neighbors—Jamaal and Latonya Taylor—she grinned and took off for her own set of stairs without bothering to double-check her own name.

Home, home, home, sang in her brain. *I made it!*

But was Puck okay?

Back on the narrow platform by her own Insta-Closet, Zola froze in the midst of reaching for the back of her mirror, to get it to slide away and let her back in. She was so close to safety. So close to being able to scramble through the Insta-Closet and back into her own bedroom. So close to being able to curl up in her own bed and act like everything was normal—like Zola *hadn't* just had the greatest adventure of her life.

But nothing was normal. Zola didn't even know what "normal" meant anymore.

Instead of reaching for her own Insta-Closet, Zola reached for her mother's.

"Mom?" she whimpered. And in that moment, she didn't feel like a brave, bold girl ready to confront her mother in her search for the truth. She was just a scared little girl afraid of shadows, and desperate to believe that her mother had all the answers.

Or maybe she didn't even care about answers. Maybe she just wanted Mom to hug her and stroke her hair and whisper into her ear, "Shh, shh, everything's okay. I'm here now. I'll take care of you. I'll fix all your problems. Don't you worry about anything."

The back wall of Mom's Insta-Closet slid all the way down, and Zola scrambled in through the opening. She meant to rush through the Insta-Closet, out into Mom's bedroom. She was focused only on getting to Mom as fast as possible.

But then the light came on in Mom's Insta-Closet.

And Zola could see what it actually held.

15

It had been a long time since Zola had been in her mother's Insta-Closet.

She had a vague memory of being a toddler or preschooler sitting on the floor of Mom's Insta-Closet. Zola had been stacking blocks into a tower while Mom got dressed. Zola could picture the red and green and blue blocks swaying and then falling onto the blond wood floor; one of the blocks skittered over behind a . . . curtain? Or a long, elaborate skirt that Mom was planning to wear? Or some cascade of fabric that Mom had ordered for an art project?

Zola couldn't remember the explanation for the fabric. But she remembered Mom saying in an unusually sharp voice, "No, Zola, let Mommy get that one." And then she'd picked up toddler Zola and put her down *outside* the Insta-Closet before retrieving Zola's block.

And was that maybe the last time Zola had been in Mom's Insta-Closet? About a decade ago?

It did seem like, after that, Mom was always up and already dressed before Zola awoke.

But now Zola stood stock-still in Mom's Insta-Closet, in front of a spill of gold-threaded, lacy fabric that Zola was certain was exactly the same fabric as the last time, ten years earlier. Seeing it as a twelve-year-old, rather than a toddler, Zola could tell now that it was definitely a curtain, not clothing. She could also read the sign pinned to the curtain at eye level: "PLEASE DO NOT RECYCLE ANYTHING IN THIS AREA. DO NOT *TOUCH* ANY OF MY POSSESSIONS!"

That was weird. The whole point of an Insta-Closet was recycling; no one would put anything in an Insta-Closet *except* to have it destroyed and returned in a new, more desirable form.

And it was automatic. Insta-Closets couldn't read or . . .

Zola remembered what Puck had said: that Insta-Closets didn't work the way she thought. That there actually were real live human beings scrambling in and out, taking out old clothes and bringing in new—just *pretending* that all the clothing was recycled in a waste-free way.

Was this proof that Puck had told the truth?

And that everything Zola had always believed about her own community—about her own *time*, even—was a lie?

Zola lost track of those questions, because the curtain

was partly open. Zola whipped it back, completely out of the way. Behind the curtain lay the oddest assortment of items: rows and rows of old-fashioned books, some with the words "Photo Album" embossed on their spines; some with titles like *Grimms' Fairy Tales* and *Little Women* and *Rebecca of Sunnybrook Farm* and *Bridge to Terabithia* and *Are You There, God? It's Me, Margaret*. Above the rows of books, pictures hung on the walls. Down on the floor, a somewhat crooked, crudely assembled wooden bucket tilted against a wobbly metal pot and an old-fashioned-looking quilt and . . . was that a *butter churn*?

Zola was a little proud of herself for remembering the historical term for such an obscure item. But she was completely baffled about why Mom would have these objects in her Insta-Closet—especially behind a sign labeling them Mom's "possessions."

"Possessions" is an old-fashioned word, too, Zola thought.

She tried to think if there was anything she owned that she would call a "possession." But why would she? Why would she care about holding on to anything when everything could always be turned back in to be replaced with something better?

It wasn't just that the bucket was crooked and the metal pot was wobbly. Or that the stitches on the quilt were zigzags, not a straight line. Many of the photos on the wall were grainy; some were faded as well. They were nothing at all like the crisp, crystal-clear, digital images that Zola could ask Sirilex to call up any time she wanted, from any moment of her life.

Zola remembered Mom saying she'd used old-fashioned paper in some art project she was working on. But that had been only a cover story—hadn't it?

And Mom keeps all her artwork in her studio, Zola told herself. *And even when she makes something with old-fashioned materials, she just takes a picture and then recycles the object. Anyhow, Mom's a much better artist than this.*

These pictures looked so old, they could have been from the book about Jessie Keyser.

Oh . . .

Zola stepped closer to the wall full of photos.

The large one in the middle, in an oval-shaped frame, was not, as she had first assumed, of some long-ago, long-dead ancestors in stiff, grim, old-fashioned clothes. Its sepia tone made it seem like it came from the early days of photography, when—if Zola remembered her history correctly—people had had to sit still for ten or fifteen minutes if they wanted the image to turn out clearly. This couple's clothing—a frilly bonnet and calico dress for the woman; a dark suit and Abraham Lincoln–style top hat for the man—did seem to belong in the ancient past. But it was so clear that the couple had been giggling together only moments before the camera shutter snapped; it was a glimpse of a sweet, spontaneous moment in time, not a pose anyone could hold for ten minutes. The man and the woman were gazing into each other's eyes with both joy and amusement; they seemed not to have a single care in the world. Or maybe it was that, in that moment, they didn't care about anyone or anything but each other.

They were so, so, so clearly in love.

Zola saw that first—before she noticed how familiar the woman's eyes were, how the woman's chin jutted out in such a familiar way, how the man's neatly trimmed beard matched other photos she'd seen in crystal-clear detail.

Despite the old-fashioned clothes and the odd tint of the photo, Zola knew exactly who these people were: they were her parents.

But why would they pretend to be from the past? Zola wondered. *Why have I never seen this picture before—in digital form, anyway?*

Without even thinking about it, Zola reached for the photo, pulling it down from the wall. Maybe she wanted to hug it. Maybe she wanted to worm her way into it somehow— maybe if she looked closely, she'd find evidence that there was also a small baby lying cozily across her parents' laps, or the slightest hint that her mother was pregnant with her when this picture was taken.

Maybe she wanted proof that, way back at the beginning of her life, her parents loved her as much as they'd loved each other.

But something was loose on the back of the framed photo. Zola turned it over—and there was a fluttery piece of paper tucked into the edge of the frame.

Zola's heart pounded as she eased the paper out. She carefully put the framed photo down on the stack of books so she could unfold the paper without ripping it. She wasn't used to the flimsiness of paper. Or maybe this page was extra flimsy, its creases well-worn. Was that what happened to paper that had been unfolded and refolded many, many times?

Now Zola could see that this paper was actually a letter. It made her think of historic artifacts, the letters she encountered in school VRs. But this letter wasn't about wars or governments or cataclysmic world events, like all the historic artifact letters she'd ever seen. It wasn't meant to be read for generations. From the first words, it was clear this letter was intended for only one other person:

> My dearest,
> This is how we saw ourselves when we fell in love, so I wanted you to have an image of our past. But we have such a future together, too—an unexplored, unimaginable future that I am certain will be even more wonderful than our most beloved daydreams!
> You know I want to do all of my daydreaming—and living and loving—with you!
> Your Beloved,
> Arthur (Formerly known as Chester)

Zola's father's name was Arthur. As far as she'd known, that was the name he'd carried his entire life, from the time he was born until he died suddenly and unexpectedly when he was thirty. What could he possibly mean by "formerly known as Chester"?

And why would "this"—the picture of them in old-fashioned clothes?—be how Mom and Dad saw themselves when they fell in love?

Zola reread the letter. This time, tears pricked at her eyes. Her father had loved her mother so much, and he'd died before Zola ever had a chance to know him and . . .

Zola put the letter down. It was too much to think about when she'd just run away from unknown danger a few minutes ago. She reached for the door of the Insta-Closet, ready to rush out into her mother's bedroom. No, not just that—ready to run into her mother's arms, to let Mom soothe and comfort her and explain everything.

But when has Mom ever answered all my questions? Zola thought. *What if this is the only chance I ever get to look at these . . . clues?*

Resolutely, Zola pulled her hand back from the doorknob. She didn't touch the letter or the picture of her parents again—it almost felt as though they were radioactive, too intense for Zola to handle. Instead, she rather haphazardly pulled out a book that had "My Scrapbook" stamped on its spine in curlicued letters. "Scrap" sounded like something

103

leftover and unimportant. She could start there and work her way up.

But when she opened it, Zola found that this book held more pictures, pinned to each cardboard page with a weird translucent overlay of . . . was that plastic? Could Mom possibly be harboring such a horrific pollutant that had been banned more than a century ago?

Zola forgot her indignation, looking down at the pictures. There was Mom—maybe at thirteen or fourteen, only a little older than Zola herself?—standing beside a light switch, surprise written across her face. Someone had placed a little paper label beside the picture, under the plastic. It said, "We have electricity now! Let there be light!"

Weird, Zola thought. *That must have just been from some school play. Of course Mom grew up around electricity. No way would she have been so awestruck by artificial light as a teenager. Not for real.*

The only way Mom could have been awestruck by a light switch was because it was so strange to physically have to turn on a light, rather than just asking Sirilex.

Then Zola remembered Puck saying that he and Zola were both growing up in fake Futurevilles, and it was really just 2023 outside, not 2193. So Mom would have actually been a teenager not in the twenty-second century, but—Zola rapidly did the math—in the 1990s.

That number gave Zola the chills. It had been 1996 when Jessie Keyser left her own fake village—Pastville, if Zola wanted to think of it that way. Or Historyville. Jessie Keyser wouldn't have seen a light bulb before 1996, either.

Could Mom secretly be Jessie Keyser the way Dad evidently had a secret second name as Chester? Zola wondered. *Mom's name is Hannah now, not Jessie, but . . .*

Her thoughts tangled, and Zola realized she was missing something obvious. She'd seen a picture of Jessie Keyser at age thirteen in the *All My Questions Answered* book Mom had left in Zola's closet. And now she was gazing directly at a picture of Mom at roughly the same age.

They weren't the same person. Mom's hair was lighter and tamer, and her eyes were bluer, and her face was more serene. *Zola* looked more like Jessie Keyser than Mom did.

But Mom and Jessie look enough alike that they could be closely related, Zola thought. *They could be . . . They could be . . .*

She turned a page, and came upon a picture of two adults and six kids, with the paper label beside it simply saying, "My family, 1997." This picture was too small, and oddly grainy. But Zola could still tell: the two oldest girls in the picture were Mom and Jessie Keyser.

So were they sisters?

16

Zola began flipping pages frantically, looking for proof. She came across a photo that was definitely teenaged-Mom and teenaged-Jessie together, alongside a younger girl of maybe six or seven.

All three girls seemed to be in clothes from the 1990s, not the 1800s: T-shirts, shorts, strappy sandals.

Jessie's younger sister, Katie, was one of the kids who got sick with diphtheria, Zola remembered. *The book said Katie was the one Jessie thought about the most, when she left her village for help.*

So did this picture prove that Katie, at least, had survived?

Zola felt a burst of happiness at that thought. But she also felt annoyed that Mom—or whoever had written the paper labels for some of the pictures—hadn't attached names to this particular photo.

It was so frustrating to have to search for answers. She wished she could just open the door of the Insta-Closet and shout out to Sirilex—or even Mom—"Is this a picture of three sisters? If not, how are Mom and Jessie and Katie Keyser related? Where are Jessie and Katie Keyser now? Why have *I* never met them?"

And that was only the *beginning* of Zola's questions.

She kept turning pages.

But Zola wasn't used to the weird system of a physical book with paper (and, ugh! Plastic!) pages that had to be painstakingly lifted and moved and placed by hand. The scrapbook slipped out of her grasp and fell against the shelves of other books. And one of the heavier pages near the back slipped out.

No—it was just a paper that had fallen out from its plastic wrapping. Not a letter this time, but a . . . a . . .

Newspaper clipping? Zola thought, feeling a grudging sense of gratitude for her history teachers, who had insisted that she learn about such an archaic method of communication.

Once upon a time, newspapers had been the main way people got news about what was happening in the rest of the world. Zola wasn't sure when that had changed—the twentieth century? The twenty-first? But there had definitely still been newspapers in the 1990s.

Oh. This newspaper clipping was dated. It said, "July 13,

2011" in small print at the top. And below that, in much larger print, were the words "Futurevilles Attraction to Open on Site of Old Clifton Village."

Zola recoiled.

Futurevilles . . . Clifton Village . . . So where I'm living right now . . . it's the site of the very village that Jessie Keyser escaped? she marveled.

She scanned the article, reading too fast and too eagerly to truly absorb the words.

". . . seen as a boon to a rural area that has been struggling economically ever since the original tourist site shut down . . ."

"Everyone remembers the tragic history of the original tourist site, which hid a darker intent. . . ."

"Investors promise that Futurevilles occupants will be treated better than original Clifton Village residents. . . ."

Then she reached two paragraphs that made her slow down. In fact, she had to read them twice to make sense of them:

> *Deice Kirone, the CEO of Futurevilles Inc., points to one particular last-minute addition to their roster as proof that residents will have good lives there: "Did you see that Hannah Keyser will be joining our idyllic community? Hannah, who's Jessie Keyser's sister and grew up in Clifton Village? She understands that it's*

more important to look toward a better future, rather
than dwelling on the past.

Hannah Keyser will be moving to one of the Future-
villes with her infant daughter. Her husband also grew
up in Clifton Village, but Arthur Seward died earlier
this year . . .

Zola almost dropped the paper. This, then, was proof. Proof that Mom and Jessie Keyser were sisters. Proof that she and Mom really were living in a Futureville. Proof, presumably, that it really was 2023, as Puck had told her.

Zola reread the article, making it all the way to the end of the last sentence this time:

". . . Arthur Seward died earlier this year in a tragic on-the-job accident that is now being investigated as murder."

Murder? Zola thought.

If she believed this article, if she believed what Puck had told her, then this newspaper article was also proof of a different sort.

It was also proof that Mom had lied to Zola about her father's death.

17

Zola slumped down to the floor. She could imagine Mom or Sirilex asking, "Are you all right? Do you need help? Are you in pain physically or mentally or psychologically?"

But neither Mom nor Sirilex could see her. Zola had no desire to be around her mother at the moment, and Sirilex . . .

Isn't trustworthy either, Zola thought.

Her head spun so badly that Zola had to lean against the bookshelves to stop the dizziness.

Dad was the only person she'd ever known who'd died. (Actually, she hadn't gotten a chance to *know* him exactly, but . . . he was the only person connected to her who'd died.) Medical care was amazingly advanced, and the world was an entirely safe place in 2193—er, in Zola's Futureville. Everyone else Zola had ever met or heard of lived long and happy and deeply fulfilling lives—that is, that was what she had always believed everyone's lives were like, before she'd met Puck.

So of course, when she was a little girl, she'd become obsessive about asking questions about her father's death. What did it mean that he was dead? Where did he go? How could someone be alive one minute and dead the next? Didn't he love her? Didn't he want to stay with her always? Why did he go away?

Mom's answers had been inadequate and unsatisfying, and Sirilex's answers had been inadequate and unsatisfying, and so had the answers Zola got from the three different grief counselors she went to between the ages of four and seven. But their stories had always *matched*: Of course Zola's dad had loved her very, very much. He hadn't wanted to leave her, ever. It wasn't his choice at all. He had just had something wrong with his lungs that nobody realized until it was too late. Even with the amazing medical care available in the 2100s, sometimes things like that still happened. It was nobody's fault. But Zola shouldn't worry about anyone else she loved dying like that—or even herself—because Zola's lungs and Mom's lungs and the lungs of everybody else she loved were perfectly fine.

How could Mom have ever told me all that with a straight face if anyone ever thought that Dad was actually murdered? Zola thought.

How could Mom have told Zola anything about 2193 or the amazing technology of Insta-Closets and Insta-Ovens or any other supposedly perfect detail of their lives when *none* of it was true?

It wasn't helping Zola to prop her forehead against the bookshelf. Her head kept spinning. She burrowed under the quilt on the floor, wrapping it around her shoulders as if she could hide from all the questions crowding her mind. The underside of one of the quilt's corners felt strangely rough, so Zola flipped it over. There were tiny words sewn— or would it be called "embroidered"?—into that corner, in stiff, dark thread.

Made by Hannah Keyser, they said. **Finished Feb 28, 1840.**

More proof that Mom grew up in Clifton Village, Zola thought dully. *Not that I need it.*

What she wanted now wasn't proof anymore. She wanted *explanations*. Reasons. She wanted things to make sense.

And she wanted to know what she was supposed to *do*.

Impatiently, she kicked out her legs, knocking the wobbly wooden bucket against the crooked metal pot. They clanged together like a mallet hitting a gong, and Zola was grateful that Insta-Closets were always soundproofed.

Or are they? she thought suddenly.

What if that was just another lie she'd been told?

Nervously, she glanced at the door that led out into Mom's bedroom. For the first time, she noticed that the door was ever so slightly ajar. Maybe it had been like that all along. Maybe Zola had accidentally opened it, just a crack, when she'd touched the doorknob earlier, when she'd longed to run to Mom for comfort.

Zola threw the quilt off her shoulders and scrambled to her feet. She needed to get out of here before Mom came to investigate.

But what if Mom or Puck or . . . or some Technologist makes it so I can never get back in here again? Zola thought. *What if Mom throws away all this . . . proof . . . so she can keep pretending it's 2193 and everything is fine?*

She grabbed the scrapbook and newspaper clipping. She also snatched up the framed picture of her parents in the strange, old-fashioned clothes.

But, no, Mom would notice right away if that was missing, Zola thought.

She put down the picture and seized her father's letter to her mother instead.

And then the door of Mom's Insta-Closet opened.

"Ohhh . . ."

Mom's voice.

But it wasn't Mom's usual voice—confident and competent and certain. Mom sounded more like Zola when Zola's emotions were soaring out of control, when she was too angry or anguished or anxious to know what to do.

Zola whirled around. In a flash, Mom stepped into the Insta-Closet with Zola and whipped the door shut behind her.

"What you're seeing here—I can explain," Mom said. Her voice was too bright now; her smile, too tense and fake. "I . . .

I could say I'm working on an art installation about life in Indiana through the ages, and . . ."

"But that's not true," Zola snarled. "Mom, quit lying to me. I know everything."

Mom's face changed as quickly as if she'd completely dropped her mask, once and for all. The corners of her mouth quivered. Her eyes flooded with tears as she seemed to take in every detail about Zola: the scrapbook clutched to her chest, the letter grasped in her hand.

"Oh, honey," Mom said. "I don't know how much you know. But whatever it is—it's not enough."

She took two steps forward, ending the distance between her and Zola. And then she wrapped her arms around Zola's shoulders, enclosing Zola in a giant hug.

And Zola let her.

18

Mom and Zola sat down together on the floor of the Insta-Closet. Both of them burrowed under the quilt from 1840. (Or, well, fake 1840. From the time period when Mom had *believed* she was living in 1840.) Zola leaned her head on Mom's shoulder now; Mom kept her arm around Zola's waist.

And Mom stroked Zola's hair, just like she used to when Zola was little.

Zola felt about four years old.

"I know you found the book I left for you about Jessie," Mom murmured soothingly. "Did you have a chance to read it?"

"Not the whole thing," Zola admitted. "But a lot. I know about Clifton Village. I know about the diphtheria. And about Jessie . . . your sister . . . going for help."

Mom nodded, accepting this. Agreeing that she'd wanted Zola to know those things.

"And now you've seen . . . these mementos of mine," she said with a wave of her hand that seemed to indicate everything from the butter churn to the photos. "Your father made that metal pot and wooden bucket. I made the quilt. By hand. It's probably hard for you to understand, when you can have any item you want, anytime you want, but . . . these were treasures to us. Precious."

Zola was enjoying feeling all safe and cozy and little-kid-ish. She didn't want to think about anything sad or dangerous right now. Anyhow, she couldn't bring up her father's death when Mom had such a wistful, longing expression on her face.

But it annoyed her that Mom acted like those "treasures" mattered so much.

Is that why Mom told me so many lies? Zola thought. *Just to hide all of this?*

Who, exactly, had Mom been hiding her "treasures" from?

"You could have told me *I* was being raised in a 'different time' village, too," Zola said. She couldn't keep the bitterness from her voice.

Mom lowered her head as if she was ashamed. As if she thought she deserved Zola's anger.

This was not how she usually acted.

"I'm sorry," Mom said. "It became too dangerous to tell." She gave a harsh laugh. "I know, I know. I should have learned from history. From my parents' experiences, and the way they weren't allowed to tell *me* the truth. Me or Jessie or Katie, or our brothers, either . . ."

"How could you have—" Zola began.

But at the same time, Mom was asking, "Does it bother you? Knowing you're always being watched?"

Zola recoiled. That was what Puck had started talking about, right before he yelled, "Run!"

"Weren't you paying attention, all those times I complained about Sirilex and the mood sensors and the security cameras?" Zola asked. She picked at a loose thread in the quilt. Was it safe to mention Puck and what he'd told her? "Didn't *that* tip you off that I hate being watched?"

Mom winced. Maybe Zola was getting better at reading her mother's face—or maybe Mom had completely given up on trying to hide her emotions.

That was definitely guilt in Mom's eyes.

"I heard you," Mom said. "I *did* listen. I just couldn't tell you the truth. I didn't *want* to keep saying that Sirilex and the mood sensors and the security cameras were good for you. But I couldn't tell you that you were also being watched by tourists. By people who wanted to know what their future would be like. Er—*could* be like."

"They don't see any more than Sirilex can, right?" Zola asked, her voice gone wobbly.

"No . . . ," Mom began. "The tourists aren't supposed to be able to see into the Insta-Closets, while we're changing. Or any bathroom, once the door is shut. The Futurevilles organizers kept *that* promise at least. As . . . as far as I know."

Zola couldn't let herself think about what other promises might have been broken.

"But these 'tourists' have been watching you and me everywhere else?" Zola asked. "Out on the street? At school? At *home*?"

"Yes," Mom said. She looked down at the quilt, too. "I'm sorry."

It *was* worse to think of strangers watching Zola, rather than just Sirilex and mood sensors and security cameras always being on the alert. Sirilex, after all, was just a highly advanced artificial intelligence. And it was supposedly only AI monitoring the mood sensors and the security tapes. Strangers would be real live human beings. Human beings who might make fun of her. Or who might decide that she was stupid or awkward or pitiful—when Zola hadn't even known they were watching.

"If it makes you feel any better," Mom said gently, "I'm sure most of the people watching you are jealous. Because they wish they had your life. Everybody in the twenty-first century would want their own Insta-Closets and Insta-Ovens. They want clean air and no climate change and no worries and—"

"But I don't really 'have' those things—I just think I do, right?" Zola challenged. "What if that's not the *real* future for the tourists, either?"

Something had flipped, with Mom telling her once again how great her life was. Zola no longer felt safe and cozy and protected, nestled against her mother's side, huddled under the quilt. Now she felt itchy and impatient and irked. And the quilt felt like just another blanket of lies, holding her down.

If Mom had lied to her so much before, how could Zola be sure that Mom wasn't still lying now?

"Mom, I know there are two Futurevilles," Zola said. "I saw the other version. The bad one. With my own eyes."

Mom gasped. The color drained from her face.

"How . . . ?" she whispered. Then she gritted her teeth and pulled Zola closer, as if she was trying to protect her even more. "Those Technologists," Mom snarled, glaring up at her Insta-Closet mirror as if her worst enemies were standing there. "The new Insta-Closet they installed for you . . . they gave you access, didn't they?"

Zola shoved away from Mom.

"How do you think I got into *your* Insta-Closet?" Zola asked.

"Oh, right. . . ." Mom grimaced. "I thought you just tip-toed through my bedroom when I was sleeping, but . . . you must have gone *between* the Insta-Closets. I see. You can do that now. They must have changed the biometric settings on your Insta-Closet mirror, to allow you access. And before you came to my Insta-Closet, you tiptoed down the stairs and . . . you only peeked out at the other Futureville, right? No one saw you there, did they? And then I guess you must have gotten scared and run right back here, and . . ."

It felt like Mom was begging Zola to lie to *her*.

"What would it matter if anyone saw me?" Zola asked. "And why are you mad at the Technologists for helping me? It's not like *you* ever gave me enough answers!"

Mom reached for Zola again, but Zola dodged her arms. Mom let her hands flutter down helplessly to rest on the quilt. When Mom looked at Zola again, her eyes were burning.

"Zola, you've been able to grow up believing that the world around you is a safe and welcoming and entirely friendly place," Mom said. "I *wanted* that for you. I wanted to spare you all the pain and fear and confusion I saw around me, once I left Clifton Village. No, it's more than that—all the pain and fear and confusion I *felt*, from age fourteen on. But with all the other mistakes I made, I'm afraid I might have left you . . . defenseless. Too innocent. Too trusting. When the Technologists showed up yesterday to install your new closet, I didn't know which side they were on. I still don't know if their intentions were good or bad. But, either way, if there are people trying to involve you in some, I don't know—would you call it a rescue attempt? Either way, that puts you in danger. And you don't know enough to navigate that danger. *I* don't know enough to figure out what to do, myself!"

Maybe this was supposed to be a confession: Mom explaining why she'd brought Zola to yet another artificial tourist village with people watching, even after seeing how badly that went in her own childhood; Mom explaining how she'd made the same kind of mistake as her own parents. Thinking she'd signed up for one kind of life for her offspring, and getting something entirely different.

But to Zola, it felt like Mom was saying she didn't trust Zola.

Like Mom thought that, because Zola had grown up believing it was the twenty-second century, and everything was perfect—she'd believed that until this very night, anyway—Zola couldn't cope with reality.

Zola would never be able to rescue Puck from danger.

And Zola would never be able to rescue herself.

Or even find out the truth about her father's death.

Zola shoved the quilt off her legs and stood up.

"Maybe I should just go back to the other Futureville," she threatened. "Maybe I *have* to see things with my own eyes, to know what's true and what isn't. Maybe that's the only way I'm ever going to find out anything."

"Zola, you don't know what you're talking about." Mom's eyes swam with tears. Her voice turned frantic. "I couldn't bear it if I lost you . . . if . . ."

She didn't say, "if I lost you, *too*," but Zola jolted, as if she'd heard the unspoken extra word. It should have made Zola more cautious, to remember that Mom had lost Dad; that Zola was all Mom had left.

But right now, it just made Zola angry.

"Right, we've established that I don't know enough—and that you don't, either," Zola said, not even trying to soften her words. "So maybe you're honestly trying to explain things to me now, but how can either of us know that you're really telling me the truth? What if what you're telling me now is just more lies?"

For a moment, Mom just stared up at Zola. It felt like punishment now, to look into Mom's eyes—Zola could see the full load of pain and fear in Mom's gaze. Mom didn't seem to be trying to hide any of it.

But then Mom turned and began digging out something from behind the lowest row of old-fashioned books. Maybe Zola's eyes were a little misty, too; she could barely see to track Mom's movements. Zola blinked once or twice, and then Mom was kneeling before her, pressing something into Zola's hands.

"*This* is how you'll find out that everything I'm telling you is true," Mom said. "This is how you can see for yourself what's really going on. And, if you're careful, you can do it safely."

Zola looked down. A rubbery headband dangled from her fingers. A rubbery, rectangular pair of eyepieces lay in the palm of her hand, bridged by an equally rubbery nosepiece.

"VR goggles?" Zola asked incredulously. "Have you forgotten that the 'V' stands for 'virtual'? They won't show me *anything* real!"

"They're not just VR goggles," Mom said. "Or, they began that way, but then I used them in an 'art project.' . . ." She giggled, a little nervously. "They'll *look* like ordinary VR goggles to everyone around you. But what you can see through them will be all too real!"

19

"How could that be?" Zola challenged. "Technologists are the only ones who—"

"Artists have to understand how things work, too," Mom said softly. "I pretended I was only doing research for the sake of my art, but . . . look."

Mom put her fingernail in a crack at the bottom of the goggles' eyepiece and pried it open. Now the eyepiece section lay in two halves, showing only emptiness where there should have been internal circuitry.

Zola changed her question.

"But why . . . ?"

"Same as you," Mom said. "I wanted to see what was real."

Zola felt a little glow—she and Mom were alike! It felt like they were a team now, not on opposite sides.

"I needed to see all the ways we were living in a prison, not a paradise," Mom added bitterly.

Zola gulped.

"But what if someone . . . notices?" she asked. "What if I walk right through the middle of someone's avatar, and they complain, and I don't hear them, and . . ."

It wasn't that it would be illegal to go around outside her house without a working pair of VR goggles. It was just that no one ever *would*. It would be like walking around naked. Or, no—like walking blindfolded, without being able to hear or smell or taste or touch, either.

It would feel like being a ghost.

Or like being in the bad Futureville . . .

Zola's stomach churned. But Mom touched a small switch on the side of the goggles. Instantly, the normal circuitry slid down out of the goggles' casing, locking into place.

"They can go back to VR mode whenever you want," Mom said, holding the goggles up to Zola's eyes. Zola peered straight through them, and all of Mom's "treasures" disappeared. Instead of seeing a bookshelf and old pictures and a butter churn, Zola saw nothing but the bland wooden wall of Mom's Insta-Closet. Mom hit the switch on the goggles again, and Mom's treasures were back.

"So I wouldn't have seen any of this if I'd come in here wearing normal VR goggles?" Zola marveled, gesturing at all Mom's treasures.

"Zola, there's a lot the VR goggles have always hidden

from you," Mom warned.

She sounded grim, but it made Zola bounce up and down on her heels.

"I want to go out and try these right now!" Zola said.

"Zola, it's the middle of the night!" Mom exclaimed, almost laughing now. "There's nothing out there *to* see right now!"

But just then the Insta-Closet rocked a little bit, side to side. The lights around the mirror flashed.

"Oh, wait—what time is it?" Mom asked. She reached behind the row of books again, and pulled out what looked like a heavy gold locket on a short chain. She touched a knob, and the front panel of the locket—or whatever it was—sprang open. "This was your father's pocket watch," she murmured. "When we were children, that was a sign of wealth and manhood, for a boy to be given his first pocket watch, and . . ."

Zola peered over her mother's shoulder, at something she vaguely recognized as an old-fashioned clock face.

"It was a sign of wealth and 'manhood,' and it wasn't even digital?" Zola asked.

But Mom had evidently made more sense of the numbers on the clock face than Zola had. She was gasping again.

"We've been talking a lot longer than I thought!" she exclaimed. "It's almost time for the show to begin again!"

"The . . . show?" Zola asked.

"That's what I call everything we do for the tourists'

benefit," Mom said, rolling her eyes in a way Zola could appreciate. "Look, especially if you want to try out those goggles today, we have to make extra sure we don't tip anyone off that there's anything going on. . . ."

Mom began giving directions, and for once, Zola accepted them without question.

She scrambled back through the mirror of Mom's Insta-Closet and back into her own Insta-Closet without even pausing on the platform in between.

Later, she told herself. *Later I can come back and explore more . . . when I know more and can be braver.*

She didn't pause in her own Insta-Closet, either. Instead, she walked straight through, into her own bedroom.

Then, as Mom had directed, Zola yawned and stretched dramatically.

"I can't believe I fell asleep in my Insta-Closet!" she exclaimed, trying to sound embarrassed and annoyed and groggy, not excited and jangly-nerved and much too alert. She tilted her head side to side. "Ugh, now I've got a stiff neck, too."

"Perhaps you will learn next time not to leave your bed in the middle of the night," Sirilex replied, as smug as ever. "Shall I do a medical scan, to see if you require treatment for that stiff neck?"

"I'll be fine," Zola muttered, making a scornful face. For once she was almost grateful that Sirilex was so annoying—

it made acting her part easier.

Zola ordered clothes from her Insta-Closet, got dressed, and sat through the usual "show" with Mom over breakfast. This was different than usual, though, because it felt like they were partners now—it wasn't just Mom saying, "Look how wonderful the Insta-Oven is; look how wonderful our lives are in 2193," and Zola growling back because that was *so* annoying to hear first thing in the morning. Now it was Mom saying her lines and Zola understanding that they were just lines, but still having to make her own replies typical, too.

Mom kept her gaze steady on Zola's face the whole time. Mom said, "Look! Your waffle appeared in no time at all!" and it felt like Mom was really pleading, "Can't you see how I was fooled? Can't you see why I thought this would be a good life for us? Can you forgive me?"

And even as Zola answered begrudgingly, "This waffle is yum," she hoped Mom could see in her eyes what she was really thinking: *It does help to have some of my questions answered. But don't you see why this always felt so weird to me, when I didn't know anything?*

Don't you see why I have to find more answers?

And why I want to help Puck and everyone else in his Futureville?

Finally it was time for the morning walk before school—outdoors, this time. When Sirilex started to give the weather report, Mom interrupted firmly, "You know, if Zola believes she can tolerate a cool and windy walk, we should let her

128

learn for herself if that's true."

Seriously, Mom? Zola thought. *Couldn't you have said something like that yesterday?*

"Oh, wait—I ordered new VR goggles for you, because I noticed your strap was sagging," Mom said, pulling the "new" pair for Zola from the pocket of her cardigan sweater. She began fitting the goggles over Zola's head, and pulled them into position.

Mom's eyes telegraphed the message, *You know these are the goggles that I tinkered with, but you'll have to pretend there's nothing different. Please—be careful! Don't react! Don't put yourself into any danger!*

"Mo-om!" Zola made herself complain. "My old goggles were fine! New goggles are always too tight at the beginning, and—"

And then Mom opened the front door.

Zola stared out eagerly. At first, the scene before her was just like yesterday's: the flowers and trees of Zola and Mom's front yard, curving sidewalks, a newly paved street, the flowers and trees of their neighbors' yards.

Mom reached out and pretended just to be adjusting the strap. But she must have flicked the switch to "real reality." Because suddenly a huge crowd of people appeared in the street: people of all ages and shapes and sizes and skin tones, all staring with undisguised curiosity at Zola and Mom.

And they were *loud*: kids shouting, "What's happening at this house?" and a man with a bullhorn chiding, "Settle down, and I'll tell you!" and someone who must be a teacher hissing, "Sshh!"

Zola's jaw dropped.

"Wh—Where—?" she began, forgetting that she *couldn't* ask where the crowd had come from, or why she hadn't been able to see or hear them before.

Mom laughed, loudly enough to cover anything else Zola might say.

"Oh, *now* you appreciate the higher-quality polarization of light with those new goggles? And the way their noise-canceling technology is just as good as the system in our house?" she teased—or, really, *pretended* to tease. In reality, Zola needed to translate Mom's words in her head to figure out what she actually meant: *Remember what I told you? Remember how I said you'd be surprised to lose the noise-canceling aspect of VR, too? You have to keep pretending that you* don't *see or hear those people. Got it?*

"I . . . I guess you're right," Zola said grudgingly. "I did need new goggles."

"Ah, my first win of the day!" Mom sounded way too amused. "I'll take it. Now, here you go—off to school!"

She gave Zola a kiss on her forehead and a little shove on the back.

"Route?" Sirilex asked, as usual.

But the voice came from behind her, from her house, rather than from the earpiece of her goggles.

That's probably for the tourists' benefit, Zola realized. *So they see and hear me communicating with my goggles.*

It wouldn't matter what walking route scene Zola ordered. Even if she said Antarctica during the Shackleton expedition or South Africa during the fight against apartheid—or a peaceful stroll on the beach—these goggles wouldn't show her anything virtual as long as she left them on the real reality setting. But it might be a *little* easier to control her reactions if the route she pretended to order was similar to what she was really going to see.

"You know, I'd like to go with the streets of my own town again," she announced, for Sirilex's benefit. "It'll help with my next social studies project."

"You don't have any upcoming social studies projects in the next few weeks," Sirilex said, sounding as suspicious as a digital voice possibly could.

"I know," Zola said. "I'm thinking ahead. Could you load the images, please?"

She paused, as if giving Sirilex time to do her bidding. She pretended to hear the soft whirring noise that signaled a download.

And then she stepped outside, and shut the door behind her.

20

Outside was . . . different.

The cluster of tourists Zola had seen from the doorway had moved on to the next house, and Zola was glad that that gave her a few moments to adjust.

Just like yesterday—when she'd seen her town only through VR, while walking on a treadmill—Zola could see trees and grass and flowers and pavement and houses. But today, nothing sparkled in her view through the real reality goggles. Nothing gleamed. Some of the flowers—tulips? Daffodils?—were flopped over on the ground, as if they'd given up. The yard next door had a large dead patch in the grass, and an unsightly heap of twisted wires and some kind of mechanical motor on a concrete pad at the corner.

Oh, yeah, Zola thought. *Because it's not actually 2193 and we don't actually have Perfect Tech, where things like heating and cooling units are so small and unobtrusive that I don't even notice them. Or they were always just disguised by the VR. . . .*

Even the sky overhead was flat and gray, not crystalline blue.

Then Zola was hit in the face with a spray of water.

"Sirilex!" Zola hissed. She opened her mouth wide, ready to scold, "How could you have forgotten to provide an umbrella? It's raining now, and I'm not protected!"

Just in time, Zola remembered: she and Mom had specifically stopped Sirilex's weather report. And any ongoing monitoring would have come through her VR goggles. But she was only seeing and hearing and feeling reality now—she just had to pretend she had VR.

So she really needed to pretend that she didn't *mind* being hit with a face-full of rain.

"Never mind, Sirilex," she muttered.

Sirilex didn't reply.

Oh, right—once I shut the door, I broke the connection with Sirilex. Without VR, I'm not linked to Sirilex here any more than I was in the tunnel or by the other Futureville.

Zola was standing right in front of her own house—the house she'd lived in for as long as she could remember. But she felt like an astronaut floating in outer space, completely lost. Completely unmoored.

"Zola!" This was a whisper from behind her. Mom's voice.

Mom had opened the door again, just a crack. "Do you need extra help? Are you too tired to go to school after getting such a bad night's sleep?"

Zola shook herself off. If she went back, Mom might never let her try the real reality goggles again. Mom—and probably Sirilex, too—would find a reason to tuck her back into bed and keep her protected and safe (and bored and ignorant and useless) forever.

"I'm fine," Zola announced, loud enough that the Sirilex connection from inside the house could hear, too. "Just taking a moment to appreciate this beautiful spring day. Nothing wrong with that, is there?"

She widened her eyes, pretending to see blue skies and gleaming solar panels and pert daisies and daffodils, stretching up toward the sun. And then she turned decisively toward the walk to school.

The rain isn't too bad, she told herself. *It's really only mist. At least the goggles keep it out of my eyes. . . .*

She tried to keep her pace steady and relaxed, like any normal morning walk. But she quickly caught up with the cluster of tourists still lollygagging in front of the neighbors' house.

"Yes, yes, step out of the way, everyone."

Zola heard the words beside her, and it took all the willpower she'd ever possessed not to whip her head to the right and gawk at all the people now gawking at her. If she'd had normal goggles on, they would have included noise-canceling

134

earbuds that made her believe she was only hearing the chirping of birds, or whatever sound effects went along with the VR.

It also took a lot of willpower to keep walking in a straight line, even as a blond-haired girl in jeans and a T-shirt barely managed to scramble from the sidewalk to the street in time.

"She doesn't even see me!" the girl exclaimed, and Zola felt proud of her acting abilities.

"She wouldn't see you, regardless." This was the official-sounding voice again—undoubtedly the tour guide. "But odds are, this typical twenty-second-century child is viewing an educational route even on her way to school. Even if she looks directly at you, what she's seeing would be a scene along the Nile or ancient trade routes in the Mojave or the glorious plumage on some bird in the Amazon. . . ."

That was like giving Zola permission to look directly at the tourists, wasn't it?

Zola stopped, turned her head, and pretended to gaze at some random Amazonian parrot. She cocked her head, as if listening for birdsong.

The girl who'd stepped out of Zola's way giggled. A dark-haired girl beside her muttered, "Is it fair for us to stare at her if she doesn't even know we're here?"

Zola decided she liked *that* girl.

"Oh, think of the people here as celebrities," the tour guide said airily. "They know they're being watched, even if they don't see us."

The tour guide was an older man with a shiny white bald head and an official-looking suit jacket with an insignia that said, "Futurevilles' Finest" on the pocket. Zola *really* wanted to glare at him and shout, "That's a lie! It's only the adults here who know they're being watched! The kids like me— none of us ever knew anything!"

But Zola kept her expression bland.

No, go with awestruck, she reminded herself. *These people think you're seeing some amazing Amazon wildlife.*

She studied the tourists, but pretended she was studying exotic birds.

About half of the tour group seemed to be kids on some sort of school trip—there was even a cluster near the front that reminded her of herself and Beatriz and Amir and Eromi, half listening to the tour guide and half whispering together under their breath. The tourist kids' clothes didn't quite achieve the same range of dressy to faux-battered that Zola might have seen in her own classroom; it looked more as though they were wearing uniforms of jeans and T-shirts and hoodies.

Behind the schoolkids, the other tourists included older people in capri-length shorts and what seemed to be Hawaiian shirts—were they retirees on vacation?

"See, Murray, we should install solar panels—it's the wave of the future," Zola heard one of the women exclaim to her partner.

"Enh, Carol, we're not going to live long enough to see this future," the man replied grumpily.

Like everyone else in the tour group, both the man and the woman were wearing goggles. Zola remembered Mom telling her that the tourists' goggles made everything look shinier and more exciting—just like the VR goggles that Zola had always worn before. But their goggles seemed a little retro—and they all had the word "TOURIST" stamped on the straps.

Zola wished she could see *exactly* what the tourists were seeing. She also tried not to stare jealously at the umbrellas many of the tourists carried.

"Does that girl realize it's raining?" a boy asked anxiously as he flipped his own sweatshirt hood over his head. "Does she feel the mist on her face, or—"

"She probably thinks it's rainforest mist," the tour guide said. "Some kind of all-around virtual sensation. Or, who knows, maybe she thinks she's walking alongside Niagara Falls. Want to find out? Remember how I told you in my introduction that if you stood close enough to any of the Futurevilles residents, you can view the same scene they're seeing through their VR goggles?"

Wait—what? Zola thought.

The boy nodded and started walking toward her.

"It should start when you're one foot away," the tour guide added. "And then if you push the 'echo' setting on your goggles, we can all see what you're accessing."

What was Zola supposed to do now?

The boy was getting closer and closer.

Then Zola knew what to do.

"Oh no!" Zola exclaimed loudly, as if responding to a Sir-ilex voice in her earbud. "Why didn't you remind me earlier? Now I'm going to be late for school if I don't run!"

She treated the sidewalk like a starting block and took off sprinting her fastest.

"Bye, birds!" she called over her shoulder, using that as an excuse to look back.

None of the tourists were following her.

To keep up the pretense, Zola kept running even after that cluster of tourists was out of sight. She darted past one group of tourists after another. It almost made her giggle to see them scramble out of her way. She veered close enough to some that, without the usual noise-canceling earbuds, she caught bits and pieces of several tour guide spiels:

". . . and this is their city hall where, as with every level of government, they've perfected the combination of being perfectly efficient and perfectly humane . . ."

". . . over there, you'll see their public transportation depot, which accommodates the needs of everyone in town . . ."

". . . yes, that *looks* like an art museum, but it's actually a retail outlet where town residents can purchase masterpieces for their home from all over the world . . . Well, yes, they'd just be digital reproductions, but even a trained expert could hardly see the difference. . . ."

Finally, Zola reached the school. Without the glow of the VR effect, it seemed a little run-down, its limestone walls a dull gray against the duller gray sky. But it still seemed to have attracted more tourists than Zola had seen anywhere else. And they all seemed to be school tour groups, all swarming on the school steps. Since Zola had to slow down for the bottleneck of everyone going into the building together, she was able to hear a tour guide's entire description of what the tourists would see.

"This is the only location in this Futureville where you're allowed to interact with the residents," this tour guide explained breathlessly. She was a heavily made-up woman about the same age as Mom. Zola could see the kids around her rolling their eyes at the woman's enthusiasm.

"How do you explain *that* if this whole place is supposed to be 'exactly what the future could look like, if we do our part now'?" a particularly snarky-sounding boy asked. Even Zola could tell he was quoting some motto. "In schools in the future, will kids from the past show up to ask questions? What do you tell the kids here about strangers just appearing out of nowhere?"

"Excellent questions!" the tour guide said with a totally fake smile. "Remember, these kids know this is a tourist attraction and they're being watched. . . ."

Zola wanted to scream, "That's a lie! My friends and I were never told any of that!" But she gritted her teeth and swallowed hard.

You can't let on that you see them, she told herself. *You can't let on that you hear them. You can't give away that you're wearing real reality goggles. Not unless you want to be caught, and get yourself and Mom both in trouble.*

"Anyhow," the tour guide continued, "in your interaction with the Futurevilles schoolchildren, they'll see you as avatars joining virtually from around the globe, not visitors from another time."

Visitors . . . , Zola thought vaguely. Then she jerked to attention. So *that* was who the Visitors were, who showed up in her classroom on Visitors' Day. No wonder they always seemed so odd!

"Yeah, but what if *she* decides to be a troublemaker?" the snarky boy asked, pointing to a shy-looking girl that even Zola could tell would be voted "Least Likely to Make Trouble" at any school. "What if Amelia starts asking questions like, 'Don't you know it's not really the future? Are you trapped here? Doesn't all this being perfect all the time make you want to play a prank on the teacher, like hiding the Smartboard remote or—'"

"Bryson!" another woman standing nearby scolded the boy. "This is your last warning. If you can't be respectful, I will personally escort you out of this park and you will sit on the bus until the rest of us are finished!"

Zola felt kind of sorry for Bryson. Maybe some of the other kids did, too, because a few of them surrounded Bryson and muttered, "Don't talk back!" "Don't make the chaperone mad again!"

But Zola also felt sorry for Amelia, whose face had flushed bright red. Nobody surrounded her to advise: "Ignore Bryson! Yes, he's acting immature, but that's on him, not you!"

Why weren't the adults offering a lesson about how impulse control isn't fully developed in preteens, so you have to be understanding and forgiving of your own failings and those of others as well, and . . .

And, okay, I never listen all the way to the end of that particular lesson, Zola thought. *But maybe it would help Bryson and Amelia?*

The tour guide shifted uncomfortably on her feet.

"No worries!" she said, too brightly. "Since the children in the classroom you'll visit will see you only as avatars, we've allowed for a time lag on all interactions. So any inappropriate questions will be filtered out—the schoolkids here will never hear them."

Well, that explains why the Visitors always seem so slow and jerky, Zola thought.

She was at the doorway to the school now, the last Futureville child in, since she'd been dawdling to hear the conversation in the Bryson and Amelia group.

"Oh, here, we'll just follow this child," the tour guide said behind her. "Don't worry—she'll be totally unaware of our presence until we're actually in her classroom."

Zola barely managed to keep herself from looking back over her shoulder and smirking.

Act normal, act normal, act normal . . . , she told herself.

She braced herself for entering the classroom and seeing it totally empty. That's how it would have to look since her classmates—and the teacher—were from all around the world, and only present virtually, as avatars themselves.

This is where I could totally give myself away, Zola thought, panicking. *How can I act normal when I can't see anyone around me? When I'm going to make it look like I'm walking right through people—and not answering my friends when they talk to me?*

She'd have to use the VR again. She'd need that to hear whatever her teacher and classmates might say and do.

Zola flipped the switch on the goggles just as she stepped into her classroom. What a relief! There were all her classmates milling around—their avatars, anyway. The classroom looked as it always did in VR: as if kids from every continent were meeting in cyberspace, all their shiny technology glowing around them.

Zola went over to stand by her friend Beatriz, who was resplendent today in a traditional Bolivian skirt and a blouse threaded through with green and red and blue ribbons along the neckline.

"I was starting to worry you might be absent!" Beatriz gushed. "I'm so glad you made it before the bell!"

"Me, too!" Zola agreed, with a relieved laugh.

The laugh would be a good way to cover her actions if she switched back into real reality mode for an instant, wouldn't it?

Zola lifted her hand, pretending she needed to scratch her forehead. She hit the switch on the goggles. And then, because she couldn't quite believe what she was seeing, she actually shoved the goggles completely above her eyes, so they covered her eyebrows instead.

It didn't matter. She still had trouble trusting what she saw. Her eyes still presented her with an impossible-to-believe situation:

Beatriz hadn't disappeared. Beatriz wasn't all the way away in Bolivia, beaming in to Zola's classroom every day as an incredibly clear avatar, thanks to futuristic technology.

Whether Zola saw her in VR or with her own bare eyes, one fact didn't change:

Beatriz was standing right in front of her.

21

So for our entire friendship—all the years we've been together in school—Beatriz must have been right here in my own town, not thousands and thousands of miles away? Zola wondered. *We could have been inches away from each other most days?*

There were other kids around her, too, but for the moment, Zola could only focus on Beatriz.

For the first time since walking out her door that morning, Zola was *furious*.

All along, we could have been talking and playing together, face-to-face? Zola thought. *Beatriz could have come over to my house after school? We could have had sleepovers together, and whispered secrets late into the night, just like kids used to do in the old days?*

Zola hadn't even realized that was something she'd been longing for.

"Beatriz!" she called. "Look at me for real! Please!"

Beatriz just kept smiling blankly.

She can't even hear me now, Zola thought. *Because of the noise-canceling function of the earbuds on her goggles. Because I'm* not *speaking through VR.*

This was unbearable. Being face-to-face with her best friend and not able to communicate was worse than thinking they were thousands of miles apart, and speaking only through VR.

Zola reached out, ready to yank the goggles from Beatriz's face. Ready to make her friend see real reality, too.

But at the last minute, she stopped.

"People's lives might depend on it," Zola thought. That's what Mom had said the day before, when she was afraid Zola might make a scene about the note in her Insta-Closet. And that was when they were at home, just by themselves.

Now Zola was at school—in front of the strange, unpredictable tourists. What if Zola did something that endangered Beatriz?

Nobody *ever* took their goggles off in public. Nobody ever touched anybody else's goggles.

Zola buried her face in her hands. This was too distressing, too confusing.

"What's that girl doing now?" someone asked behind her. One of the tourists.

Zola had to think fast.

"Oh, these new goggles!" she exclaimed. She remembered a line she'd heard in history VRs about early twenty-first-century games. "I need to reset the VR boundaries."

Quickly, she pulled the goggles back over her eyes, and waved her arms a few times, turning slowly in all directions for good measure.

But she still had the goggles on the real reality setting, so she could still hear the tourists and tour guide behind her.

"Let me explain what you're seeing," the tour guide was saying. "In the future, kids will be grouped together in school not by geographic locations but by their educational needs and personal learning styles. This classroom brings together children from all around the globe, who all benefit from being together. In a sense, you could say they *are* each other's global studies teachers."

Not true, Zola thought. *Not exactly . . .*

But she managed not to say that out loud.

Bryson, the kid who'd been so snarky before, wasn't so good at staying silent.

"So, what, you've got Futurevilles all over the world?" Bryson asked. "Dang, why didn't our school spring for a field trip to the one in the Caribbean? A little beach time, a little—"

"Bryson!" the chaperone hissed. Her face flushed. "No interrupting! That's—"

"It's okay," the tour guide said quickly. "He's helping me introduce my next point."

She kept a tight smile on her face.

"Our friend here with the inquiring mind"—the tour guide gestured toward Bryson—"probably already knows that right here in Indiana is the only place you can see a Futureville. Maybe someday we will have Futurevilles all over the planet. Wouldn't that be wonderful? But we can still get the feel of the global classroom of the future right now. For the most part, as tour guide, I don't want to ruin the illusion that you have stepped into the future by telling you how we 'work our magic,' as it were. But I do want to tamp down any further unnecessary questions." She fixed Bryson with a stern gaze. "It's true that all the kids in the classroom actually live right here in this Futureville. I mean, in reality, these kids are neighbors. After hours, when all the tourists have left, of course the kids get together. In person. Their lives outside of school are probably not that different from yours. But isn't it gracious of these children to depict the world of the future every day for kids like you?"

Now it took every ounce of self-control Zola possessed not to scream out, "That's a lie! I never get to see my friends except virtually! We're *never* truly face-to-face! At least, not without *thinking* that we're hundreds or thousands of miles apart . . ."

She couldn't listen to any more lies from this tour guide right now. She took a step forward, bringing her closer to Beatriz, who looked confused.

What had Zola missed in the conversation with Beatriz?

Zola flipped back into VR just in time to hear Beatriz say, "Hello? Zola, did you walk to school in your sleep today? And you're still sleeping?"

Maybe the VR had made it look like Zola was just standing there, doing nothing.

"Got a lot on my mind today," Zola muttered. "Sorry. What were you saying?"

"I was just telling you how beautiful the sunrise over the Andes looked today," Beatriz said.

"Yeah, I've seen that in VR," Zola said wistfully. "But someday it would be cool to see it for real. Don't you think?"

Wouldn't that be like an invitation for Beatriz to admit that she didn't actually live any closer to the Andes than Zola did?

She didn't want to get Beatriz in trouble, but . . . Beatriz was her best friend! How could they keep lying to one another?

Good grief, Zola thought. *Who knows where Beatriz has been told I actually live?*

She leaned her head closer than usual to Beatriz, because maybe they could just whisper back and forth; maybe they could bypass the VR. Zola pulled out the earbud from her left ear and raised the goggle from her left eye even as she kept everything in place on the right. That way, she could hear and see reality and VR all at once.

But that meant that she could hear her own voice coming out of Beatriz's VR earpieces. Only, Zola's words had been twisted and reshaped. Instead of "Someday it would be cool to see that for real," the words being fed into Beatriz's ears were, "We're so lucky to have VR show us everything. It's as good as being there for real."

Zola jerked back and stared—with *both* eyes—straight at Beatriz. And it was so odd. Zola's right eye, the one covered by a VR goggle, saw Beatriz's expression light up. Her right ear heard Beatriz giggle again and agree, "You're right. We are so lucky to live in 2193."

But Zola's left eye, the one that she'd uncovered, saw the corner of Beatriz's lips droop downward. How had Zola never noticed that Beatriz looked so lonely?

Zola had to strain to catch the actual words Beatriz spoke. Were they, "Yes, I wish we could meet for real someday"?

And it was in English, too, Zola thought. *Not Spanish or Quechua. We never needed Insta-Translators to speak to each other.*

It was so unfair how Zola and Beatriz had been kept apart and lied to. The VR even made it seem like they were lying to each other.

But it also made no sense. If the tourists were told the kids got together all the time—and they were only acting and pretending to need VR during school hours—why didn't that really happen?

Zola felt her heart lurch. She recognized the loneliness on Beatriz's face. Her own face probably looked the same a lot of the time.

Her *real* face, anyway.

Zola missed whatever Beatriz said next, both the fake and real words.

"Sorry," Zola apologized again. "I'm spacey today. Didn't get enough sleep last night."

But who could say what Beatriz actually heard? Zola didn't dare to dart her head close to Beatriz again. Not without calling attention to herself.

For a moment, Zola just stared at her friend—that wouldn't seem too weird, would it, since Zola had just said she was spacey? Zola was getting even better at looking around with both eyes, and still managing to separate the two views. In reality, Beatriz wasn't wearing a traditional Bolivian skirt and beribboned blouse. Her outfit *was* colorful, but the reds and blues and greens bled together more like an abstract painting than a traditional South American weaving. Her hair wasn't pulled into a thick braid over one shoulder, but was springing out in a torrent of curls that made Zola think of the difference between 1800s Clifton Village Jessie Keyser and the 1990s version.

At least when Jessie saw her Clifton Village friends with braids and calico dresses, that's truly what they wore, Zola thought ruefully. *At least she and her friends could whisper together for real.*

But they had also been infected with diphtheria. On purpose.

Zola held back a shiver, remembering Puck telling her that she was in danger, just like him.

But he didn't say anything about disease . . .

He hadn't had time to tell her exactly *what* danger she and her classmates were in.

Resolutely, Zola looked around, hoping to pick up on more clues in her classroom.

Off to the side, Amir and Eromi were actually wearing jeans and T-shirts that could have helped them blend into one of the Futureville tour groups, rather than anything representing their supposed lives in Egypt and Sri Lanka. And . . . they looked lonely, too.

But it's 2193, Zola thought automatically. *Everybody's happy all the time because . . .*

No. That wasn't true.

Zola had no idea what any of her friends were really thinking and feeling, because she only ever saw them in VR.

And the VR lied. All the time.

All of Zola's friends were actually strangers. She didn't know or understand them any better than she knew the odd tourist kids at the back of the room.

Her heart in her throat, Zola glanced back at the tourist kids again, to see what they had noticed. Who could say what the VR was showing them?

But no one in the tourist group was even watching Zola and her friends. They were circled around Amelia and Bryson and the chaperone. Clearly something had happened.

Zola inched a little closer to the tourists to hear better.

"But I didn't pull Amelia's hair!" Bryson was protesting.

"It just got caught on—"

"You were standing too close!" Amelia countered. She didn't look meek and mild anymore. She looked fierce.

"That's it, Bryson," the chaperone said, tugging on his arm, pulling him away from the other students. "I'm taking you out to the bus."

Zola heard everything in real time, but it took her brain a moment to catch up. The chaperone was behaving so oddly. Why wasn't she asking Sirilex for a replay of the scene from a moment before, so she could be sure she was treating both Amelia and Bryson fairly?

Oh, right, Zola thought. *Mom said the tourist goggles are different than ours—they don't have Sirilex.*

And the chaperone didn't even ask Bryson or Amelia or the other kids how the misunderstanding made each of them feel. That left the whole group to poke each other and whisper and point. It was hard to tell what anyone was learning from this experience.

No, no, don't focus on any of that right now, Zola told herself. *Think . . . think . . .*

The chaperone was taking Bryson out to the school bus.

The bus was apparently *outside* of the Futurevilles. Or, if it wasn't outside now, it would be driven out when the entire school group left.

What if I follow the chaperone and Bryson? Zola thought. *What if that's how I find a way out of the Futurevilles for myself?*

22

"Oh no!" Zola said aloud. She hadn't figured out her whole plan yet, but she thought that was a good start.

"What's wrong?" Beatriz asked. Her face wrinkled into a concerned squint that stayed the same whether Zola looked with her left or right eye.

"I, uh . . ." An excuse occurred to Zola like a gift from above. "I'm getting a low battery signal on my VR goggles, even though they're brand-new. Ugh, now nothing's working. Hold on. Let me go get a backup pair. . . ."

She dashed toward the classroom door, right behind Bryson and the chaperone. Hopefully Beatriz and all her other classmates—and the teacher, too—would just think that Zola would reappear once she'd replaced the battery. Of course, Beatriz and her other classmates also thought they were only together virtually, anyhow.

But who else would be paying attention to where I go and what I do? Zola wondered.

Automatically, she opened her mouth to ask, "Schoolilex, can you tell me . . ." She caught herself just in time.

"Schoolilex, I'm just going to run home to order another pair of goggles from my Insta-Closet," she muttered.

Would that work? *Was* anyone watching her besides the tourists and the AI framework that kept the entire town running?

She was out in the school hallway now, and nobody stopped her. There was no one in sight except Bryson and the chaperone, and they were already turning the corner ahead of her. Zola slowed her pace, so it wouldn't be obvious that she was following.

"Ha ha, why didn't I ever think of this before?" she muttered, just in case someone was listening. "What a great excuse to get out of class! I'll have to remember this the next time we have a test!"

That would help cover for her actions, wouldn't it? Especially if she followed Bryson and the chaperone in a different direction than back toward Zola's house?

She also didn't want anyone to notice that she was still wearing her goggles with one eyepiece shoved up over her eyebrow. So she yanked the goggles fully back into place, and set them completely to real reality mode.

Zola rushed around the corner just as the door out of the school building was swinging shut behind Bryson and the chaperone. Now she sped up, because there were so many directions they might go once they got out to the sidewalk. She hurled herself through the door behind them, and came close enough that she could hear Bryson whining, "Mo-om! You embarrassed me in front of my friends!"

He's calling her "Mom"? Zola thought. *The chaperone is Bryson's own mother?*

"And you embarrassed me," the chaperone said, jerking Bryson around to face her directly. "Look, I thought it'd be *fun* to chaperone your field trip. Do you act like this at school all the time?"

Zola missed hearing Bryson's reply, because she was so stunned. She stopped in her tracks.

A mother would tell her own child he's embarrassing? Zola wondered. *An adult would say that to a kid?*

That was so cruel. It wasn't cruel for a kid to say a parent embarrassed him—kids were just learning. Parents understood that.

"We'll have you stay on the bus until lunchtime," the chaperone told Bryson. "You can think about all the ways you disappointed me."

That was horrifying, too. Zola felt a little sick to her stomach. She felt a stab of fear. Maybe she didn't want to keep following Bryson and the chaperone. Maybe she didn't want to see anything of the world outside her Futureville.

But what if this is my only chance?

The chaperone went back to tugging Bryson forward, and

Zola kept going, too.

"I can walk on my own," Bryson said sulkily. "You don't have to treat me like a little kid."

The chaperone shot Bryson a look that was almost kind.

"I know it's hard being twelve," she said, more gently than before. "I do remember that."

So maybe the chaperone isn't a completely terrible person? Zola thought.

This was confusing, too.

The chaperone and Bryson were walking away from the school now, back toward the public plaza in front of city hall. Zola crept behind them, even as she kept pretending she couldn't see or hear them.

But maybe she wasn't as good an actress as she'd hoped. They'd barely gone a block when Bryson asked, "Why's that Futureville girl following us?"

"She's not," the chaperone said. "Weren't you listening before? Her goggles block every view of us. It's like, some VR invisibility cloaking thing."

But even the chaperone turned to look at Zola. If Zola kept walking, she'd run into them.

She pretended to be fascinated by the giant tulip bed along the sidewalk.

The chaperone and Bryson started walking forward again. While they weren't looking, Zola inched closer to make sure she could still hear them.

"Whatever," Bryson grumbled. "I still think the people here are creepy. It's like they're trapped in a video game or something." He spun into an imitation: he robotically took two steps forward, turned as if he were following a line on the ground, took two more steps, and turned again. He could have been a mime making a perfect box. Then his shoulders slumped and he slipped back into his more-normal saunter, trailing along behind the chaperone.

"You're pretty good at that," the chaperone said admiringly.

Is that really how we look to them? Zola wondered. She remembered laughing at the history VRs of twenty-first-century kids with their clunky video game goggles and jerky movements—but she'd never thought that her own motions could look the same from the outside. She wanted to tell Bryson and the chaperone, "You know, you're seeing *us* through goggles, too. The virtual versions you see aren't necessarily accurate, either!"

Oops—she'd accidentally gotten too close again. Both Bryson and the chaperone shot her a worried glance as they stepped into the wide-open public plaza in front of city hall.

"What if she tackles us and steals our tourist goggles?" Bryson asked. "Didn't that tour guide say the goggles are our tickets in and out of this creepy place? And they're the only way we can even *see* the exit signs?"

What? Zola thought. *What exit signs?*

She barely managed to stop herself from gazing all around. Or from totally freaking Bryson out by grabbing the goggles from his face. That would show him not to make fun of her and her friends!

But that would also give away that she could see him.

Bryson turned and kicked his foot toward her, high in the air, like someone attempting karate or tae kwon do without any training.

"Stay away from me, creepy girl!" he yelled.

Once again, it took a lot of acting on Zola's part not to react. She turned her automatic flinch into a pretense that she was hearing some command through her goggles.

"No, Sirilex, I am not playing hooky from school! I'm going after new batteries for my goggles!" she called.

The chaperone snatched Bryson off the sidewalk.

"Don't you ever think before you act?" she demanded. "Don't you remember that whole lecture about how it is *your* responsibility to stay out of the residents' way, and if you touch any of them, you will be thrown out of the park instantly?"

"You're already throwing me out of the park," Bryson grumbled.

"But there's also a huge fine for touching the residents," the chaperone countered. "You know that would come out of your allowance, right? For approximately the next ten years."

"Whatever," Bryson muttered.

The two of them went back to walking forward, with Zola following as closely as she dared. Strangely, they seemed to be heading straight toward the blank wall at the back of the plaza. They didn't slow or turn even when they were just a step away.

And then something truly bizarre happened. A panel of the wall in front of them just slid away. Zola got a quick glimpse of bright lights and signs—"ENTRANCE," "GIFT SHOP," "CAFETERIA," "GUEST DROP-OFF"—and lines of people snaking through a maze of roped-off areas. And then both Bryson and the chaperone stepped through the open space.

Right after that, the panel slid back into place. Bryson and the chaperone had disappeared, and Zola was staring at nothing but a blank white wall.

That . . . was the exit, she thought numbly. *They could tell, and even with my real reality goggles I couldn't see any labels.*

She couldn't help herself. She'd stopped caring about anyone noticing that she was acting strange—or that she was following Bryson and the chaperone.

She dashed right after them.

23

One second later, Zola smashed into the wall.

"Ow, ow . . ." Zola clutched her nose, which had taken the brunt of the impact. She gingerly felt the ridge of cartilage beneath the scraped skin.

Okay, it's not broken, she told herself. Or bleeding. She lifted her hand a little higher, to the nosepiece of the goggles, which had been painfully slammed into the bridge of her nose. But she was lucky again—the goggles weren't broken, either.

Don't you ever think before you act? she thought ruefully, the same question the chaperone had hurled at Bryson. She'd heard the chaperone say only tourist goggles worked for leaving the Futurevilles. And Zola had still run straight into a wall, thinking she could get out anyway.

And now I've probably tipped off everyone around me that

I can see the tourists, that my *goggles aren't the VR kind I'm supposed to have. . . .*

Mom was going to be so mad at her. No, it was worse than that—Mom was going to be so disappointed.

And scared.

Zola whirled around, trying to think of some excuse to explain her strange behavior.

Science experiment about testing the properties of solids? No. Acting class? Maybe . . .

Dozens of tourists were milling about the plaza, the giant open space between the city hall of Zola's town and the wall she'd just smashed into. But absolutely none of the tourists were looking in Zola's direction. Instead, they seemed to all be gazing toward a spot to Zola's right, farther down along the wall. Someone over there was screaming.

Please let it not be because of me. Please, let it not be someone who's going to come over and arrest me and . . .

Zola could just barely make out words in the screaming.

"No! No! Too tight! Hurts!"

It sounded like a kid.

All these people are just standing around, and some little kid is in pain? Zola thought incredulously.

Forgetting her own problems, Zola dived through the crowd.

Beside a second seemingly blank stretch of the wall, a little kid was flailing about on the ground. A man and a woman—undoubtedly his parents—were crouched beside him.

"Caden, buddy, we talked about this," the mom was saying. "You *have* to wear the goggles to see all the fun things in this Futureville."

"*I'm* wearing my goggles," the man said. "Don't you want to be like Daddy?"

"Hu-u-urts!" the boy wailed, kicking and pounding his fists on the ground.

"Maybe you could adjust the strap," a woman said, off to the side.

"With a kid like that, throwing tantrums, the best strategy is to just walk away and deprive them of attention until they calm down," another woman advised.

"When I was a kid, I would have been spanked for acting like that," a man muttered.

What does the word "spanked" mean? Zola wondered. *And why isn't Sirilex chiming in to tell the parents what they should really do?*

She guessed this proved that the tourist goggles didn't have a Sirilex connection. But it seemed like in an emergency like this, Sirilex should find a way to speak *somehow*.

She edged a little closer, pretending she was only examining the archway over the blank wall behind the screaming boy. Now that she thought about it, this archway matched an archway over the section of blank wall where Bryson and the chaperone had disappeared.

So maybe one side's the entrance and the other's the exit? she wondered.

The little boy's screams grew louder. The mother tried to pick him up, but he shoved her away. Then he began yanking at the goggles.

"No, buddy," the dad said. "Leave those on, or we'll have to go back out of the park. If you just calm down, we can—"

The little boy managed to pull the goggles off his face.

"Bad goggles!" he screamed.

Then he hurled them away. The goggles sailed through the air, and Zola knew instantly: *they're going to hit me.*

There was no time to step out of the way. No time to react at all.

The goggles *thwonk*ed against Zola's rib cage. Instinctively, Zola doubled over. She clutched her hands over her ribs and her stomach and the little boy's goggles. Around her, she heard seemingly everyone in the crowd of tourists let out a gasp.

And then a siren began sounding throughout the plaza. Zola could hear it through the little boy's goggles.

Everyone was still watching her.

What do I do? What do I do? Zola thought frantically.

And then she knew.

24

"*Ow!*" *Zola exclaimed, straightening up* even as she rubbed the place where the goggles had hit. This required no acting at all—it really did hurt. But then she added, "Something bit me!"

She raised her hands to her face, letting the little boy's goggles slide down her right sleeve, out of sight. She pressed her fingers against her ear, as if listening intently.

"What's that, Sirilex?" she asked loudly. "You say I should go home and let my mom look at my injury, make sure I won't have an allergic reaction? Okay!"

She took off running, and the crowd of tourists parted before her. She'd hoped nobody would be watching her by the time she reached the other archway—and the other stretch of blank wall she now knew to be an exit. (At least, it was an exit if you had tourist goggles—which she did now! She did!) But lots of tourists were still gazing curiously after her, even as others watched the family with the goggle-throwing, screaming child.

Okay, plan B, Zola thought grimly.

She kept running, following a route that really did lead home. Once she reached her own house, she burst in the door and called out, "Mom! I need your help! There's something wrong with my goggles—it showed me a VR where some terrible insect *bit* me!"

Zola yanked the goggles from her head. She waved them at Mom—but used her other hand to clutch her right sleeve, holding the precious tourist goggles out of sight.

Mom squinted at Zola, clearly confused.

"Something . . . bit you?" she repeated.

"Yes! Come into my Insta-Closet with me, and help me get the *right* goggles this time!"

Mom's eyes seemed to beg, *Is this necessary? Can't you stop drawing attention to yourself?*

"A VR insect bite would cause no *actual* pain," Sirilex chimed in. "Zola, you are letting your imagination run away with you."

You have no idea, Zola thought.

"Sometimes a girl just wants her mother's help," Zola said, with stubbornness she didn't have to fake.

Mom followed Zola into Zola's bedroom. They both stepped into the Insta-Closet, and Zola slammed the door.

"This is going to trigger so many alerts," Mom said. "We probably only have about five minutes before—"

Zola drew the tantrum-throwing little boy's tourist goggles out of her sleeve.

"We can escape now," she said. "You and me. Together."

The Insta-Closet was too small for Zola and Mom to fit in comfortably together. But Mom still drew as far away from Zola as she could, pressing her back against the wall.

"Oh, Zola," Mom murmured, the color draining from her face. She reached out and touched the word "TOURIST" on the strap. "Oh no. What have you done? Did you . . . did you *steal* those? Off some tourist's face?"

"No! I got lucky!" Zola waved the goggles at Mom. "*We* got lucky! Some kid just threw them at me!"

"Oh, Zola," Mom repeated. Her face was so pale now that Zola was afraid her mother might faint. "We've got to get rid of those. Before we get caught. There's no way anyone would let us just walk out of here, either one of us, wearing those." She gazed around frantically, as if fearing a thousand security cameras might be watching her every move. "And your life here is so good—why would you ever want to leave?"

Zola wanted to shout, "Mom, we're in the Insta-Closet! No one can hear us! Are you acting and lying again? Or are you really that terrified?"

She genuinely couldn't tell.

Mom grabbed the tourist goggles from Zola's hands.

"Don't throw them away!" Zola gasped.

166

Mom turned the goggles over and over in her hands. She touched a button at the side. And then it was like the goggles were a living thing that suddenly fell asleep.

Or a robotic toy that had just been turned off.

Oh, Zola thought. *Mom was afraid of the mic on the tourist goggles. That's why she said that thing about how good our life is here.*

"Mom!" Zola exclaimed. "You *were* lying before, weren't you?"

Mom shook her head warningly. She *still* didn't want Zola to talk—or to tell the truth. Was she still afraid of the goggles?

Or just afraid of everything?

Now Mom gazed around again, but more calculatingly. She drew something from under her own shirt.

It was the old-fashioned book about Jessie Keyser, *All My Questions Answered.* Mom had evidently found it where Zola had left it, in her bed. Mom held the book out to Zola as if to say, "You'll need this. Take it with you."

"I don't understand," Zola moaned. "What are you trying to tell me?"

Mom flipped over to a blank page at the back of the book. She took out an odd, old-fashioned writing device—a pen? A pencil?—that she had evidently hidden inside the spine of the book.

Zola leaned over Mom's shoulder to watch what she wrote:

> Our only chance is if you escape through the other Futureville. Go through one of the tourist exits there. The authorities won't expect that.

Mom kept her hand slanted over the words, so Zola could barely see each letter as Mom formed it.

"Oh!" Zola exclaimed. "I understand! Come on, then!"

With one hand, she reached for Mom's arm. With the other, she reached for the Insta-Closet mirror.

But Mom was shaking her head again. Mom was adding to the words she'd already written:

> This only works if you go without me.

25

Mom was the one who opened the mirror. Mom was the one who gently helped Zola out onto the platform between the Insta-Closets. Mom slipped the book into Zola's hands and whispered, "This will help." And then the opening closed again, with Mom still in the Insta-Closet and Zola alone in the near darkness two flights of stairs above the tunnel.

For a moment, Zola could only stand there, frozen in place. She could imagine Mom stepping out of the Insta-Closet in the opposite direction, out into Zola's bedroom. How long did they have before Mom would be answering the front door, to smile with fake pleasantries and lies for some . . . bad-guy Technologists? Guards? Security forces? Zola didn't even know how to picture the enemy. Whoever they were, how long could Mom hold them off?

What if Mom lies like a champ, and they still *find me*

cowering here on this platform? Zola wondered. *What if I fail without even trying to escape?*

It was that thought—that she couldn't let herself fail without trying—that got Zola's feet moving. She scrambled down the stairs, taking them two at a time.

At the bottom, she found the tunnel changed from the night before. Before, it had been deserted, and so darkly shadowed that it was a wonder Zola hadn't run into a wall. Now the lighting was still dim, but she could see dozens of figures in ragged clothes running back and forth and up and down the neighbors' stairways carrying trays of food and bundles of clothes. These were the people from the other Futureville, Zola realized. The ones like Puck who actually delivered all the items that were supposedly recycled or created by all the Insta-Closets and Insta-Fridges and Insta-Ovens in Zola's Futureville.

So Puck was telling the truth about that, Zola thought.

She didn't have time to worry too much about that right now. What mattered now was that, if she ran through the tunnel, she'd fit right in.

Or not, she thought, glancing down at her orange shirt and matching tiger-striped shorts. It wasn't just that they were so brightly colored—they were also conspicuously *new*.

Maybe I can convince one of the runners to stop for a minute and trade clothes with me?

She saw a door ajar off to the side—maybe she could duck in and change.

Zola crept over to the door and pushed it open a little wider to reveal . . .

A wonderland.

What other word could there be for a giant room full of every type of clothing Zola could ever imagine desiring, in every color and style? It was like falling into a rainbow. But it was also . . . ridiculous. What need would Zola ever have for a ball gown with alternating tiers of skirts? Or sixteen versions of the same ball gown, in sixteen different shades?

How was this not the most *wasteful* thing ever, that her Futureville had all this ready and waiting, just on the off chance that she might someday order it from her Insta-Closet? Even worse—could there be a storeroom like this beneath every house in her town?

Focus, Zola told herself. *Hurry.*

She didn't have to ask anyone to trade clothes. She just had to find the "stylishly ragged" section of this room and grab something made for her.

She waded through the racks of clothes until she reached a section with piles of distressed jeans and baggy T-shirts with artfully torn holes. She yanked a pair of pants and a shirt from the piles and pulled them on over her glaringly orange outfit. She also grabbed a fashionably ragged messenger-style bag, shoved the *All My Questions Answered* book inside, and slid the strap over her shoulders and across her chest.

Better, she thought. *Now run!*

She was in such a rush her ears started ringing. Maybe

she was hyperventilating. Maybe she was about to faint. She opened her mouth to ask, "Sirilex, what's wrong with me?" before she figured out the sensation.

Her ears weren't ringing because of anything internal, anything about her own body.

Her ears were ringing because picking up the clothes had set off some sort of alarm. An alarm that made her whole body vibrate as though she was being hit with waves of sound, without her actually hearing it.

Okay, okay, no big deal—I was getting out of here anyway, she told herself. *Just run faster!*

She shoved her way through the racks and piles of clothes.

Once I'm out in the hallway again, I'll be safe, she thought. *I'll blend in. No problem. I'll just run to the other Futureville and get out through one of the tourist exits and . . .*

It helped to tell herself what she was going to do. It helped to think how relieved she'd feel once she made it to safety.

She ran sloppily, frantically. She knocked over neatly stacked piles of clothes and flung racks together like bumper cars from one of the old-fashioned amusement parks she'd seen in VRs.

And then the door was in sight, right ahead of her.

Faster, faster, faster . . .

Zola flung herself toward the doorway, ready to yank the door open.

But just as she did that, someone shoved the door open from the other direction, to dash in from outside. Zola was in midair when she tried to squirm away, to dodge. Her legs tangled with the other person's legs; her shoulder and the messenger bag slammed into the moving door and ricocheted back.

Zola fell to the ground.

And the other person fell on top of her, pinning her in place.

26

"*Let me go! Leave me* alone!" Zola wailed, trying to wriggle away.

"Stop! Zola—shh! It's me! You know me, remember?"

It was Puck. The boy from the night before.

Zola still shoved him away but didn't scramble to her feet instantly.

"What are you doing here?" she demanded. Science class had taught her to identify all the ways she was in panic mode. Adrenaline had to be coursing through her veins. She darted her head side to side, looking for danger everywhere. Her body felt like it was still vibrating with the invisible, soundless alarm.

Puck hit a square black device attached to the waistband of his ragged jeans.

"I'm one of the people who supplies the Insta-Closets and

Insta-Kitchens for you and your mom, remember?" he said. "And I just saved you, turning off that alarm."

Zola no longer felt like she had a drum beating against her breastbone.

"What good is a soundless alarm?" she asked.

Puck tapped his ear. Now Zola saw that he had something small and white stuck in it: an odd strip of . . . that was plastic again, wasn't it?

"*I* heard the alarm all right," he said, wincing. "That's supposed to keep anyone from my Futureville from stealing from your storerooms."

"Oh," Zola said. She kept peering around anxiously. "Puck, I'm escaping. You . . . you can come with me."

Zola had met Puck only the night before. She barely knew him. But somehow it made her feel better, not to have to run away all alone.

But Puck only grimaced.

"Yeah, right," he said. "You really don't know anything, do you? There's no way to escape."

Zola had stuffed the tourist goggles up her sleeve again, alongside the other pair. She let the edge of one of the eyepieces slide out ever so slightly, barely into view.

"Puck, I have tourist goggles," Zola said. "They'll let us see the exits. They'll let us *use* the exits."

Puck's eyes widened.

"You do? Then maybe . . . maybe . . ." He scrambled to

his feet, and held out his hand to help Zola up, too. "Let's go before they catch us!"

Zola didn't need to take his hand. She was already springing up.

"Oh, er, wait—" Puck dashed over to the wall, and picked up something wrapped in a ragged cloth. Or, no—it was a backpack, so battered and old that it *looked* like nothing but ragged cloth.

"What's that?" Zola asked.

"My lunch," Puck said. "It's . . . never mind. Let's just go before we get caught!"

They ran back out into the long hallway of the tunnel. Puck stayed close to the wall, where the shadows were darkest. Zola ran alongside him, the messenger bag thumping against her hip. Every so often, she cast a worried glance over her shoulder.

Was Mom able to lie convincingly when the Technologists or security guards or whoever showed up? Zola wondered. Or is someone chasing us even now?

It was too hard to tell, when the light was so dim, and when so many people were running around, anyway. The dark figures streaming past Zola and Puck went by so quickly that Zola only got glimpses. They mostly seemed to be carrying breakfasts: mounds of synthetic scrambled eggs, triangles of flaxseed toast. . . .

"They keep us hurrying so much, nobody has time to

talk," Puck muttered bitterly. "None of *my* people are going to stop us."

"That's . . . good . . . for us . . . isn't it?" Zola countered. She'd been running so fast for so long now. She longed to stop and catch her breath. But she kept running anyway. "What about . . . are there guards? Security cameras watching you work?"

"At the end . . . but . . . I'll disable the security system," Puck said. He was panting, too. "We all . . . know how to do that."

That made Zola feel a little better.

But what if Mom couldn't lie well enough? What if people are waiting at the end of the tunnel—they're going to let us run all the way there, and get tired out, and then *they'll grab us?*

Zola decided not to mention that worry to Puck.

They reached the spot where Zola had tripped the night before. She lifted her feet higher, pushing off more emphat ically with her toes. She was glad she'd chosen high-quality running shoes from her Insta-Closet this morning. Or—she corrected herself—ordered them from her secret storeroom of clothes and shoes, that she'd never known about before.

Puck darted toward the wall. He hit a button that opened up what seemed to be an old-fashioned control panel. Zola had seen screens like that in history VRs from the twenty-first century. She couldn't make sense of any of it, but Puck's fingers danced across the panel as if it were a digital piano and he was a musical virtuoso.

"Thanks," Zola said. She bent forward, trying to draw in enough air to fill her lungs. "My mom . . . she didn't tell me . . ."

"She wouldn't have known about this," Puck said.

"Why didn't . . . last night . . ."

Zola was panting so hard, she couldn't get her complete thought out. But it seemed that Puck understood what she wanted to know: If there were security cameras at the end of the tunnel, why hadn't Zola gotten in trouble for her forbidden visit to the other Futureville last night?

"I shut off the security cameras last night, too," Puck said. "I did that as soon as I got the notification from your Insta-Closet that you'd stepped through the mirror . . . just in case."

"Oh," Zola said. "Thank you for that, too."

She felt so weird, finding out that she'd had to rely on his help so many times. She wanted to tell him, "Look, I'm an independent kid! I *thought* it was just technology taking care of me—AI systems delivering my clothes and food. . . . At least I was smart enough to bring the tourist goggles, remember?"

But Puck was already turning away from the control panel. Its bright glow faded back into the wall.

"Okay," Puck whispered. "Anyone watching this security scene for the next five minutes will see only a loop of the *past* five minutes, when nobody was moving in or out of the tunnel. So we just have to creep out and blend in as fast as we can with whatever's going on in my Futureville. . . . Just follow me. We're on my turf now."

Zola gritted her teeth and nodded.

Puck edged toward the mouth of the tunnel. Zola stayed right behind him. She could see the sky outside now: it was just as gray and grim as the sky her real reality goggles had shown her back in her own Futureville.

Well, duh, she told herself. *It really is the same sky.*

Puck darted from the end of the tunnel toward the straggly bush where he and Zola had hidden the night before. Zola kept her eyes trained on Puck's back as she tiptoed behind him. She reached the bush and grabbed one of the branches to keep it from hitting her in the face. Maybe she looked like she *needed* to hold on to the branch to steady herself, because Puck said, "This bush will show up on the security cam footage when it starts again, so we can't stay here longer than a few seconds. . . . Come on!"

He launched himself down the hill. Zola took off after him.

And that was when she heard the first gunshot.

27

Zola screamed and threw herself to the ground. She recognized the sound of gunfire from history VRs in school, when she'd seen depictions of war so she'd know how evil it had been.

But those were VRs! I knew it wasn't real! I'm not wearing VR goggles now! I'm not wearing goggles at all! This! Is! Really! Happening!

In VRs, the fighting was always distant and remote. Abstract. Zola never saw any blood. But now when Zola lifted her head ever so slightly, she saw a man ahead of her suddenly clutch his chest and sink to the ground. His grimy white shirt turned red beneath his hands.

And then Puck was right beside Zola on the ground, hissing in her ear.

"Zola! This is all an act! For the tourists! It's fake!"

Zola blinked.

"I mean, it's good if you keep acting terrified, but you don't have to be terrified for real," Puck whispered. "There's a whole pack of tourists over there, and when they turn to go, we can just follow them. . . ."

Zola looked around again. The bleeding man was squirming on the ground.

No, he's convulsing, she thought.

Then she noticed that while the man had his head turned away from everyone else, he winked almost merrily at Puck and Zola. His "blood" made a trail in the dust, flowing toward a crowd of people who were still shrieking and recoiling. All of them wore goggles—*Tourist goggles,* Zola told herself.

"That'll serve you right, for stealing my family's wheat and barley seed!" a woman screamed at the man from one of the houses. "You know our crop failed last year, and my children ain't had enough to eat ever since!"

"But my children are starving, too!" the bleeding man struggled to yell back. "And if I die, they'll . . . they'll . . ."

He stopped talking. His arms and legs stopped twitching.

But his head lolled back toward Puck and Zola again, and Zola saw him roll his eyes at them as if to say, "How could anyone believe this cheesy overacting?"

Still, Zola looked toward Puck. He was so skinny, his bony elbows sticking out from his ragged sleeves.

Could it be true that people here really don't have enough food? Zola wondered.

A swarm of people in filthy, ragged clothes emerged from the tumbledown shacks. Like the bleeding man, they all wore battered-looking goggles. But their faces were all so dirty that it was hard to tell.

Zola saw a man in a blue blazer step to the front of the crowd of tourists. He was dressed exactly like the tour guides back in her own Futureville.

Wonder what he's telling the tourists about what they just saw? she thought.

Then she remembered: she could find out. She slid out the tourist goggles she'd been hiding in her sleeve. Holding them off to the side, out of sight of the tourists, she turned them on.

"Don't put those on yet!" Puck hissed at her. "Someone will see you, and everyone knows actual tourists aren't allowed in this field! Wait until we can slide in with that group!"

"I just want to listen," Zola muttered back.

She lifted the goggles toward her head, and pressed the earpiece close, all the while pretending she was only holding her hands over her ears, still in shock from witnessing the fight.

At the front of the group of tourists, she saw a little boy step toward the tour guide and ask a question. His words came through her earpiece clearly.

"Don't those people over there know they should wash their face every day?" the boy asked anxiously. It was odd that *that* was what he was worried about, when he'd just supposedly witnessed a gunfight.

"Those people don't have enough clean, sanitary water to wash with," the tour guide said, shaking his head sadly. "They don't even have enough clean water to drink."

"They can have *my* water bottle!" the little boy said, lifting one from a backpack.

The tour guide beamed at the little boy.

"That's so nice of you," he gushed. "But, remember, they're only actors, showing you what life *could* be like in the future, if we don't take care of our planet now."

Beside Zola, Puck whispered, "The next thing the kid's going to say is, 'Oh, I will take care of our planet! I promise! I don't want *this* to be *my* future!'"

From Zola's earpiece, she heard, "Oh, I will take care of our planet! I promise! I don't want *this* to be *my* future!"

She peered at Puck in surprise.

"The kid's a plant," Puck muttered. "I played that role for a whole year, when I was five. Only time I ever had nice clothes and goggles—though the goggles were fake. There was food involved, too, as a reward. Or a bribe. Twinkies. That's what the food was called. Mmmmm . . ."

Zola's head spun. She wasn't wearing VR goggles, tourist goggles, or the real reality goggles Mom had given her. And she still wasn't sure what she could and couldn't believe with her own eyes.

The crowd of dirty-faced people surrounded the bleeding

man on the ground.

"Any of you'uns steal from me, you'll get the same treatment!" the angry woman yelled from her shack.

"Come on," Puck whispered, rising into a crouch. "The tourists are about to go on to the next viewing area, and we can sneak up behind them. You might want to . . ." He motioned smoothing back his hair. He actually spit into his hands and used that to press down a wayward cowlick at the back of his own head.

"Ugh, that's—" Zola caught herself before she let the word "disgusting" slip out, too.

"No choice, if we're going to try to look like tourists," Puck said. He spat into his hands again, and wiped off a streak of dust from his face. Then he tucked his shirt into his pants. The shirt was more holes than fabric, so tucking it in didn't improve its looks.

"Here," Zola said, worming her way out of her artfully torn shirt and handing it to Puck. She still had her original bright orange shirt on underneath. She used her fingers to brush her hair back—*she* wasn't going to use spit! She opened her mouth to say, "Sirilex, could you tell the Insta-Closet to give me a hair clip?" but stopped herself just in time.

The cluster of filthy people blocked her and Puck from the view of the tourists now, so this was a great time to run over behind them. But Puck was frozen in place, holding her shirt.

"We're being stupid," he said. "*I'm* not going to blend in with the tourists, whether I wear this shirt or not. I don't have the right kind of goggles! The only kind we have here are ragged and nasty—they tell the tourists they're for the air pollution and the harsh sunlight. But, really, it's so we can be ordered around through the earpieces. If I'm with the tourists, everyone would see that I don't fit in! You'll have to go without me!"

First Mom, then Puck, Zola thought. *What is it with everyone acting like I have to do scary things alone?*

"Can't you just . . . ," she began—on the verge of saying, "Can't you just order a decoy pair from your Insta-Closet?"

But Puck didn't have an Insta-Closet. In reality—*real* reality—neither did Zola.

"Here," Zola said, pulling the "reality" goggles from the pocket of her shorts and holding them out to Puck. "These will do, as long as nobody looks too closely at you."

"Oh," Puck said. He looked back and forth between the shirt and the goggles. "You'd let me, um, you'd let me . . ."

Zola swallowed hard.

"I need your help," she admitted. "I can't do this without you."

28

It turned out that the tourist group Zola and Puck joined was far away from any exit. With the tourist goggles on, Zola could see glowing red signs saying "EXIT THIS WAY." But she and Puck didn't dare make themselves conspicuous by just running in that direction. So they had to follow along with the agonizingly slow tourists, even as Zola wondered, *What if Mom* didn't *manage to lie convincingly, and someone's going to show up here any minute, to punish Puck and me? Or what if all the tourist goggles are tagged and individually identified, and someone in a security office somewhere is tracking my every move, as long as I have these goggles?*

The tour guide in the blue blazer droned on at the front of the group. His face looked more and more hangdog as he talked about how this Futureville had no government anymore, no one officially in charge at all, so people just fought back and forth over their dwindling resources.

"It's every man for himself," the guide said, looking sadder and sadder. "And every woman and child for themselves, too. No one takes care of anybody else. If one person manages to plant an apple tree that actually matures enough to produce apples, their enemies come by and pick all the apples and throw them away before they're even ripe. Just to be mean! Just to make sure that their neighbor doesn't have it any better than them!"

"That's not true!" Puck muttered beside Zola. He was standing close enough that he could hear the guide's narration coming out of Zola's earpiece. "It's the people running our Futureville who destroy whatever we grow! If we didn't have some people secretly taking care of one another, out of the tourists' sight, *none* of us would survive!"

"Okay, shh," Zola said, because others in the tourist group were turning around to look at Puck.

Will they notice that Puck looks too skinny and starving to be a tourist? Will they notice that his clothes aren't quite right—and his hair is plastered in place with spit?

But Zola probably didn't look right as a tourist, either. Her orange shirt was too bright and fluorescent. She couldn't seem to master stepping forward and then stopping whenever the tour guide indicated—she was used to VR scenes where she got to set her own pace.

The tour guide talked about pollution. He talked about how the weather was too extreme in every season now—just look at how the sun beat down today, when it was only April!

(Zola's goggles felt painfully hot on her face when he said that. But she noticed that some of the kids ahead of her in the group only laughed at that special effect.) The guide talked about how people had fallen into a cesspool of cultural and racial and religious strife and hatred rather than working together for the good of all humanity. Just then—definitely on cue—groups of people came out of the Futurevilles shacks and began punching and kicking each other.

"I . . . can't watch this," Zola whispered to Puck. "How could anybody watch this?"

But some of the kids in front of her began chanting, "Fight! Fight! Fight!" as if it were all an entertaining show. A tall, thin man in the crowd—definitely a teacher—tried to shush them.

"It's all fake, remember?" Puck whispered back to her. "Fake blood, fake bruises . . . Those guys know how to make it *look* like they're punching each other really hard, but they're actually not."

"So what I saw last night—the people around the bonfire, the kids stealing the cans of, uh, 'pop'—was that fake, too?" Zola asked hopefully.

"Um . . . no," Puck admitted.

The group moved on.

At long last, they came to a giant square of crumbling cement, where other tour groups stood clustered around their own guides.

"And now you have reached the end of our tour," the guide for Zola and Puck's group announced. "After you pass through the exit, you will see the goggle return receptacles on your right. Please place your goggles in the bin for sanitation and recharging so they'll be ready for the next tourist. Remember, 'reduce, reuse, recycle' is one way we're going to avoid having *our* futures turn out like this Futureville!" He chuckled as if he'd made a joke.

The tour guide started giving instructions for finding the bathrooms, the route to the other Futureville and—what he seemed to care more about—the gift shop, the snack shop, and the cafeteria. Zola tuned him out and tried to catch Puck's attention. She tilted her head, tapped her goggles, and drew her arms in close to her body. She hoped Puck would understand her body language—she was trying to say, "Only my goggles will work to open the exit. Yours won't. So you'll have to stay close beside me while we're exiting. We don't want the door to shut between you and me."

Puck reached out and grabbed Zola's hand. Zola jolted.

"Is this okay?" Puck whispered. "I thought . . . we just can't be separated."

"Uh, yeah . . . it's fine," Zola whispered back.

But what a strange thing, to hold someone's hand, for real. (Someone's besides Mom's, that is.) And to know it was for real. And . . .

"Zola? Are you ready?" Puck asked.

The crowd around them surged toward the exit. Zola and Puck were like stones in a river, the current flowing past them.

Zola took a deep breath.

Through her goggles, she could see the words "EXIT HERE" glowing in front of her. When she stepped forward, those words were replaced by a longer phrase: "GOOD-BYE FROM THE FUTURE YOU'LL WANT TO AVOID! And then: YOU ARE RETURNING TO THE PRESENT, WHERE YOU STILL HAVE A CHANCE TO CREATE THE FUTURE YOU WANT TO LIVE IN. CHOOSE WISELY! MAY **YOUR** FUTURE BE FABULOUS!"

A blank wall stood in front of Zola and Puck. They both stepped forward, in sync, and the wall slid open, just as it had for every tourist in front of them. Zola clutched Puck's hand; he clutched hers. They each took another step, together.

And then they were in another world.

29

Unlike the sterile serenity of Zola's Futureville or the dirty, falling-apart strife of Puck's, the scene they stepped into now was full of gaudy colors and bright light and bustling activity. Now Zola could see the same kind of giant signs she'd gotten only the quickest glimpse of before: "SNACK BAR," "GIFT SHOP," "PARKING LOT," "THIS WAY TO THE FUTURE YOU'D *RATHER* HAVE . . ." Below the signs, tourists were *everywhere.* They stood in lines; they leaned against walls. They licked ice-cream cones and aimed bright red ketchup bottles at foods Zola had seen only in history VRs: Hot dogs. French fries. Hamburgers.

For a moment, Zola could only blink in awe.

"We did it!" Puck whispered in Zola's ear. "Those tourist goggles worked! We're out!"

He let go of her hand and . . . hugged her.

Okay, Zola thought. *It is also really weird to be hugged for real by someone besides Mom.*

Puck was already pushing himself away.

"I'm sorry!" he exclaimed. "I forgot—I've heard enough from your Futureville to know it's not right to just hug somebody without being sure you have permission, and, well, you know, things aren't ideal where I'm from. . . ."

If Zola and Puck had been in a VR, Zola would have had time to think about what Puck was saying. She would have had time to give her own answer. The scene around them would have faded to dimness while they discussed this situation.

But *nothing* faded around them. The giant room full of tourists practically vibrated with color and lights and motion. And it buzzed with other people's chatter—kids whining, "Can't we go to the snack bar now? *Puh-lease?*" and teachers or chaperones commanding, "My group—over here! We'll go out to the bus together!" and older couples conferring: "I'll hit the gift shop and get something for the grandkids while you go to the bathroom. . . ."

Zola felt like her ears were overloaded. Along with her eyes and brain.

And then someone grabbed her arm. Hers *and* Puck's.

"Hold on, you two!"

It was a stern-looking woman in a dark blazer that was even more severely tailored than the tour guides' uniforms. Zola's heart sank. How could they have been caught already?

She peered at Puck, hoping he could read the signal in her eyes.

We'll just have to take off running, she thought. *If we both break away at the same time and run in opposite directions, surely one of us will get away.... One of us will get to safety....*

But Puck, oddly, was saying, "Yes, ma'am. Sorry, ma'am."

"Goggles?" the woman demanded, her hands outstretched now. "Didn't you hear your tour guide say exactly one minute ago to return your goggles when you left that Futureville?"

"Oh, right." Zola fumbled with removing her goggles and handing them over. "I just didn't see where—"

The woman rolled her eyes and pointed behind her, where a huge sign said, "GOGGLE RETURN HERE."

"Kids," the woman muttered. "Maybe you'd do a better job of noticing things around you if you weren't too busy hugging and kissing your boyfriend. On a school field trip, even!"

"We weren't—" Zola began. "I mean, we aren't—"

Zola saw Puck dart behind the woman's back. He bent down and acted like he was dropping his goggles onto the jumble of other pairs. Only because Zola was watching him closely could she tell: he was really tucking them under his shirt.

"We'll remember to follow the rules next time," Puck said, stepping forward again to smile sweetly at the scowling woman.

"You better," the woman grumbled.

Puck slid his arm through the crook of Zola's elbow and tugged her forward.

"I have never been treated like that before," Zola muttered. "All kids—all *people*—should be treated with dignity and respect, and—"

"Zola, we have to blend in with the tourists until we're away from this whole area," Puck whispered. "You can't go around righting every wrong you see along the way."

"But in VRs—" Zola began.

Puck's face was patient, as if he was just waiting for her to remember: *We aren't in a VR. Everything we see around us now is real.*

The consequences for every single one of their actions would be real, too.

"What if we just stood in the middle of this room and screamed for someone to call the police?" Zola asked. "What if we got all the tourists to listen to us, and told them everything we know about how the Futurevilles residents like us are in danger, and—"

"And why would they believe you instead of the people who run our Futurevilles?" Puck countered. "Don't you think the owners have paid off the police around here? That's how things would work in *my* Futureville!"

Not in mine, Zola thought.

But they weren't in either of their Futurevilles now. They were in the real 2020s, when society could tip in either direction.

"You read that book about your aunt Jessie Keyser, right?" Puck asked. "What did *she* do to get help for the kids in her village?"

"She got out and found a pay phone so she could call for help," Zola said. "She arranged something called a news conference, and—"

Puck's face glowed.

"If it worked for her, it'll work for us," he said. "Sometimes history repeats, right?"

"I hope so," Zola said.

She was a little vague about exactly what a "news conference" might be—something about calling newspapers and TV and radio stations? But surely people would help her and Puck figure it out once they got farther away from the Futurevilles.

The two of them fell in line behind a group of schoolkids heading for glass doors at the opposite side of the room. Through the huge wall of windows, Zola could see a row of large yellow vehicles—was that what school buses looked like in real life? Zola had only ever seen them in ancient-history VRs.

"Sirilex, are those—" Zola began, and broke off. She looked around guiltily. What if just saying the word "Sirilex" was dangerous? In Zola's Futureville, that was all she had to do to get the attention of the AI system—what if the Sirilex network extended out even into the tourist area?

What if she'd just done the equivalent of telling Sirilex,

"Hey, look, I'm not where I'm supposed to be!"?

At least no one around her seemed to be paying attention.

"Yeet!" a kid yelled beside her, extending his arm high over his head.

"I asked for a *straight* line, people—would you call that straight?" a teacher scolded.

"Next time we take a field trip, I vote for Kings Island," one girl was telling another.

It's too loud in here for anyone *to hear what I said*, Zola told herself. *Even Sirilex.*

She had to hold herself back from putting her hands over her ears. She'd never heard such a high decibel level before. The earpieces of her VR goggles always protected her precious ear canals from such a damaging situation.

She had to stop herself from asking Sirilex to turn the volume down. But at least this time she managed to do that before saying Sirilex's name.

"Should we . . . hold hands again so we don't get separated?" Puck asked—even though he practically had to shout in Zola's ears so she could hear him over all the noise.

She glanced his way. Puck was from the other Futureville, where people did horrifying things like wasting metal cans, burning bonfires, and beating each other up. But even his face had turned pale, as if he was just as overwhelmed and frightened as Zola was.

"Sure," Zola said. "Sounds like a good idea."

She slipped her hand into his. It felt like this was something much younger kids would do—say, kindergarteners on a playground. But Zola didn't care. It helped.

The kids ahead of them were pushing their way out the door, heading into the fresh air just beyond. Zola and Puck followed along.

As soon as they stepped outside, one of the buses in front of them started up with an unbelievably loud roar of its motor. A cloud of exhaust floated toward them. Puck sniffed.

"Diesel fumes?" he muttered. "They still use diesel in the 2020s? They really are headed for turning into my Futureville!"

Zola inhaled too deeply and began to cough.

"This is a disaster!" she told him. "In a VR, we'd have to report this instantly, and—"

Then she forgot about the exhaust fumes. Because she saw something even more terrifying out of the corner of her eye, off to the left. That direction was a no-go. She looked to the right. Same. She tried to back up into the tourist center, but the crowd of schoolkids flowing out the door just shoved her back into place. She started sprinting toward the nearest bus instead. She tugged Puck along with her.

"Come on!" she told him. "We've got to hide! Now!"

30

Zola's foot caught just the edge of the bottom step of the bus's entryway. She struggled to keep her balance, leaping onto the next step up.

"No running on the bus," a bored voice said ahead of her.

It wasn't even an AI voice—it came from a large woman enthroned in front of a giant black circle.

Is she the driver? Zola thought. *A human driver, not automated? And that's a steering wheel?*

But the driver wasn't even looking directly at Zola. She didn't seem to care what Zola did, as long as she didn't run.

Zola rushed down the aisle of the bus, just walking fast, not running. She kept her face turned away from the windows at the side.

"What are you doing?" Puck whispered behind her. "Why did we have to get on this bus?"

"I saw a tour group that saw me in *my* Futureville," Zola said. "These kids named Bryson and Amelia and their chaperone . . . they were coming from opposite directions. And . . . they would have remembered me." She reached the back of the bus and ducked down into the last row of seats. "Check and see if they're still there. Especially if they're looking this way. Bryson has brown hair, and he's wearing a green-and-blue-striped shirt. The chaperone's a worried-looking woman in yoga pants. Amelia has, like, super-black hair, and she's wearing pink. . . ."

Puck plopped down in the seat beside Zola and peered out the window. Zola crouched down even lower.

"No, I don't—" Puck began. He craned his neck, looking all around. Then suddenly he jerked his head down. "Zola! They're getting on this bus!" He barely peeked over the padded green seatback in front of them. "And they're headed this way!"

Zola moaned.

"We've got to hide even better, then," she muttered. "That Bryson kid in particular, he'd yell about how I was one of those 'creepy' people and how did I escape and . . ."

She slid down lower, cramming herself into the small space between the bottom edge of her seat and the back of the seat in front of them.

"I call back seat!"

That was definitely Bryson's voice.

Zola groaned and crawled *under* the seat in front of hers.

"Should I do that, too?" Puck bent forward to ask her.

It was too late. From her position under the seat, Zola could see Bryson's bright red sneakers just a few inches from her nose.

"You a new kid or something?" Bryson asked, clearly talking to Puck. "Don't you know? That's my seat. Get out of here."

Zola thought about how Puck was so short and scrawny, and Bryson . . . Bryson was the kind of kid who'd pull a girl's hair.

Am I going to have to jump out and defend Puck? Zola wondered.

But what if she did that, and Bryson started yelling for the chaperone or the teacher or the bus driver to kick Zola and Puck off the bus?

In the VRs, the choices were always so simple. It was always "Do the right thing and be rewarded, or do the wrong thing and fail." Zola had been outside her Futureville for a grand total of probably ten minutes, and it felt like there were a thousand choices at every turn.

And *none* of them were clearly right or wrong.

"Oh, hey, I didn't know," Puck told Bryson. Puck flexed his knees like he was going to get up. Then he sat back down. "But I gotta tell you. When I sat down here, the seat was kind of wet. And it smelled like pee. Are you *sure* you want to sit here?"

Zola saw Bryson's shoes shift slightly.

"You know what?" he asked. "I got turned around. *That's the seat I was sitting in on the way over here.*"

His shoes turned toward the seat across the aisle. Zola could tell by watching his feet that he'd slid all the way over beside the window.

He didn't see me, Zola told herself. *He can't see me now.*

Her heartbeat slowed to more of a normal rate. The engine of the bus rumbled beneath her.

But how did Puck know to act like that with Bryson? How did he know it would work?

"All right, kids," a woman shouted from the front of the bus. "Settle down. When we get back to school, we'll discuss what we just saw. But you might want to think about these questions now. What choices do *you* think led to the differences between the two Futurevilles? What kind of a Futureville would you design, if you were in charge? What kind of a future are your current choices leading toward?"

Zola heard Bryson's voice call out the first answer: "Reform school!"

"I *want* to live where there's trash everywhere!" another kid said.

"Who cares about the environment?" another yelled. "We mess up Earth, we'll just move to Mars!"

Zola froze, her face pressed hard against the rubbery floor of the bus. It'd been bad enough to see Puck's Futureville, with all the fighting and filth. But at least she'd known that part of it was just for show, just an act for the sake of the tourists.

What if the 2020s were even worse?

31

"Zola! It's just humor! Those boys are only joking around!"

Zola dared to scoot her head ever so slightly out from under the bus seat. Now she was peering up as Puck bent down, pretending to tie his shoe.

"Oh," Zola said. She squinted up at him. "How did you know that upset me?"

"I know more about your Futureville than you know about mine, remember?" Puck whispered. "I know . . . nobody has a sense of humor in any of your VRs!"

That was true. Zola wanted to defend her own Futureville by arguing, "But Beatriz and my other friends and I—we make fun of the VRs a lot! We laugh together all the time!"

But did they really? Zola only saw her friends virtually, so how could she be sure what any of them thought or felt or did?

The bus picked up speed.

"Puck!" Zola called. "Are we out of the Futurevilles parking lot yet?"

Puck checked the window, then bent back down again, as if his *other* shoe were untied, too.

"I see trees and grass, and, Zola—it's *green* grass and *green* leaves on the trees and . . . things aren't brown and dead all over the place, like back home, where they make things look bad on purpose. It's beautiful! Zola, is this what the 2020s are really like outside our Futurevilles?" he whispered excitedly.

"I wish I could look out, too," Zola muttered. It felt like she was going to have to peel her face from the floor—the floor seemed that sticky. "But, Puck, watch everything. Maybe that will help us figure out more about what to do next."

Puck straightened up. Now Zola's only view was of shoes again. Shoes and the floor.

"Sirilex—" she started to ask. But of course there was no answer. And there wasn't room to pull out the *All My Questions Answered* book to read any more of it. She'd have to wait to find out anything else about pay phones or news conferences.

The bus swerved and turned and sped up and slowed down and sped up again. Zola had no way of knowing for sure, but it felt like as much as an hour could have passed before the bus stopped for good, and the teacher voice called from the front again, "Okay, everyone, go to your fifth-period class."

From her position on the floor, Zola could see kids scrambling out into the aisle, walking toward the exit. She let out a soft sigh of relief when Bryson's shoes walked away.

Puck's face reappeared above Zola.

"Should we go into the school and look for a whatchamacallit—the pay phone?" he asked.

"Do you think someone there would help us?" Zola asked. "A teacher? A principal?"

"Why would a stranger help us?" Puck's face turned into a puzzled squint.

"Because people are kind and—" Zola was still whispering, but her voice suddenly seemed too loud. It was because the surrounding noise had dimmed to almost total silence. From her vantage point on the floor, Zola looked down the aisle again—it had become one long, empty stretch of black rubber. Besides Zola and Puck, the only kids still left on the bus were up by the front door, about to get off.

Then Zola heard the bus driver's voice, echoing from the front: "Bus nineteen, checking in. Yeah, I don't have time to go back to the bus garage before kindergarten pickup. I'll just park in our usual spot. Hey, I saw that the gas station has two-for-one Gatorade this week—anybody else want some?"

"Puck!" Zola exclaimed. In her excitement, she barely remembered to keep her voice to a whisper. "Jessie Keyser found a pay phone at a gas station! Maybe we can find one there, too!"

"What's a gas station?" Puck asked.

"Um, it's where people fueled up their motor vehicles, before pollution-less cars were invented . . . maybe we should try to hold our breath when we get there?"

The bus rumbled to life again. Zola had to clutch the legs of the seat to keep from sliding back and forth. Apparently the bus driver liked driving a little more wildly when she thought she was alone on the bus.

But it was barely five minutes before the bus pulled up to a stop and the driver shut off the engine. Puck peeked over the edge of the seat and then out the window, and reported the driver's every move to Zola: "She's off the bus now. She just shut the door. We're in, like, a whole sea of—I think it's called blacktop? It's beautiful, too! So smooth and perfect! Anyhow, now the driver's walking toward a little building. . . ."

Zola sprang out from underneath her bus seat. She attempted to brush off her shirt and jeans, but the sticky stuff from under the seat had left a dark stain.

"Wait, Puck, I need to swap out my clothes in my Insta-Closet before . . . ," Zola began.

Puck glared at her.

"Oh, right," Zola muttered. "Never mind."

She too concentrated on peering out the bus window. Now the bus driver was circling around to the front of the little building Puck had described.

"Let's get out of here while she can't see us!" Zola exclaimed.

It took them a moment to figure out how to operate the door at the front of the bus—Zola wasn't used to things that operated mechanically like that, instead of sliding apart automatically. But Puck pointed to a long metal stick attached to the door. He pulled on it, and the door sprang apart.

And then they both scrambled down to the ground.

Puck hadn't been lying about the blacktop seeming like a giant sea. It stretched on and on and on, with the little building—the gas station?—in one corner, and an enormous flat building taking up the entire opposite side of the blacktop. The flat building was labeled with two red circles—one completely inside the other—and the word "TARGET" in large red letters. Was that some kind of store? It was nothing like the small, cozy shops of Zola's Futureville.

It disturbed Zola to see how many motorized vehicles were zipping across the blacktop. Where were all those people going? Yellow lines marked off spaces across the blacktop, as if sometimes hundreds of cars converged here all at once.

"Shouldn't we go around the other side of the gas station, so the bus driver doesn't see us?" Puck asked anxiously.

Zola realized he was thinking strategically while she was just looking around and marveling.

"Good idea," she said.

They darted over to the side of the gas station building and crouched down to peek in the windows. The bus driver stood in front of a counter now, with a bottle of unnaturally blue liquid in each hand.

"She'll recycle those when she's done, won't she?" Zola asked Puck.

"Oh, if only we'd had good strong plastic bottles like that in my Futureville," Puck muttered.

How could she and Puck look at the same objects and have such different reactions?

The bus driver pushed her way out of the door of the gas station. Zola and Puck waited until the woman had rounded the corner of the building, out of sight, and then they darted in through the door themselves.

"Remind me what a pay phone would look like so I can help find it?" Puck whispered in her ear.

"Um . . . ," Zola said uncertainly. It wasn't as though the book about Jessie Keyser had explained. Whoever had written the book had acted like everyone reading it would know. And maybe everyone in the 1990s would have known about pay phones.

"We'll have to ask," she told Puck. She opened her mouth to say, "Sirilex . . ." but of course that wasn't going to work here. She pointed toward the man standing behind the counter.

"You think it's safe to ask an actual *person*?" Puck hissed, clearly distraught. "What if he's dangerous? You can't just go up to people and think they're going to be *nice*!"

"What other choice do we have?" Zola muttered.

The man was watching them now. He scowled and pointed to a sign that said "Shoplifters will be prosecuted to the full extent of the law."

What were shoplifters?

Zola shoved that question aside and tried to stay focused.

"Hello," she said, stepping up to the counter. She smiled pleasantly at the man, as if he were a Helpful Clue Source in a VR (even though Helpful Clue Sources never scowled, and certainly not in a way that made their grizzled eyebrows into one long caterpillar across their forehead, like this man's). "Could you tell me where your pay phone is?"

The man guffawed.

"What is this, some kind of a prank? One of those scavenger hunt things where kids have to ask ridiculous questions?" he asked.

Zola wasn't sure what he meant, but at least he'd stopped scowling.

"Okay, okay, I'll be a good sport about it," the man said. "Get out your cell phones, and you can record my response for proof. Want me to play up the old-man angle, like, 'Eh, what's that? I don't think we've had a pay phone here since the last century! Even I barely remember what they looked like!'" He hunched over as he said that, and made his voice sound even more ancient and crochety. Then he straightened up and jerked his jaw back and forth, making his face look rubbery. "Or do you want sarcasm? How's this: 'Kiddo, you are clearly a time traveler from—what? The 1980s? Let me clue you in. Cell phones are where it's at nowadays. I bet you can even buy one over at that Target. Electronics department, you know?'" He pointed dramatically over his shoulder.

"Cell . . . phones?" Zola asked numbly. "Are they a different kind of pay phone?"

"Oh, you're good at this!" the man said. He was beaming at her now. "I see an acting career in your future!"

"Come on," Puck said, tugging on her arm.

"Oh, were you *secretly* filming me?" the man said. "Already got everything you wanted? Hey, I've got a right to half your profits if you post this on TikTok or YouTube and make any money!"

Puck was practically sprinting for the door now, pulling Zola along with him.

"You're welcome!" the man called after them. "Come back and let me know when you post it, so I can tell my grandkids to look for it! Would you believe they put me in *their* TikToks sometimes? They call me TikTok Grandpa!"

As soon as they were out the door, Zola whipped her gaze to Puck.

"What was that about?" she asked.

"The tourists *are* always talking about cell phones, not pay phones," Puck said, squinting back at the gas station in distress. The TikTok Grandpa waved at them, but it might have just been another act. "Once that man realizes we weren't joking, what if he reports us to the people from our Futurevilles?"

"He . . . won't, because . . . because we'll be able to find a pay phone and call a news conference first," Zola said weakly. "Er, I mean . . . a cell phone?"

"Should we try that Target place?" Puck asked.

"I . . . guess?" Zola agreed.

The stretch of blacktop between them and the Target place seemed to go on forever. The bus—now with the bus driver back on it, drinking her blue liquid—also lay between them and the Target store. But the driver was staring down at some rectangular object in her hand, so they felt safe just dashing past. And then they had to keep walking and walking and walking to get across all the blacktop.

"In a VR, nothing this boring would stay the same for so long," Zola told Puck. "There'd be more variety in our view, to keep us interested."

"Isn't it enough to keep us interested, thinking we might get caught at any moment?" Puck grumbled.

"No, there'd be a pretty flower over there, or a bird swooping down with a secret message in his beak or . . ." Zola thought about what she'd seen of Puck's Futureville, with everyone dirty and bedraggled and desperate. "Never mind."

They finally reached the end of the blacktop and stepped onto the sidewalk in front of the Target place. Doors swished open before them.

"Now, that's how things *should* work," Zola said. "I'm feeling better about the 2020s already."

"Shh," Puck said, glancing around as though they might have stepped into a war zone VR, and needed to stay wary.

But the few people they could see nearby paid no attention to Puck and Zola. A row of funny red four-wheeled vehicles lay before them, and a woman was plopping a toddler into one of them. Were the carts play areas for little kids? Off to the side, people in red shirts stood by what seemed to be old-fashioned cash registers with odd conveyor belts. And beyond that, a vast space seemed to hold even more varied clothes and other items than the storeroom beneath Zola's Insta-Closet.

"Whoa," Zola breathed. "I've never seen so many *things* in one place in my entire life."

"Neither have I," Puck whispered. "It's like your storeroom and your mom's storeroom and your neighbors' storeroom . . . everything together all at once!"

"We'll have to ask where the phones are," Zola whispered back.

"All this asking questions is dangerous," Puck said, planting his feet stubbornly in place. "It'll make people remember us." He pointed toward the back wall of the store, far, far off in the distance. "Look, it says 'Electronics' back there, and the gas station guy said that was where we'd find phones. . . ."

"Okay, okay," Zola agreed.

It seemed to take almost as long to get to the back of the store as it had taken to cross the blacktop. But partly that was because there was too much to look at now, rather than not enough.

Finally they reached the area of the store under the word "Electronics." The back wall of this area was completely covered with screens, all carrying the words "Get your Target gift cards now!" Then a rectangle labeled "Target gift card" shimmied and danced across each screen.

It was hypnotic.

"That's a cell phone," Puck said.

Zola tore her gaze away from the dancing gift cards and the wall full of screens. Puck was pointing at a small object that seemed to be chained to a counter in front of them.

"I've seen the tourists use them to take pictures," Puck said. "Some of the adults in my Futureville talk about how great it would be if we could just steal one of the cell phones, but . . . you know. Too many security cameras around us."

And none of those security cameras saw Puck and me join the group of tourists? Zola fretted. *Or saw us leaving the Futurevilles?*

"Okay, great," she told Puck, trying to hold back her fears. "Do you know how one of these things work?"

"Don't you?" Puck asked. "It's *your* Futureville that has all the technology!"

"We don't use phones!" Zola protested. "Those are, like, ancient technology. Our VR goggles connect us to anyone we want to talk to, anywhere in the world. Or, well, that's what they always told us. . . ."

Puck touched the screen of the little phone. A picture appeared of what seemed to be a partly eaten black apple.

"We can just ask that boy over there—" Zola began, pointing to another counter, where a kid who looked barely older than Puck and Zola was hunched over something . . . maybe a cell phone of his own?

"No, we can't ask anybody for anything!" Puck complained. "If we were real 2020s kids, I'm pretty sure we'd know how to use a cell phone!"

"But we aren't, and we don't," Zola countered. "So—"

"We're just going to have to steal it, and figure it out on our own," Puck said, peering around furtively.

"Steal?" Zola hissed at him. "Stealing's wrong!"

"Not if it's for a good purpose," Puck said. "We can explain later. But . . ." Now he was staring up at the ceiling and the corners of the giant room. "Where do you think the security cameras are? How should we break this chain?"

Zola gaped at him in horror as he tugged on the chain holding the phone in place. Then she glanced quickly toward the teenager behind the other counter. What if he'd heard Puck?

But the teenager was looking in the other direction, at a man who'd stepped up to that counter.

"Any chance I can get you to switch those TVs to the game?" the man asked. "You're a basketball fan, right? I thought I'd be home by now. But I'm waiting on my wife, and it's killing me to just watch on my phone."

"If it's a customer request, we're allowed to make that change," the teenager said. Zola couldn't see his face, but his voice made it sound like he was beaming with joy.

The wall of screens off to the side suddenly transformed

into dozens of views of basketball players dribbling up and down a court.

"This is great! They're distracted!" Puck whispered.

"But it's not like *security cameras* would be distracted by a sports game!" Zola whispered back.

The man and the teenager were talking about something called March Madness and Indiana's chances. They cheered when a basketball player in red and white sank a basket.

Zola didn't know what to do.

But suddenly the repeated scenes of the basketball game disappeared, and an official-looking woman appeared on all the screens instead.

"Here's our noon news updates," she said. "We've just learned that two kids are going around posing as disgruntled employees of the Futurevilles, and spreading bizarre lies about Morgan County's largest employer. It's not believed that they are dangerous, but if you encounter them, the Futurevilles Corporation would like to warn you: you can't believe a word they say."

And then, multiplied again and again on the wall full of screens, a picture appeared of Zola and Puck exactly as they looked right now: Zola in her orange shirt; Puck with his hair slicked down with spit.

Puck's hand shot out and grabbed Zola's arm, yanking her down to the floor.

"Hide!" he whispered.

32

"They know we left," Zola groaned in a whisper. "The security cameras were watching us all along. . . ."

But why had the people running her Futureville—and Puck's—let them get out at all? Had they just not wanted to make a scene by capturing them in front of all the tourists?

But now they're announcing publicly that we've escaped? How does that make sense?

Zola kept her back against the glass base of the counter. But she turned and peeked through the glass toward the man and the boy.

"Go back to the basketball game!" the man shouted angrily at the screens.

"They didn't see us," Puck whispered. "We're okay."

"But how can we call a news conference now—or get help from anyone—if the word's gotten out that everything we might say is a lie?" Zola whispered back.

The woman whose face was repeated again and again on the wall full of screens kept talking about how many jobs the Futurevilles had brought to the area, and how the company had been ranked the top employer to work for every year for the past dozen years.

"We attempted to talk to Futurevilles critic Dr. Jessica Keyser about this latest information, as it seems she may be related to one of the children," the woman added. "But a spokesperson at the Indiana University Medical School said she was not available for comment."

Beside Zola, Puck was yanking off the shirt she'd given him. Then he shoved it at Zola.

"What are you doing?" Zola whispered.

"Trying to make us look different than those pictures!" Puck whispered back. "Cover that orange shirt!"

Zola started to object, "Won't somebody notice that I'm just wearing the shirt you were wearing before?" But Puck was right—her orange shirt was as bright as a flare. The one he was pulling over her head was a bland pale yellow, and completely forgettable.

Then she got her closest look yet at the ratty, faded T-shirt he'd had on beneath.

"But, Puck!" she complained. "Your shirt says 'Future-villes' right on it!"

It did. The stenciling was peeling off, but Zola could just barely make out the words "Which Future Do You Choose?" above an arrow that split in two directions. It also held the words "Futurevilles, Indiana."

"I know!" Puck whispered through gritted teeth. "They give us the leftovers that don't sell in the gift shop—we're supposed to be wearing these ironically. Don't worry. I'm turning it inside out. Let's get out of here!"

As soon as Puck had reversed his shirt, they both stood up. Zola started to dash forward, but Puck caught her arm.

"We'll look less conspicuous if we walk," he muttered.

He was right about that, too. But it was excruciating to stroll casually when Zola longed to run her fastest.

"Keep your head down," Puck advised. "Maybe let your hair fall over your face so the security cameras can't identify you?"

Zola bit her tongue to refrain from telling him, "The security cameras already saw us! That's not going to help!"

She let herself cast one glance over her shoulder, to make sure neither the teenager nor the man by the counter were following them.

They were back to watching the basketball game.

Puck and Zola strolled down the long, broad aisles of the Target store. They stepped out the front door.

Should we go back to the bus? Zola thought. *Back to the school, and follow my plan to ask for help from a teacher or the principal?*

But the school had sent its kids to visit the Futurevilles. Why would anyone at the school believe Zola and Puck instead of the Futurevilles people?

The bus was gone, anyhow. Zola could see only a long stretch of empty blacktop where the bus had been parked.

Beside Zola, Puck froze in place on the sidewalk.

"Oh no," he moaned under his breath.

"What?" Zola asked.

"More security cameras," Puck whispered. "Everywhere around us. On all those light posts out in the parking lot . . ."

Zola hadn't even noticed the light posts. In a VR, if that had been an important detail, the posts would have glowed extra bright, to draw her attention.

How's anyone supposed to know what details around them are important, outside of a VR? Zola wondered. *Or without Sirilex pointing out what matters?*

"So the 2020s are like our Futurevilles," Zola groaned. "There's nowhere to hide."

Puck jolted as if Zola were the Helpful Clue Source in a VR, and she'd just said something unexpected and brilliant.

"Oh, but we do have places to hide in our Futurevilles," Puck muttered. "Your Insta-Closet."

"Yeah, right." Zola rolled her eyes, as if Puck were as ridiculous as Zola's mom. "I don't see one of those around here. And, you know, Insta-Closets aren't as private as I thought."

"But where people hide in *my* Futureville . . ." Puck swiveled his head all around, gazing at the sky. No—he was trying to gaze at whatever lay behind the Target store. He grabbed Zola's hand once again. "Yes! Come on!"

"Where are we going?" Zola asked, even as she followed

him around the corner at the side of the store.

Puck paused only long enough to grin in her direction. He seemed genuinely delighted about . . . the clump of trees and bushes in front of them?

"Where are we going?" he repeated, drawing her forward. "The uncharted wilderness."

33

"'The uncharted wilderness' sounds like something my mom would say," Zola protested. "That's just some land no one's taking care of, or nobody pays attention to, or . . . okay, I get it."

"Right. If nobody cares, nobody's watching," Puck said gleefully.

He shoved his way into a thick part of the underbrush. Wincing, Zola followed. It was impossible to avoid being jabbed by sticks. Cobwebs clung to her hair, and something dark—mud? Pollen?—smeared across her shirt.

In a VR, she thought, *there'd be a path*.

In a VR, the trees would also be soaring and majestic, and the underbrush would be something picturesque—ferns, maybe. These trees were scraggly and misshapen. Some of the underbrush even had thistles and thorns that pulled at Zola's clothing.

It was nothing like a VR.

"If someone's looking for us, they'll see from the parking lot security cameras that we came in here," Zola said. "So it won't matter that there aren't cameras tracking our every move inside these woods."

"*Is* someone actually looking for us?" Puck asked. "Or are they just waiting for us to . . . make a mistake?"

"Sirilex, what mistakes do we need to avoid in this simulation?" Zola asked aloud, before she could stop herself. She clapped her hand over her mouth. "Oops."

They were past the worst of the underbrush now. Zola couldn't even see the parking lot when she glanced back.

"Don't worry," Puck said in a hushed voice. "I don't think anybody's listening to us here."

"But what are we going to do?" Zola asked. "We can't stay here forever! We don't even have any food!"

Puck sat down on a fallen log.

"Well, that last part's not true," he said.

He pulled his backpack to the side so he could yank on the broken tab of the zipper. He made a big enough opening that he could pull out something squished in a brown paper wrapping.

"Peanut butter sandwich," he said, holding it up. "We can each have half."

It looked pre-chewed. But Zola's stomach rumbled unpleasantly, and she wasn't going to make a fool of herself in front of Puck by demanding an Insta-Oven gourmet meal.

"Oh, that's right," Zola said. She begrudgingly took the mushed mess Puck slid into her hand. "You were smart enough to grab your lunch before we ran through the tunnel."

"What I learned in my Futureville is, you don't leave food behind," Puck said.

Zola took a tentative bite. The sandwich tasted better than it looked. But that wasn't saying much.

"Your mother made it for me," Puck said. "She hides food in her Insta-Closet for us to eat whenever she can."

"*My* mom?" Zola asked. Before she could think about it, she added, "Don't you have parents of your own to take care of you?"

Puck stared down as if the answer were in the mud beneath his feet.

"Not parents who care about me, or want me around," he said.

"What? That's—" Zola choked back the word "impossible." She had to remind herself once again that she wasn't living in some perfect 2193. And that Puck had experienced a very different "future."

"Even if they did care, they don't have enough food themselves," Puck said, with a shrug that didn't hide his hurt. "Or enough of anything."

Zola sat down on the log beside Puck.

"I'm so sorry," she said. "But I don't understand. It looked like all sorts of people were paying to go into your Futureville,

223

just like mine. They tell the tourists we're only acting. They tell the tourists that kids in my Futureville get to hang out with their friends any time they want, after we're done 'acting' for the day. And I don't think the tourists in your Futureville would be happy if they knew you really were starving. Or close to starving. Or . . . neglected in any way. I mean, that's—inhumane! It's got to be illegal, even in the year 2023!"

Puck looked ashamed, as if it were his fault that he didn't have enough food.

"Maybe you just think the 2020s are better than they really are," he muttered. He gulped down a particularly large clump of peanut butter. "I heard you sometimes, when you were doing a VR on the other side of a wall from me. When your mother thought I could get a little education, too. I heard you say things like, 'Nazis, leave those children alone!' and 'Martin Luther King, Jr., *I'll* join that protest with you!' And I thought, I just need to get you on my side, and you'd change everything. You'd make sure things are better and fairer in *both* our Futurevilles. And then I thought, if only I could escape, everything would be okay. And then you and I got out, and I thought, if only we can call a news conference like Zola's planning . . . that way we can get all the help we need."

"Doesn't seem like that's going to work, either," Zola muttered dejectedly, through a mouthful of peanut butter.

"Maybe . . . maybe we should just sneak back into our Futurevilles?" Puck asked. "Where at least we know they'll keep feeding us?" He looked down at his last bite of sandwich. "At least, someone will?"

"You mean, give up?" Zola asked incredulously.

The bark of the downed tree they were sitting on dug into her legs. Mud squished beneath her shoes. Peanut butter oozed unpleasantly between her teeth. Sweat dribbled down her forehead, but her cheeks felt clammy.

Zola longed for a clean change of clothes from her Insta-Closet. She longed for better food from her Insta-Oven—and definitely something cold to drink from her Insta-Fridge.

But most of all, she wished everything around her was just another VR. In a VR, the light would be glowing or dimming to let her know which details around her she should focus on or ignore. She'd be able to know for sure if Puck himself was a Helpful Clue Source or if she needed to be distrustful of anything he'd told her, anything he suggested.

As it was, every sensation around her seemed to be asking for equal attention: the pain in her legs, the quicksand feeling around her feet, the sticky peanut butter, the alternating sweat and chills. And then there were other details she couldn't seem to shut out, either: the memory of the woman on all the screens back at the Target, saying neither Zola nor Puck could be trusted. The odd way the man in

225

the gas station had acted, claiming they owed him money if they posted video of him on TikTok. (What did that even mean?) The way a corner of the book she'd been carrying in the messenger bag kept poking her side. Zola couldn't even shut out the constant traffic noise coming from beyond the little stand of trees she and Puck were hiding in. Why were 2020s cars so *loud*?

She opened her mouth to ask Puck that question—maybe he'd know. Maybe there was at least one thing she could stop wondering about. But just then, the traffic noise got louder. Was a car driving particularly close to their hiding place? Or . . . multiple cars?

Zola stood up and tiptoed over to one of the bushes near the parking lot they'd escaped. She peeked out through the leaves.

A car was idling there. This was a classic situation from a VR—in a VR, Zola's job would have been to jump out and say, "Hey! You're polluting! Shut off that car engine!"

But Zola was stopped from doing that. Because she could see the word written on the side of the car: "POLICE."

A second later, she heard a woman's voice saying, "Yeah, we had a report of a sighting of the suspects at a Target. We're going in to grab the security footage now."

34

Zola whirled toward Puck. He'd heard the police officer, too. The anguish and fear on his face probably matched Zola's own expression.

Zola held up her hands, hoping he could understand: *What do we do now?*

Outside their stand of trees, Zola heard the police officer add, "Yeah, I parked over on the side, so if the suspects are still in the area, they won't see us."

Then Zola heard footsteps—footsteps going in the opposite direction.

Zola dared to whisper to Puck, "They don't know where we are."

"Let's keep it that way," Puck whispered back.

Zola hunched over, trying even harder to stay hidden behind the bush. But it was hopeless. In a moment the police officer would probably see all the security footage. Zola and Puck wouldn't be able to stop that. And their stand of trees was so small—if they tried running anywhere else, they'd surely end up on some security tape again.

Puck pointed up.

"If we climb . . . ," he whispered.

Zola saw what he meant. The police would probably assume they'd run as far from the Target as they could. If they simply climbed one of the trees and got out of sight that way, maybe the police would leave without finding them.

Puck grabbed a broken-off branch and dragged it across the mud, erasing his footsteps. Quickly, Zola grabbed another branch from the ground and did the same with her own. Then Puck held out a hand, like he was offering to boost her up into the nearest tree.

"Are you kidding?" Zola muttered. "I'm taller than you. I should be giving *you* a boost!"

"Oh, right," Puck said. "I just thought . . . I wasn't sure you'd ever climbed a tree for real before."

"Lots of them, in VRs!" Zola assured him.

So Puck scrambled up the tree first. And then Zola had to struggle to figure out where to put her feet, where to put her hands.

Climbing a tree for real wasn't like climbing one in a VR. The branches on this tree weren't evenly spaced, like in a VR. They also weren't uniformly thick enough for Zola to trust that they would hold her weight.

But she couldn't complain to Puck when she'd acted so confident.

The branches shook beneath her feet. A few times, she started to step on a branch, and changed her mind, deciding it was too risky. Her upward progress was much, much slower than Puck's. But finally, she joined him near the top of the tree. He nestled in one crook of branches; she nestled in another, right beside him. Then Zola made the mistake of looking down. They were far above the ground.

"That's real, too," Puck said. "The distance. Don't fall."

For a moment, Zola felt dizzy. Then, through the leaves, she saw the police officer coming around the corner of the Target again. No—two of them, a woman and a man. The woman seemed to be in charge.

"You check back in those trees, but I bet they're long gone," the female cop said.

The male cop stepped over toward the clump of trees. He shined a flashlight toward the underbrush. But he didn't look up.

And then both cops got back in the car and drove away.

Zola let out a deep sigh.

"You were so smart!" she told Puck. "I'm so glad you figured out where to hide, even thinking to erase our footprints. . . ."

"It's just what I would have done back home," Puck said, with a modest shrug. But Zola noticed that his face flushed, as if he was both embarrassed and pleased by her compliment.

Zola eased one foot onto a lower branch, starting to climb down. Puck reached out a hand to stop her.

"No, wait—they could just be faking us out," he said. "They might come back."

Zola gaped at him, and Puck sighed.

"That's also something that could have happened back home," he muttered. "Zola, I was so scared you would think the cops might be on our side—that they would be people you could go to for help."

"Not when I heard them call us suspects," Zola said. "I'm not *that* naïve."

Puck looked skeptical.

"How long do you think we should wait?" Zola asked.

"Maybe an hour?" Puck suggested. "Or . . . maybe until dark, when we can creep out without being seen."

"That's hours away!" Zola protested. "How could anyone hide in a tree for that long?"

"People find they can do all sorts of things when they're in danger," Puck muttered back.

Zola sat and waited. The bark jabbed into her arm. Her back started to ache from sitting sideways.

Maybe five minutes had passed.

"You're the one who told me I was in danger, back in my Futureville," Zola said. "You're the one who asked for help, who said we should run away. You . . . and my mom."

"And you really only trust me because you trust your mom," Puck said, as if he'd figured out Zola long ago.

Zola narrowed her eyes at Puck.

"How can you be so sure I trust my mom?" she challenged.

"You left your Futureville, didn't you?" Puck retorted. "You're here in this tree with me, aren't you?" Puck let go of the branch he was holding on to just long enough to shove his messy hair back from his face.

At least this time he didn't use spit.

But it was annoying that Puck had figured out Zola's motivations before she'd figured them out herself.

"I trust . . . that my mom *thinks* everything she's told me is the truth," Zola said. "And I trust that that's how it is for you, too."

"Ditto," Puck said.

"What, um, what danger was I in back in my Futureville?" Zola asked in a small voice. There hadn't been time to ask that before. They'd both been too busy running away. "What danger would we have been in if those police officers had arrested us?"

She was treating Puck like a Helpful Clue Source in a VR. Or like Sirilex. She *wanted* him to know everything. Not just how to climb trees.

But Puck frowned.

"I don't know . . . exactly," he said. "But don't you see how your life was getting smaller and smaller? How they were trapping you in your own home?"

"I went to school!" Zola protested. "Though . . . I guess there were more and more days when Sirilex said I should only join from the treadmill at home. And . . . I only saw things through my VR goggles, regardless."

"So it was the same whether you were there in person or whether you were on a treadmill at home," Puck said.

He was right.

And outside of school, almost everything else was virtual, too. Except for when she was in her Insta-Closet.

Or arguing with Mom, she thought ruefully.

"My life was no different from any other kid's in my Futureville," she told Puck. "We were all taught that fear was a thing of the past, that, that . . . that we were *safe*."

"And yet, people were disappearing," Puck said.

"What?"

Puck shook his head, as if reluctant to tell.

"I was waiting until we had help," he said. "Until I could tell the whole story to someone who could fix things."

"Right now, it doesn't seem like you have anyone to tell *except* me," Zola countered.

That was something she would say in a VR, to get a hesitant Helpful Clue Source to trust her. The words came out automatically.

But somehow, they also felt true.

"You mean that people from your Futureville were disappearing, right?" she gently prodded.

"No—yours," Puck said. He gripped the center branch between them even more tightly. "On your street, there are

232

five empty houses now. At least, I think they're empty. Your mom says she never sees anyone going in or out of them anymore. And all the people from my Futureville who used to supply the Insta-Closets and Insta-Kitchens for those houses, they don't have jobs anymore. So now there are more people from my Futureville who don't have enough food. Because, mostly, it's people from your Futureville giving us food."

Zola's head spun. How could she have been so ignorant of everything going on around her?

All those VRs I spent my time on, she thought. *All those problems I solved in a pretend world. Because I thought all the problems in the real world had already been taken care of . . .*

"Maybe people are just leaving my Futureville because they want to," she suggested. "Maybe it's nothing . . . diabolical. Just a choice."

"Think about how your mother acts," Puck said. "Don't you think she'd leave, too, if she had a choice?"

Zola thought about the pinched look her mother's face got when she talked about the Insta-Closet or the glories of their Insta-Oven or Insta-Fridge. She thought about Mom saying, so bitterly, "It's almost time for the show to begin again!"

She thought about how fearfully Mom had reacted when Zola found the "help us" note in her Insta-Closet.

She thought about all the things she'd been annoyed with about Mom that . . . weren't a choice.

"It's like you and your mom were both trapped in a prison,

233

just as much as everyone in my Futureville," Puck said. "And you didn't even know it."

"Because everyone told me my life was perfect," Zola muttered.

A breeze rustled the leaves around them, sending Zola's hair streaming out behind her. It was the kind of breeze that might have occurred in a VR. One that signaled, "Things are changing. You're figuring things out. . . ."

Maybe VRs and the outside world weren't *completely* different. Maybe the breeze was a sign, in its own way.

Maybe Puck and I can still succeed, Zola thought. *Maybe . . . Maybe . . . Maybe . . .*

Maybe the idea for what they could do had been lurking in the back of her brain all along, and she just had to stop running long enough to notice it.

Zola eased the *All My Questions Answered* book out of the messenger bag.

"It sounds like there is *one* person who would believe us," she said. She held up the book. "Jessie Keyser. Who's . . . at the Indiana University School of Medicine."

"But where is that?" Puck asked.

"Oh, we can just ask—" She stopped before getting to the word "Sirilex." She frowned. "In VRs from the twenty-first century, sometimes we have to go into libraries to get answers to specific questions. Maybe we can find a library?"

"Libraries would have security cameras, too," Puck muttered sulkily.

"I think we're just going to have to risk it," Zola said. "So if you think we should wait at least an hour before coming out of these woods, let's spend it reading the rest of Jessie's story. Mom did say the book would help me. Want me to read aloud? Whispering, of course . . ."

Puck shrugged and nodded.

Zola squirmed over a little, so she could circle her elbow around the center branch and still leave both hands free for turning pages in the book. But that meant that the bark dug into her knees—could there be any less comfortable place for reading than crouched in a tree? She lifted the book a little higher, so its pages were in the sunlight, rather than in the shadows from all the leaves. She tried to turn to the page she'd left off reading the night before. But actual, physical, made-of-paper books were more fragile than the ones she'd encountered in VRs. This book was more than twenty years old. And she'd treated it roughly, cramming it into the messenger bag and letting it slam around while she hid under the bus seat, dashed away from the police, and climbed the tree. The spine of the book cracked when she opened it. She fumbled the book, almost dropping it, and smashed some of the pages together when she caught it again.

"Did you break that?" Puck asked.

"No!" Zola protested. "It's just the glue—or whatever holds it together—it's not working very well."

Something slipped out of the bottom of the book's spine.

Were the pages coming out? Were real, actual, physical books *that* delicate?

Zola saw that the paper slipping down wasn't a neatly cut rectangle like all the other pages of the book. It was more like a wad of paper folded over and over, and barely peeking out from the book's binding.

Holding her breath, Zola pulled it out completely. She closed the book again, laid it in her lap, and gently unscrolled the folds of paper on top of the book's cover.

"It's a letter!" Zola gasped. "A letter . . . from Jessie Keyser!"

35

Sept. 3, 2011

Dear Hannah,

You know I've tried as hard as I can to talk you out of moving to the Futurevilles. And I know you have stopped listening to me; I know nothing I can say or write will change your mind. But please know this: always, and no matter what—I still love you. You will always be my sister, and Zola—this child I've barely gotten a chance to know—will always be my niece. You are family, and . . .

But, no—I vowed I wouldn't use this space to try again to change your mind. Because I don't want you crumpling up this letter and throwing it away. I want you keeping it. I want you looking at it again when you're not so grief-stricken and heartbroken and angry. I want you remembering the "I love you no matter what" part above everything else.

And . . . I hope you know you always have a way to escape, if I am right about the Futurevilles, and you are wrong. Believe me, I would rather be wrong. This is not about one-upmanship. You and I have always made different choices. You liked our childhood in a way I didn't; I know there's a part of you that grieves the simplicity of Clifton Village and its rules—maybe even a part of you that resents me for ending that setup and ruining everything you were taught to value. But no matter what happens, you can always come to me for help. I will keep my house on Crooked Creek Vista; even if I'm not there, I will always leave messages there for where you can find me.

This is silly—I am acting as though cell phones don't exist, as though internet searches are impossible. It is not the 1800s; people can always be found. You and I, of all people, know how difficult it is to hide in the modern world.

And I know you would tell me you can still get mail from inside the Futurevilles; you will come out for vacations and holidays. You would tell me I will see you soon. But do this for me. Keep this letter with you in your Futureville. Keep it hidden. And if

you need me, know that I will always be there for
you in a heartbeat.

I love you. And Zola. Always.

Your sister,

Jessie

P.S. If it is Zola who needs this—little baby
Zola grown up; imagine that!—then here is the
information you need to find me:

Jessie Keyser

1802 Crooked Creek Vista

Indianapolis, Indiana

(317) 555-8230

Below that was a map: Futurevilles as a messy blob at the bottom, a line labeled "Route 37" going north, and then a spidery series of turns leading to 1802 Crooked Creek Vista inside a giant circle labeled "Indianapolis."

"*This* is what Mom meant about the book being useful," Zola exclaimed. "It wasn't that she thought we should use a pay phone and call a news conference like Jessie did in 1996. She meant for us to discover this letter and go to Jessie for help! *Aunt* Jessie!"

Puck was peering doubtfully over her shoulder.

"That letter's from twelve years ago," he said. "Twelve years is a long time. What if your aunt gave up on your mom ever contacting her again? What if she moved away, after all?"

"She wouldn't have," Zola said. "She promised." She pointed to the spot in the letter that said, "No matter what happens, you can always come to me for help."

Puck's face didn't light up, as Zola expected. Instead, he winced, as if he thought promises could be broken as easily as they were made.

Or maybe it was another problem he was thinking of.

Now Zola was the one wincing.

"Ohhh," she moaned. "This map shows how to get from the Futurevilles to Jessie's house. But . . . we're not starting from our Futurevilles. We don't even know *where* we are now!"

In a VR, there'd be a useful map overlay to add. Or she could ask a Helpful Clue Source for exact geographic coordinates.

How did people navigate anywhere in the real world? How did anyone keep from becoming completely lost?

Puck shook his head. But he did it in a merry way.

"Sure we do," he said. "Don't you remember how I looked out the window while we were on that school bus? We already came north on that Route 37. Zola—we're in Indianapolis now!"

36

Neither of them could bear to wait a full hour before climbing down from their tree and sneaking out of the tiny wooded area behind the Target. Zola flipped through the rest of the *All My Questions Answered* book, but she was really only skimming. All she had to do was get to her aunt Jessie's house, and then, she was sure, her questions would be answered, and everything would be fine. So there was no need to read carefully.

"You think it's safe now?" Zola asked Puck as she turned the last page. Had fifteen minutes passed? Had twenty?

"Probably about as safe as it's ever going to be," Puck muttered.

Zola couldn't understand why he didn't seem as overjoyed as she felt.

"Look, we'll watch out for security cameras," she said. "And police cars. And we won't talk to anyone until we get to Jessie's. We'll be fine. This is just like a VR where we've finally unlocked all the rules we have to follow, and now all that's left is getting to the destination."

"There might be—" Puck began. Then he shook his head. "You know what? You're right. This is all fine. Let's go."

They both climbed down the tree without falling. Puck knew how to retrace the route back to the giant road labeled "37." But it took a long time. And he insisted on hiding as much as possible whenever there were trees or bushes or buildings. Or, in areas that were completely open, he insisted on strolling casually, as if they were two normal 2023 kids out for a normal walk. Unremarkable. Unnoticeable.

They reached a stretch that was all concrete, with only shallow ditches on either side of the road, and Zola protested.

"Puck, we don't look normal regardless. Nobody's out walking except us. Kids are in school, and the adults . . ." A red car zipped past them, blaring an odd sound like a goose honking. Maybe whoever was in the car thought they were in the way? "Adults are all in cars."

Puck had already grabbed Zola's arm, jerking her to the side.

"I see that," Puck muttered, through gritted teeth. "But there's a different way to walk, where you're acting like *you* think everything you're doing is absolutely normal and not worth anyone else noticing. You don't go around like this." He swung his head back and forth, his eyes wide, peering around as if he'd never seen a street or a car before in his life.

"You're saying that's how I've been acting," Zola said. Her voice came out sounding injured. Her hands balled into fists, without her even planning it. Who did he think he was— her mother? Her friends never treated her that way. *Beatriz* would never say such a thing. Not even her teachers corrected her this harshly.

Oh, right, Zola thought. *I never talk to my friends for real, only through VRs. I don't see my teachers face-to-face, either.*

Puck sounded like Mom—because Mom was the only person Zola ever related to in person, without the distancing effect of the VR goggles between them.

Without the possibility of distorted reality that the VR goggles had, either.

Zola didn't actually know *what* Beatriz or her other friends had said to her over the years.

Puck's face did not look like something out of a VR. The corners of his mouth ticked down; his eyebrows wrinkled up. He looked, all at once, as if he was ready to fend off punches if she decided to raise her fists—or to give her a comforting hug if she sagged down to the concrete in despair and defeat.

Real people were *complicated*.

"You can still look around," Puck said gently. "Just not so . . . obviously."

"Got it," Zola said.

They kept walking. Zola could see houses off to the side. She could see trees off in the distance. She could see more concrete and grassy ditches ahead of her.

Everything around her was so . . . blah.

"It's all so beautiful, isn't it?" Puck asked, looking around a little too obviously himself. "Those houses don't look like any of them would have leaky roofs. The trees are green, not dying. This road . . . there's not anywhere that it's crumbling and falling apart. And those cars are all shiny and new, not rusted-out and sputtering. . . ."

He's comparing everything to his Futureville, Zola thought. *I'm comparing it to mine.*

She opened her mouth to say, "If you think this is beautiful, you should see where I live! Or you should see the VRs I've seen of Table Mountain or Paris in the springtime or Shanghai along the Huangpu. . . ."

But how did she know that any of those places were really the way they looked in VRs?

For that matter, how could she still think of her hometown as beautiful, when she understood so little about it?

"Yes," she told Puck, her voice as gentle as his had been moments earlier. "This is nice."

They trudged onward. Zola caught a glimpse of blue in a field off to the side—was it a pond? A creek?

"Puck, aren't you thirsty?" she asked. "We can get a drink over there."

She pointed. But Puck pulled back on her arm just as urgently as if she'd been about to step in front of another car.

"It'd be polluted," he said. "It'd make us sick."

"But in the 2020s, environmental laws changed, and all streams and waterways became so clean that . . . oh, right," Zola sighed. "We don't know what really happened in the 2020s. Or . . . what's happening."

She was thirsty, and getting thirstier by the minute. She was hungry, too. Half of a mashed peanut butter sandwich was not enough for anyone for a nourishing lunch before a long walk.

But I wouldn't have even had that, if it hadn't been for Puck, she thought.

She clamped her teeth together to stop herself from complaining. Or from automatically calling out to her Insta-Oven or Insta-Fridge that were now miles and miles away.

Or from calling out to Mom.

Did Mom ever get out of our Futureville to see Jessie—or anyone else in her family— after Jessie wrote that letter? Zola wondered.

Had Mom *liked* everything about their Futureville in the beginning? Had she expected to still have vacations and holidays with her family? Or was she glad to be away from them?

It made Zola's heart ache, that she didn't even know answers about her own mother.

Once Zola and Puck finally reached the bigger road— Route 37—it felt even stranger that they were walking along as cars and trucks sped past them. Zola and Puck took to darting close to stores and fences to seem less obvious.

One of the stores they neared had a big sign in the window that called out "COLD DRINKS! SNACKS!"

"Puck—let's take a break here," Zola suggested. "That's such a small store, surely they wouldn't have security cameras. And I don't know about you, but I could use a snack right now! And a drink."

Even without Sirilex's constant monitoring, she could tell that her electrolytes were getting low. And even without a single mood sensor around, she could tell that a break and a drink and something healthy to eat would bring her spirits up.

"Do you have any money with you?" Puck asked. "Or are you suggesting theft again?"

"Theft—no!" Zola protested. "That's wrong! And money . . . what are you talking about? I'm sure they would have biometric screeners that would automatically charge our accounts the cost of whatever . . . Okay. Never mind."

"Not used to being a suspect on the run, are you?" Puck said with a grin that almost looked merry.

Zola didn't have a good answer to that.

It was hours later, and the light was dimming, when they finally turned onto a winding street whose corner-post sign said, "Crooked Creek Vista." It was in a neighborhood of small, tidy houses. To Zola's eyes, the whole area looked quaintly old-fashioned. But she didn't say this to Puck.

He'd switched into a mode of peering around cautiously without moving anything but his eyes.

"Do you think someone's going to stop us?" Zola whispered. "Do you think they knew where we were headed, and were just . . . toying with us, letting us get this far?"

That was something that had happened to Jessie Keyser when she had escaped from her fake village to go for help.

"Don't know," Puck muttered.

Once again, Zola longed for Sirilex to give them answers.

But what good was Sirilex when so many of its answers were lies? she told herself.

Certainty was useless when what you were certain of wasn't actually true.

They reached 1802 Crooked Creek Vista, a brick house with green shutters. A yellow car sat in the driveway. Puck casually put his hand on the hood of the car.

"Still warm," he reported.

"That's horrible," Zola gasped. "Engines shouldn't give off warmth. That's a waste of energy, and—"

"This is the 2020s," Puck reminded her. "I don't think they've figured out how to prevent that yet. I just meant . . . if this is Jessie's car, she just got home."

Zola noticed that he didn't add, "Or if it's someone we should be afraid of, they've just arrived. They're waiting for us."

But somehow the expression on his face seemed to say that, anyhow.

The two of them crept toward the front door.

In a VR, I'd need to try to get ahead of Puck, Zola thought.

Because he's smaller and might need my protection.

But this was real life, and Zola couldn't quite bring herself to be that brave. She did at least walk alongside him, up the sidewalk, past a patch of tulips and daffodils and pansies. . . .

When they got to the front door, Zola saw that it was open just a crack. Silently, she pointed so Puck would notice, too.

Puck made a face that seemed to say, "That's lucky!" He pantomimed what he seemed to think they should do: push the door open just enough to slip inside, and then crouch down immediately, so they could hide until they saw who was actually in the house. Zola nodded.

If it's really Jessie who's here, I would recognize her, Zola thought. *And we can explain. If it's someone else—someone we don't want to meet—we can just creep back out.*

Puck eased the door open, and Zola peeked in. She could see a gray couch and a stretch of hardwood floor. No people. That was all she let herself glimpse before she edged her way in, into a shadowy space by the door. Immediately she started bending her knees, trying to get down and completely out of sight.

And then she heard a scream. And barking.

"Who are you? Get out of here! I've got an attack dog! Bru—sic 'em!"

37

Something large and furry launched itself toward Zola and Puck.

"No, no! Don't hurt us!" Zola screamed.

Beside her, Puck was crooning, "Nice doggy. Good boy. Or girl. That's right—I've got peanut butter on my hands . . . you like that, don't you?"

Incredibly enough, the large, furry creature had started licking Puck's fingers. Then the dog whimpered and pressed its floppy-eared head against Zola's hands as if it just wanted to be petted.

"Okay, the 'attack dog' part was kind of an exaggeration, but . . . you are intruders, and you have exactly one second to either get out of here or tell me why I shouldn't call 911, and—"

It was a woman's voice. But the woman had dodged over behind a wall, so Zola couldn't see her.

"Jessie?" Zola called. "*Aunt* Jessie?"

The woman peeked around the corner.

This wasn't Jessie Keyser.

Zola would have expected Jessie Keyser to look a lot like Mom. Or like Zola herself, only grown up. One rainy afternoon when she'd been bored, Zola had had Sirilex show her images of what Zola might look like at various ages: twenty-two and forty-five and ninety-two. . . . It had been comical to think of herself at ninety-two—and, anyhow, Sirilex had assured Zola that she would *never* actually look that ancient in real life, since age-erasing medical treatments were already available. Zola had played around with different ages and hair color and eye color and hairstyles and clothing styles— and then she'd gotten bored with that, too, because none of it mattered. Nothing she changed made a difference to her essential Zola-ness. No matter what, she still had the same snap to her eyes, the same glow of curiosity on her face.

Even at first glance, this woman also seemed like someone who was fully herself in any setting. She was tall and had close-cropped dark hair and brown skin; she wore blue jeans and a purple windbreaker. And even though the dog had completely failed at scaring off Zola and Puck, the woman still looked confident that she could take control of the situation.

She looked like the type of woman who could take control of any situation.

But a transformation came over her face when her eyes met Zola's.

"Oh," she gasped. "Oh my." She put her hands to her face. "I think I'm going to have to sit down for this one."

She took four steps forward and sank down onto the couch. She lowered her hands a little to peer out at Zola again, as if she'd half expected her to vanish.

"Are you all right?" Puck asked.

The dog whimpered, and galumphed over from begging for attention from Zola and Puck to lay its chin comfortingly on the woman's lap.

The woman shook her head, as if trying to clear it.

"After all this time . . . I never expected *this*," she said. "For you to just walk into Jessie's house when Jessie's not even here. . . . And then for me to see you, and have it feel so much like I'm going back in time, and I'm just a kid visiting hokey Clifton Village . . . and meeting Jessie for the first time. . . ."

"Then this *is* Jessie's house?" Puck asked, as if trying to extract the important information.

"And you know her?" Zola added. Then she was annoyed with herself—in a VR, she'd have points taken off for asking such a pointless question. Clearly this woman knew Jessie Keyser. She was in Jessie's house. "You met her when she was still in Clifton Village?"

"Technically, as she was leaving it . . ." The woman moved the dog aside, rose from the couch again, and held out her hand. "I'm Nicole Stevens."

"Nicole Stevens?" Zola repeated. "*The* Nicole Stevens? From the book?"

She pulled out *All Your Questions Answered* and held it up.

"There's a woman named Nicole in there?" Puck asked. "You didn't read me that part."

"A *girl* named Nicole," Zola corrected. "The only tourist Jessie met that she really liked."

Nicole lowered her hand to clutch the couch. Zola realized belatedly that she or Puck really should have shaken Nicole's hand—such a strange and archaic custom!—or at least apologized for not doing so. But Nicole acted like she had more important things on her mind.

"You had that book all along?" Nicole asked. "That means . . . your mom kept it? She was allowed to keep it and share it with you? So you've known for years that—"

"My mom had the book, but she always kept it hidden," Zola explained. "I didn't know about it until yesterday."

Puck put his hand on Zola's arm.

"Maybe you shouldn't reveal everything until you're sure . . . ," he murmured.

"Oh, I'm sure we can trust Nicole Stevens," Zola said. "Jessie trusted her!"

Puck flashed Zola a glance that seemed to ask, "But can we trust that this woman really is Nicole Stevens? Can we trust that anything anyone tells us is true? Especially when you know now that people have been lying to you your entire life?"

He had a point.

"Where *is* Jessie?" Zola asked. "How soon will she be home?"

Nicole pulled out a small rectangular device that Zola recognized now as a phone.

"She's away on a camping trip, and I've been dog-sitting for her. We trade off like that all the time," Nicole said. "But I'll call her right now—I'm sure she'll want to rush home immediately. Be ready for the squeals of joy!"

Nicole's fingers danced over the screen of her phone, then she held it up to her ear. Zola edged closer, so she could hear, too. She was ready to squeal for joy herself at the sound of her aunt's voice.

But three odd, tinny notes of music sounded from the phone instead—*do do doooo*—and then a robotic voice said, "The number you have reached is no longer in service."

"What?" Nicole said, holding the phone out from her ear and staring at it in disbelief. "That doesn't make sense!" She stabbed a finger against the screen. "Maybe if I just try again . . ."

But before she could do anything else, her phone began blaring out different music. With a puzzled frown, Nicole touched the screen and lifted the phone to her ear.

Whoever was on the other end now had a softer voice, so

Zola could hear only Nicole's side of the conversation.

"No, she's not with me. . . . She didn't tell me anything about . . . Yeah, same." Nicole's eyebrows shot sky-high. "That's impossible! She loves working there! And, anyhow, that's not how she'd do it, even if . . . Yeah, you do that." Her gaze flicked toward Zola and Puck. "Let me know the minute you hear anything."

She lowered the phone. Her eyes seemed almost glassy with shock.

"What was that about?" Zola asked. "Who were you talking to?"

Nicole blinked.

"That was Jessie's boss," she said. "Jessie just quit her job. By email. And then she said that, from now on, she can only be reached by snail mail."

Zola couldn't quite remember what email and snail mail were, but they sounded bad.

"And that means . . . ," she began cautiously.

"You think someone's lying," Puck said, as if he'd caught on to what was really important. "You think someone's just pretending to be Jessie, and making it so no one can reach her."

"But why?" Zola asked, totally bewildered now. "Why would anyone want to—"

"To make it so you don't meet your aunt?" Puck suggested.

Now Zola felt like she was going into shock.

254

"You think this is because of the Futurevilles," she said. "You think . . . Is Jessie in danger now, too?"

"I don't know," Nicole said. She clenched her teeth. "But something's really wrong. And we have to fix it."

38

Everything was messed up and confusing, but Zola knew one thing: she *liked* Nicole Stevens.

Nicole had needed only a moment to be shocked and horrified by what she was now calling "the lies about Jessie." And then she'd swept into action. She'd locked the front door behind Puck and Zola. She'd taken the dog's face in her hands and put her nose against the dog's nose and said, "Sorry, Brunhilda, no long walk for you. You're just going to have to run around the backyard on your own for a little bit."

As soon as the dog was released to the outdoors through a sliding glass door, Nicole rifled through a purse sitting on the table.

"First things first," she said. "I can prove I am Nicole Stevens. So you'll know you can trust me."

She pulled out a piece of—yikes, was that *plastic*? Again?

This time, it was a card with one large and one small picture of Nicole, and the words "Indiana USA Operator License."

The card did indeed announce that Nicole was Nicole Stevens. And that she was five foot ten, and had been born on June 2, 1983. Which . . . made her the same age as Jessie.

"That doesn't prove anything," Puck countered. "Just that you could pay for some sort of ID card *saying* you're Nicole Stevens. Someone's out there pretending to be Jessie. So you could be just pretending to be Nicole."

"Fine," Nicole said. She lifted the *All My Questions Answered* book out of Zola's arms. "I'm a little embarrassed to still know this, but you can find me on page one hundred eighty-two."

Nicole flipped over to page 182, which showed a picture of two girls, one Black, one white, with their arms around each other's shoulders. The words below the picture said, "Jessie became pen pals and then good friends with Nicole Stevens, the girl she first encountered in the tourist area of Clifton Village. Nicole, a budding historian, was happy to catch Jessie up on 'news' of the Civil War, the emancipation of slaves, and the civil rights movement."

Nicole wrinkled her nose.

"Yeah, the way things were described back in the 1990s when a Black girl and a white girl were friends—it just doesn't age well, you know?" she muttered.

Nicole rolled her eyes. Somehow that was all it took for

Zola to see the resemblance to the girl in the picture with Jessie. Even though the girl in the picture was smiling.

"Puck, this is the right person," Zola said. "We can trust her."

"If you say so," Puck said, a little grumpily.

"And who are you?" Nicole asked him. "I can figure out this kid"—she pointed at Zola— "but you . . ."

Puck and Zola gave a quick version of who he was and how they'd met and everything else that had happened since Zola found Puck's note in her Insta-Closet. Nicole looked more and more concerned as Puck described life in his Futureville. And as Zola told about never seeing anyone outside of VR anymore except her mother.

"So we knew we needed to come to Jessie's house," Zola finished up. "But now it sounds like we've got more problems than ever, if Jessie's . . . unreachable. It sounds like we can't go to the police or call a news conference, but . . . how do you think we can fix all this? And maybe rescue Jessie, too? Do you know what 'messages' she'd left here for Mom or me?"

"Not entirely," Nicole said. "I know Jessie has a little box at the back of her house where she left a note for your mom or you, with a special phone in it—she thought that was enough so you could always reach her! But there are so many unknowns in your story. Were the police at that Target really looking for you, or were they just actors hired to seem like cops? Or were they real cops looking for someone else? How did the Futurevilles people know you'd come looking for Jessie? How far did they go in making her unavailable? Did they kidnap her? Or . . ."

Nicole winced, as if she couldn't go on with that thought.

Just then, her phone dinged. Nicole looked down at it, her frown deepening.

"What?" Zola asked.

"Jessie's boss checked with the police to see about reporting an identity theft," Nicole said. "She's going to keep trying, but . . ."

Zola leaned forward and read over Nicole's shoulder: "Their first response was, 'She's an adult. She can cancel her phone service and quit her job if she wants.' Seriously?"

"So it's hopeless," Puck said.

His shoulders slumped. His eyes stayed downcast. And Zola felt as dejected as he looked. How could any of them survive this? It was bad enough to be in danger. But how could they cope with not knowing how to fix things?

Or—not knowing much of anything?

"No, no—not hopeless," Nicole said, rising from the overstuffed chair she'd been sitting in while Puck and Zola told their story. "I may not have all this figured out, but I know where we can look for answers."

"Where?" Zola asked.

"Come on," Nicole said.

She led Puck and Zola down a hallway to a closed door,

and then down a dark flight of stairs.

"Um, I don't like this," Puck whispered behind Zola. "Not at all."

"Hold on, I'm finding the light switch," Nicole said. "Light will help."

"Sirilex, please . . . ," Zola murmured, before she remembered that that would do no good.

And then Nicole must have discovered the light switch, because suddenly everything was bright and glowing around them. And Zola could see again.

And she could see . . .

. . . they were back in the Futurevilles.

39

Oh, wait—not really, Zola realized, instantly correcting her first impression.

Directly in front of her were giant pictures from her Futureville. There was Mom, holding a cup of coffee. Mom working on an art project. Mom showing Zola how to ride a tricycle when Zola was maybe two or three . . .

Tears flooded Zola's eyes, and she had to look away.

But her glance to the side revealed a scale model of both Futurevilles, resting on a set of sawhorses.

When Zola looked in the opposite direction, she saw a wall full of papers and string and . . . were those actual newspaper clippings? Cut out from an old-fashioned newspaper?

"Jessie calls this her 'Crazy Conspiracy Theorist Lair,'" Nicole said. "She made fun of herself, because she knew how all of this looks. I assure you, by day, Jessie is a respected scientist and doctor. Or . . . she was. And will be again, because her boss didn't believe that 'resignation.' But Jessie also spent the past twelve years trying to figure out how to reach out to her sister Hannah, who . . . might as well have joined a cult. This is where Jessie keeps her research."

"What's a cult?" Zola asked.

"Uh, usually it's a religious group, I think, but not always—it's any extremist group that brainwashes its members and expects absolute devotion and . . . cuts them off from contact with the outside world," Nicole said.

"But why?" Puck asked. "Why would anybody do that to another human being?"

"Money, power . . . and sometimes because the people who set up the cult are true believers themselves," Nicole said. "They *think* they're doing something good, but it turns evil."

"Which reason was it with the Futurevilles?" Zola asked.

Nicole held up her hands helplessly.

"That's the big question, isn't it?" she asked.

Zola drifted toward the wall of news clippings and scrawled notes. She couldn't concentrate enough to read anything start to finish, but headlines and random phrases jumped out at her:

CHOOSE YOUR FUTURE: PERFECT?
OR PERFECTLY AWFUL?

NEW TOURIST ATTRACTION
TO FOCUS ON THE FUTURE,
INVITE INTROSPECTION—
AND BRING JOBS TO WORKERS NOW

... expected to bring attention and outside dollars to an economically depressed area of the state still suffering from the closing of Clifton Village in the late 1990s ...

... just as tourists will get to switch between seeing both a hopeful and a horrifying vision of the future, the residents of the Futurevilles will trade off depicting life in each scenario.

"In reality, all of them will get the luxuries and comforts of the 'good' Futureville," according to the news release. "But they will periodically get the dramatic fun of play-acting the devastation of the 'bad' Futureville ..."

Zola recoiled.

"Puck, did you see this?" she asked, pointing at that particular clipping. "This means you were supposed to have the same kind of life as me. We were supposed to take turns pretending to live in your Futureville and mine!"

"Yeah, well, that didn't happen, did it?" Puck muttered.

Zola saw that a page thumbtacked beside the news article had four words scrawled across it in handwriting that must have belonged to Jessie: *This was a lie!*

"In the early years, Jessie went to the Futurevilles again and again," Nicole said. "And she paid other people to go there, and she kept track of where various residents were spotted, day to day. She tried to get someone from the news media to investigate, but it didn't seem important to them. And . . . when Jessie kept harping on it, it made her seem like a crackpot."

Zola had never heard the word "crackpot" before, but she could figure out what it meant.

"So Jessie acted like the scientist she'd been trained to be and kept gathering evidence, in hopes that eventually she'd have enough to prove her . . . well, I was going to say 'theories,' but really it was more like . . . suspicions," Nicole said. "Or fears."

"But she didn't want to be right," Zola said, remembering the letter she'd seen from Jessie to Zola's mother. "She *wanted* to believe that Mom and I were fine, and"—she glanced at Puck—"and nobody was being hurt. And that all of us could leave anytime we wanted."

Nicole frowned. Her eyes looked especially sad.

"Well, that would have hurt Jessie, too," she said, stepping closer to the wall and Zola and Puck. "Because if everything was fine in the Futurevilles, that meant Jessie's own sister never wanted to see her. And never wanted her daughter—you—to grow up knowing her family."

Zola flinched. She almost felt responsible for hurting Jessie, too. But that wasn't fair.

"*I* wanted to meet Jessie," she said. "As soon as I found out she existed. It's just that . . . Mom never thought it was safe to tell me until yesterday."

Nicole didn't reply. She was staring at another section of the wall.

"This is new," she muttered. "When did Jessie figure this out?"

Zola rushed to Nicole's side, to read over her shoulder.

In this section of the wall, there were fewer newspaper clippings, as if the news media had lost interest in the Futurevilles in recent years. But Jessie's scrawled notes continued.

Nicole was staring at a piece of paper where the handwriting started out neat, but got messier and messier:

> What if the Futurevilles are like Clifton Village in more ways than I thought?
>
> CV was a tourist attraction hiding an illegal, unethical medical experiment.
>
> What if the Futurevilles are doing that, too?
>
> Counterargument: There's no sign of medical experiments in the Futurevilles. I've looked.

But what if the experiments aren't medical in the same way?

What if they're just psychological?

What if the isolation was the point all along???

"Zola," Nicole said slowly. "Before you met Puck, how long did you say it'd been since you'd seen anybody but your mother face-to-face, not through VR goggles?"

"I guess . . . years," Zola said. "If ever." She was so used to VR goggles—and things like the Picture Walls—that it was hard to remember what was real and what wasn't. Even her memory of playing in the snow as a three- or four-year-old— had that been actual or virtual?

She looked again at the picture of Mom with toddler Zola on a tricycle. Neither of them wore goggles. So there *had* been a time in Zola's life before goggles.

But that was the only outdoors, goggle-less picture.

"They always said school had to be VR, to connect with people all over the world," Zola told Nicole. "But everything else became virtual, too. VR goggles were just . . . automatic."

Even when Mom wanted to let Zola see what her Future-ville was really like—with the tourist groups strolling through—Mom hadn't told her to go out without goggles. She'd given her goggles that *looked* like a normal VR pair, but could show reality, too.

But that was just because Mom didn't want me to be caught without goggles. . . .

Why had that mattered so much?

Why had Zola not even thought to ask why that mattered so much?

Because . . . I've been brainwashed?

"Hold on—the people in *my* Futureville haven't been getting more isolated," Puck protested. "They keep making us live more and more crowded together. They keep making us run around more, taking care of the people in *your* Futureville. . . ."

"Every experiment needs its control group," Nicole said with a grimace.

"But which Futureville is the experiment, and which is the control group?" Zola asked. "And what can we do about it?"

Nicole laid a gentle hand on Zola's shoulder.

"I think we have to blow up that particular experiment," she said.

"Blow up?" Zola repeated. "You mean, hurt people? Use explosives and cause pollution?"

"Sorry—I was using a figure of speech," Nicole said. "I meant, end your isolation in a dramatic way." She held up her phone again. "Because I'm going to call everyone I know to come and help."

40

Zola sat on the couch in Jessie Keyser's living room, with Brunhilda the dog nestled comfortingly beside her. Periodically, the dog nudged Zola's shoulder with her nose—not in a "Get up and do something!" way, but more as if to say, "I understand. This isn't what I expected right now, either."

Who knew dogs could be so sympathetic?

Without Brunhilda, Zola might have run screaming from the room. Because . . . she was surrounded.

A woman and two men stood to her left, all wearing medical scrubs and badges identifying them as doctors, and the woman was arguing, "But any reputable scientific study would require that the children's parents had signed releases—do you think they forged the paperwork?"

"Or do they even care about passing off their studies as reputable?" one of the men countered.

In front of her, Nicole was leaning down with a little kid—

a seven- or eight-year-old?—who had twisted braids and skinned-up knees and a neon-green dress that looked like something Zola herself might have chosen from her Insta-Closet. And Nicole was telling the little girl, "Yes, I know you really want to meet your cousin, but she's not used to having a lot of people around, so let's wait a bit on that, okay?"

Cousin? Zola thought. *I have a cousin?*

But of course she could have cousins. Her mother and Jessie had had three brothers and another sister. There were lots of possibilities.

Zola wanted to stand up and say, "Oh, hey—I'm fine. Glad to meet you! What's your name?"

But before she could do that, she got distracted by the conversation to her right, where Puck was telling a crowd of women who looked like any one of them could be Nicole's mom, "I always knew we weren't being treated fairly. I always knew something had to change. . . ."

"Amen," one of the women said.

"From the mouths of babes," another agreed.

Someone tapped Zola on the shoulder.

"Overwhelming, huh?"

A man sat down beside her. He had messy brown hair and greenish eyes, and something about him seemed familiar.

"So, I'm your uncle Andy—Hannah and Jessie's little brother, and, also, Nicole's husband—lucky me, that Jessie introduced us. . . ."

"I have an uncle?" Zola squeaked.

"More than one," Uncle Andy began.

"And . . . doesn't that make Nicole my aunt?"

"Yes, and I'm a little hurt that Nicole didn't point that out sooner, but . . . honestly, there's so much family news you and your mom need to catch up on, none of us know where to start," Uncle Andy said. "The first step is just making sure none of this is too much for you. Would you like to move to another room and have people come in one by one to talk to you? Rather than having the whole IU med school over there holding a colloquium, and all the church grandmas over there ready to offer sympathy, and the family cabal back there"—he pointed over his shoulder—"and all my tech bro—and sis!—friends over there . . ."

Zola hadn't even noticed the group of people who all seemed to be wearing khaki pants and polo shirts—both the males and the females. They were sitting on the floor by the fireplace, all of them hunched over laptops and cell phones.

The idea of sitting in a quiet room and only having to pay attention to one person at a time sounded *divine*.

But Zola shook her head stubbornly.

"That's too slow," she said. "I want to find out what happened to Jessie as soon as possible. And I want to get my mom out of danger as soon as possible. And . . . to set everyone free. From both Futurevilles."

Uncle Andy raised an eyebrow and gave her a sympathetic half frown. It was almost the exact same expression that

Zola's mom used when she was sympathizing with Zola—
even though Uncle Andy's half frown slipped down into a
beard, and that certainly wasn't the case with Mom.

Zola wished this was some "Explore Family Resemblances"
VR, and she could just mute everything else around her and
talk to Uncle Andy about what everyone in the family looked
like, and how they acted similarly, and . . .

And that's not really important now, is it? she asked herself.

Except it kind of was. The family resemblance made her
think that she could trust this man she'd never met before.

*But did Mom want to get away from her entire family when
she went to our Futureville? If so, why did she give me the book
with Jessie's letter?*

"Can I at least get you something to eat?" Uncle Andy
asked. "One of your other uncles, Nathan, is actually a gourmet chef now, and his solution to every problem is food. So
there are lots of choices over there. . . ."

He pointed back toward Jessie's kitchen.

Zola had been starving on her walk with Puck, but somehow she wasn't hungry at all now.

"No, thanks," she said in a small voice.

The dog licked her chin, as if she could tell that Zola
needed more comfort than ever.

And Zola started listening to the conversation behind her,
from the group of people Uncle Andy had described as the
"family cabal."

"Jessie's resourceful," someone was saying. "She could handle Clifton's crooks when she was thirteen—she'll be fine now. She can outsmart anyone."

"But she knew Clifton Village inside and out," someone else argued. "She only knows the Futurevilles as an outside observer."

"Still, has anyone observed that vile place as much as she has in the past twelve years?"

Yes—Puck and me, Zola thought. *And Mom.*

But she still collapsed against Brunhilda's fur, as if even thinking about Mom weighed her down.

"Jessie left Clifton Village all by herself," Zola said to Uncle Andy. "I had Puck to help me and now this entire room—er, house—full of people, and we still haven't managed to get anyone to safety. We even have the internet now, and Jessie didn't know it existed, back in 1996. Why can't we fix this?"

"I don't think that's a fair comparison," Uncle Andy said. "You're not dealing with the same set of problems. And Jessie would be the first to say that that whole media fixation with 'Thirteen-year-old girl singlehandedly saves entire village' wasn't accurate. She said almost everyone she met helped in some way. And that, really, the most useful thing she did was just catching diphtheria herself, and proving her story that way."

"Then could Puck and I prove we've had people doing

psychological experiments on us?" Zola asked.

"Psychological experiments are harder to prove than medical ones," Uncle Andy said regretfully. "And the media now is a lot more . . . splintered . . . than it was back in 1996."

Zola slumped back against the couch. All the conversations swirling around her were giving her a headache. In a VR, she'd put everyone on mute and freeze them midsentence to give herself time to think.

But real life, she was finding, wasn't that much like a VR.

Puck came over and sat down on the other side of Brunhilda the dog. Was he overwhelmed, too?

Zola watched him bury his face in Bru's fur.

"This is pointless," he complained.

"All these people want to help," Zola said. "They're *trying.*"

"Or they just want some of that crab dip back there," Puck muttered, sitting back up to point over his shoulder. "Or they don't have anything better to do on a Tuesday night. Or they think it's exciting, that Nicole called them for help. This reminds me of all the grown-ups in *your* Futureville, who would give the people from my Futureville extra food or clothes. They acted like they wanted to be nice. But they'd also say, 'Sorry we can't actually change how this is set up.' And 'Please don't tell our kids that their Futureville is a lie. We don't want our kids to worry.'"

"That's what my mom told you," Zola said glumly. "She was afraid that your note would put me in danger."

"Well, to be fair, it *did*," Puck said with a teasing grin.

For a moment, Zola concentrated on nothing but running her hands through Bru's fur. In a VR, there would be no reason to focus on petting a dog, because it never felt quite right. Maybe by the time of the real 2193, VR technology would be good enough for that. But Zola almost hoped that that would never happen.

It seemed important that this was real. That she was petting an actual dog, not just an imaginary one.

It . . . almost felt like putting a VR on pause for a moment to give herself time to think.

"Wait a minute," she said to Puck. "Did you say other grown-ups in my Futureville were giving people from your Futureville food or clothing? Other people besides my mom were helping in secret? Even though it endangered them?"

"Yeah, sure," Puck said with a shrug. "Like I said, that became the only way we had enough food that nobody starved."

"How many people did that?" Zola asked. "Just two or three? Or . . . lots?"

"Lots," Puck said. "Most of them, even."

Zola bolted to her feet, her mind whirring.

"I know what to do!" she announced. "I just figured out a plan!"

The entire room fell silent. People paused with crab-dip-covered crackers halfway to their mouths. The doctors stopped arguing. The tech experts looked up from their laptops. Two of the church ladies stopped midhug. And the little girl who was probably Zola's cousin peered up at her admiringly.

This might as well have been a paused VR. Except that everyone else in the room was still breathing. They were still *real*.

"What?" Nicole asked. "What's your plan?"

"We're going to need everyone's help," Zola said. "But it starts with . . ." She swallowed hard and looked down at her hands. She was afraid. But that didn't make her change her mind. "Puck and I are going to have to go back to our Futurevilles."

41

THIS WAY TO YOUR FUTURE → →
BUT WHICH ONE WILL YOU CHOOSE?

Zola shivered as she saw the Futurevilles sign by the highway.

"If we had come up with a single other plan that anyone thought would work, we wouldn't be doing this," Nicole said from beside her.

It was the next morning, and Nicole was driving Zola and Puck back to their Futurevilles.

"Wish we'd come up with a plan that didn't involve riding in a car that runs on *gas*," Zola muttered.

"At least it's a hybrid," Nicole offered ruefully. She shot Zola a sympathetic look. "But, Zola—your Futureville isn't wrong about the environment being a big concern. There are lots of things you'll have to sort out when all this is over. You've been lied to, yes, but not everything you've been told is a lie."

"Maybe just focus on the essentials right now?" Puck offered from the back seat.

The environment is essential! Zola thought.

But she understood what Puck and Nicole meant. For now, she needed to separate out short-term goals and long-term goals.

The short-term goal was rescuing people who were in danger. Right now. In 2023.

Mom. Aunt Jessie. And everyone in both Futurevilles . . .

"Let's take care of some practicalities," Nicole said. "Like money. I went to the ATM this morning while you were both sleeping and got some cash."

They'd all three spent the night at Jessie's house, because Nicole wanted to be there in case Jessie just happened to show up.

She hadn't. Nobody had heard from her since the strange message about quitting her job. And there still seemed to be no way to reach her.

Zola had thought there was no way she'd manage to sleep, but she'd dropped right off the instant her head hit the pillow, and Nicole had had to wake her in the morning.

Because they wanted to be at the Futurevilles as soon as they opened.

Now Zola had to think hard about what Nicole might be talking about.

"Money?" she repeated. "*Cash?* Do you mean people still carry around coins and dollar bills in the 2020s?"

"Well, we don't use it very often," Nicole hedged. "But I don't want my credit card tipping off anyone."

"Any more than we're going to tip off people when Zola and I show up on the security cameras, going back in pretending to be tourists?" Puck asked.

"We can't help that," Nicole said, frowning as she turned, following the arrows pointing toward the Futurevilles. "We're just going to have to hope that Zola is right, and that's what the Futurevilles people *want* you to do."

"Everybody else is in place, right?" Zola asked anxiously. "They all know their part?"

"Absolutely," Nicole assured her. "Everything's set."

The scenery outside the car had changed now that they'd turned onto the driveway toward the Futurevilles visitors' center. They were surrounded by a giant woods full of towering trees.

"It's funny how *this* part of the Futurevilles looks about the same as it did when this road led to Clifton Village," Nicole said. "It's just that the trees are taller."

"Because a healthy planet in the future would include areas of pristine forests," Zola suggested.

"And having the Futurevilles shut off from the rest of the world like this kept them isolated," Puck countered, glowering at the trees as if they were to blame.

"Both could be true," Nicole said.

Signs began popping up at the side of the road with questions about various years, as if they were driving toward the future:

2035: Is the internet free now? And available everywhere?

2045: Does every person on the planet have access to enough food and clean water every single day of their lives? Have starvation and diseases of poverty been completely eliminated?

2055: Is all menial labor now handled by robots?

2065: Has war been abolished yet?

2075: Are all energy sources renewable now?

2085: Do we have our carbon footprint under control now?

2095: Have humans visited other planets yet?

"They're not very subtle, are they?" Puck said glumly. "The answer to all those questions is yes for the buildup to Zola's Futureville, and no for mine."

Nicole shot him a sympathetic look.

"If the Futurevilles were doing nothing but getting people to think about the future, that *would* be a good thing," she said.

"But that's not the only thing they're doing," Zola said, scowling.

They came out of the woods to find the parking lot for the Futurevilles. It was a stretch of blacktop that seemed even more endless than the parking lot back at the Target store Puck and Zola had visited.

Having so much of the Earth covered by blacktop heats up the planet, Zola thought anxiously. *It prevents the growth of trees, and the oxygen they would release into the atmosphere, and . . .*

She reminded herself that she couldn't let herself worry about that right now.

Nicole pulled up beside the curb outside the visitors' center.

"Are you sure you don't want me going in with you?" she asked. "I'm fighting against every one of my mom instincts, letting you out here. We could adjust the plan a little and—"

"It has to look like Puck and I are giving up," Zola said firmly. "Like we can't imagine doing anything but going back to the lives we've always had. If you go with us—"

"I know, I know." Nicole took one hand off the steering wheel to give a resigned wave. "That changes everything. It's just . . . this is hard."

Tell me about it, Zola thought.

Her stomach churned, as though the pancakes she'd eaten

for breakfast—made by Puck, because it turned out he was a better cook than either Zola or Nicole—were leapfrogging over one another. Zola's brain churned, too, calculating, *What if someone stops us from even going in? What if there's some glitch and the rest of our plan fails completely?*

She got out of the car. Puck did, too.

And then Zola wanted to stand there waving goodbye to Nicole and watching her yellow car disappear back into the woods. But Puck nudged her and whispered into her ear, "Act defeated. Act desperate. Act . . ."

"Yeah, yeah, got it," she said.

She let her shoulders slump. She bowed her head.

And then she trudged off toward her future.

42

The Futurevilles visitors' center was every bit as crowded as it'd been the day before. Puck and Zola did their best to blend in with a group of schoolkids at the back. But Zola couldn't quite figure out how to imitate their casual carelessness. None of them were acting like someone in a VR. They didn't seem to be thinking about the Futurevilles at all.

"I think he likes you," a girl directly in front of Zola was telling the girl beside her.

"Not as much as Ben Kohlberg likes you!" the second girl teased.

"When's lunch?" a boy beside them asked.

Our plan depends on kids like this caring about people besides themselves, Zola thought in a panic. *What if they don't? What if they're not even capable of doing that?*

She reached out and clutched Puck's hand. Whether their plan worked or not, there was no turning back now.

"We have a choice." Puck spoke without even moving his lips. "We can pretend to be part of this school group, and just hope they wave us in with everyone else. Or we can go stand in line and buy tickets like we're supposed to, with the money Nicole gave us."

He tilted his head to the side, indicating a long line that snaked through several roped-off aisles.

"Are you going to say that not buying a ticket would be like theft and we have to follow the rules?" he asked.

Zola didn't want to wait in line. She wasn't even sure there was *time* to wait in line.

"It's not theft," she muttered back to Puck. She was not as talented as he was at talking so secretly. She didn't have his experience. "We've been donating practically every moment of our lives to the Futurevilles without even knowing it . . . and given what we're going to do next, the cost of two little tickets isn't going to matter."

Puck grinned.

"Way to go, Zola," he said. "Now you're thinking like me!"

The kids in front of them—the ones talking about boys and lunch—surged forward, and Zola and Puck fell into step along with them.

"Here are goggles for you . . . and you . . . and you . . . ," a bored-looking woman chanted as she handed them to each kid in turn.

She didn't even look at Zola and Puck.

It's working! Zola thought as she pulled the goggles over

her head and adjusted the strap. *We're getting away with this!*

"Group A, your guide is ready," a man who looked like a teacher announced to the entire group.

One of the girls in front of Zola elbowed the other. "Aren't we in group A?"

The other girl spent a moment doing nothing but chewing gum.

"Let's go in Ben Kohlberg's group instead," she said. "No one's keeping track."

Opportunity! Zola thought.

She nudged the gum-chewing girl.

"My friend and I will go in group A for you, in case anyone's counting," Zola said.

"Why would you do that?" Gum-chewer asked suspiciously. "What's in it for you?"

"We, uh . . ."

"Just want to get this over with," Puck finished for her.

Gum-chewer shrugged.

"Here," she said.

And then she and her friend handed Zola two tickets.

Zola had to resist the urge to high-five Puck.

The two of them rushed toward the guide starting to lead group A toward a metal turnstile.

"Wait—you didn't give us *your* tickets," the girl called after them. But the gum-chewer countered, "That doesn't matter. They wouldn't be the right tickets for Ben's group, anyhow. We'll just say we lost them."

Gum-chewer and her friend will be fine, Zola thought.

She slowed down to go through the turnstile with Puck at the same pace as the other kids around them. Gum-chewer was right: no one actually looked at their tickets.

After the turnstile, the wall in front of them slid open, and Zola and Puck and the other kids were back in the public plaza of Zola's Futureville.

Home, Zola thought, and behind her goggles, tears pricked her eyes. She was back home, but nothing was the same. *She* wasn't the same.

"Welcome to 2193, when human society is finally perfect." The guide's voice sounded through the earpiece on Zola's tourist goggles. He had a slight Southern accent and a tone of awe. "Fear is a thing of the past. Pain is a thing of the past. Crime is a thing of the past. Racism is a thing of the past. Sorrow is a thing of the past."

He paused dramatically for an instant, as if to let all that sink in.

"Everyone here is happy and fulfilled and living meaningful lives in harmony with their neighbors and their environment," the guide continued. "Come on. Let's go see."

Beside Zola, Puck was rolling his eyes.

Was I truly living a meaningful life of harmony here? Zola wondered as she automatically joined the rest of the group trailing after the guide. *Or did I just think that because I never actually interacted with anyone except Mom?*

And she'd rolled her eyes constantly at Mom. In contrast

to everyone else in Zola's life—all the people she only related to virtually—Mom was annoying and maddening and frustrating and demanding and ridiculous.

And real.

And even when Mom was at her worst, Zola always knew that Mom loved her.

She didn't know anything about how anybody else felt about her.

Except, maybe she did know about Puck now. He made fun of her, but it seemed like he also cared about her.

And so do Nicole—Aunt Nicole!—and Uncle Andy and all those other people who gathered at Jessie's house . . . who are standing ready to execute our plan even now. . . .

Zola flicked her gaze toward the huge decorative clock in the center of the plaza. It was only 8:35. They still had time.

She tuned out most of the rest of the guide's narration as they walked past city hall and the transportation depot and the row of quaint stores. It didn't matter. All she had to do was blend in until they got to the residential areas.

But beside her, Puck was wide-eyed, peering around at all the perfect buildings, the artful landscaping, the glorious blue sky with only a few decorative white clouds. (At least, it looked glorious through the tourist goggles.)

"I didn't know," he whispered to Zola. "I never actually *saw* your Futureville. I didn't know you had all this and still . . . you left it because I asked for help? And your mom risked losing all this to help me?"

"It only looks good on the surface, remember?" Zola whispered back.

Were they endangering themselves just by whispering that? Were their murmurs picked up by the microphones attached to their goggles?

"I mean, yeah, I thought it was a good idea to leave, but I found out it was an even better idea to come back," she corrected herself.

Puck shot her a startled glance, but then seemed to understand, *Oh, right. Zola is just acting. Pretending. Because we're back in a Futureville, and we can't be real anymore. At least . . . not yet.*

The guide seemed to drone on forever, describing the purpose of every building they passed. But finally he led them into the residential area.

And then the group was right in front of Zola's house.

"Here's a home where a girl about your age lives," the guide began. "Maybe you would like to watch and listen as she and her mother begin their day. You can do that if you switch the setting on your goggles to—" Zola saw the guide jolt back, as if he'd just received startling news over his headset. "Oh, wait, never mind. I just got word that this family is running a little behind because the girl took longer than usual to figure out what she wants to wear today—I'm sure that happens sometimes in your household, too. Even in 2193, kids are still kids!"

He turned and began to walk to the next house over. The

other kids trailed along.

But as soon as everyone was facing the other way, Zola and Puck raced toward the front door of Zola's house.

"Sirilex, open the door for me," Zola said softly—the first test of how the next stage of their plan might go.

The door swung open, and Zola breathed a sigh of relief even as she and Puck scrambled into the house as quickly as they could.

Puck slammed the door behind them. They both yanked the goggles off their faces.

And then Mom appeared from the kitchen, crying out, "I don't care what anyone does to me. I don't regret—"

Her gaze fell on Zola and Puck, and she put her hand over her mouth, stifling a sob.

"No," she moaned. "No. You two were supposed to be safely away from here. You were supposed to—"

"Mom, we have to hurry," Zola said, dashing toward her mother. "We—"

A change came over Mom's face—a transition Zola now recognized as Mom going into acting mode.

"Why, Zola, look at you! Did you forget to order clothes from your Insta-Closet? So you're wearing yesterday's instead?" Mom asked. To an outsider, her voice might have sounded teasing, but Zola could hear the ache beneath each word. "Is this some tween absentmindedness kicking in?"

"I—I need your help with my Insta-Closet," Zola said.

"Nothing I ordered looks right."

"Of course, honey," Mom said. "You know you can always come to me for help."

That . . . is actually true, Zola thought. *That's the part that Mom really wants me to know.*

Puck stayed glued to Zola's side as they rushed with Mom toward Zola's room and her Insta-Closet. Mom didn't even glance his way now.

It's not because she doesn't care about him, Zola decided. *It's because he's so completely out of place in our Futureville that she has to pretend he doesn't exist.*

All three of them smashed themselves into Zola's Insta-Closet. It had been crowded enough the day before when it was just Mom and Zola in the Insta-Closet—even though Puck was skinny and slight, he still barely fit in the leftover space.

But as soon as Zola pulled the door shut behind them, he touched the mirror and scrambled out through the opening that appeared as it slid down.

"Puck, wait!" Mom called after him. "Both of you—didn't you understand? Didn't you see I was trying to let you get away? And never come back?"

If there'd been an underpinning of regret and sorrow in her words before, now her voice practically throbbed with pain.

"Mom, it's okay," Zola said. "We've got a plan."

"I had so many plans over the years," Mom said sadly. "So many I thought would work and then . . ."

Puck was hesitating on the platform behind the mirror.

"Puck, *go*!" Zola insisted. "I'll tell Mom everything."

"There's one thing you can't tell her," Puck said. "Because you don't know." He squared his shoulders and peered directly at Mom. "No matter what happens next, you need to know this. I think of you as my mother, too. I *am* grateful for all you did. And everything you tried to do." And then he grinned. "But you were wrong about me not telling Zola."

He touched the back of the mirror. Even as it slid up into place again, Zola could see him begin to scramble down the stairs.

And then the mirror was closed again, and Zola could see nothing but a reflection: her and her mother, huddled fearfully together. In the mirror image, Zola saw her mother turn toward her. Mom had tears streaming down her face now.

"Yesterday—after I thought you were safe—I finally went in search of answers I'd wondered about for the past twelve years," Mom said. "I found out who was really behind starting these Futurevilles. And my worst fears were realized. It was a lot of the same people who set up Clifton Village."

Zola felt a jolt of fear in the pit of her stomach. Those people had made children sick and let them die. On purpose.

"But those men were arrested!" she protested. "They went to prison!"

"And then they got out," Mom said. "They changed their names. Including . . ."

"Including who?" Zola asked.

"Your grandfather," Mom whispered.

43

"*My grandfather?*" *Zola repeated numbly.* "You mean, your father?"

"No, your *other* grandfather. Your father's father."

Zola had barely ever thought about possible relatives besides Mom—and her dead father—before she'd read the book about Jessie Keyser. Having other relatives just wasn't . . . part of her Futureville. But now she had both a good side of the family and a bad side?

"None of this makes sense," Zola complained. "Did Dad know? Before he . . ."

She couldn't say the word "died" right now. Or "accident," and certainly not "murder." She couldn't ask any of the questions flooding her mind. Mom's eyes already held too much pain.

But maybe Zola's questions showed in her own gaze.

"Your father . . . ," Mom began. She winced and bit her lip. Then she looked back over her shoulder and shrugged, as if it was too late to do anything but talk as quickly as possible.

"I have to go back to the beginning," Mom said. "To the end of Clifton Village. It was so confusing to leave when I was fourteen. Just a little older than you—maybe you can understand, now that you've been outside."

Zola thought about how disorienting the outside world had been. But that was partly because everything seemed so primitive, so stuck in the past.

"Weren't the 1990s better than Clifton Village?" Zola asked. "I mean, no more churning butter, no more emptying chamber pots . . ."

Mom gave her a sad smile.

"You would think that," she said. "And that was how my brothers and sisters felt. They were young enough that they saw everything as an adventure. They *loved* being what they called 'modern.' They were thrilled with every new technological discovery. But I was old enough that I felt completely . . . shaped . . . by Clifton Village. In the early 1800s on the Indiana frontier, a fourteen-year-old girl was practically an adult. She was supposed to be thinking about getting married and having babies and keeping house and nothing else. And, when I was fourteen, that's all I wanted. I was already in love."

"With Dad," Zola whispered. It was a comfort to say that,

to have that be something she recognized from her life story. She knew her parents had loved each other, regardless of where they'd come from or what time period they'd lived in.

"Yes," Mom said. "He was the son of the richest, most powerful man in the village—and I'm ashamed to say that that mattered to me, too. But then when Mr. Seward turned out to be one of the evil men plotting to introduce diphtheria to our community . . . well, that was confusing. But I still loved your father."

Zola gulped. She could handle this latest news. She knew how.

"Because it wasn't Dad's fault, what his father did," Zola said. "*He* wasn't involved in any of the evil."

This was a guess, but it was such a relief when Mom nodded. Zola was sure: Mom wouldn't get that sad, longing look in her eye at the mention of Dad's name, if he'd been evil.

"Of course not," Mom said firmly. "When the news came out, your dad went from being proud and adoring of his father to . . . horrified and ashamed. He'd even been *named* after his father, and so he changed his name, from Chester to Arthur—it was a joke between us, when we found out there was a president named Chester Arthur. . . . He did that for me. And then when we got married, he took my last name instead of me taking his, and we agreed that any children we had would be named Keyser, not Seward—oh my, that was by far the most 'modern' thing I could ever conceive of, back then!"

"Okay . . ." Zola couldn't see why names mattered at a time like this. "But . . ."

Mom held up her hand, as if she wanted Zola to be patient.

"Mr. Seward—Arthur's dad—was livid. He and your father stopped speaking to one another. We didn't visit him in prison. We didn't welcome him home when he finished serving his time and was released. And then he vanished, as far as any of us knew. So we also didn't know Mr. Seward was involved with the effort to reinvent Clifton Village as a Futureville. We didn't know it would turn evil. We just saw this Futureville as . . . possibility."

"Why, Mom?" Zola exploded. She thought of all the history VRs she'd seen. She thought of all the times she'd wondered, *What if this was real, and I actually could make a difference?* "Even if you didn't know how it would all turn out, why in the world did you want to come *here*? Knowing the problems of the twenty-first century, why didn't you try to fix them? Why did you just want to *pretend* they were all in the past?"

Zola hadn't even known she was angry with her mother about *that*.

Mom's face drooped with sadness.

"Knowing all the problems of the twenty-first century, I just saw it as . . . overwhelming," she said. "I thought the only way I could help was by showing people a possible future. People I . . . wouldn't even have to talk to or see. But Arthur and I weren't *sure* what we wanted. Up until you were born, we'd kept our lives as much like Clifton Village as we could. Arthur made wood furniture. I sold baked goods. We used modern equipment in our jobs, but we came home each night to candlelight, to homemade quilts, to . . . even an outhouse, not indoor plumbing."

Zola tried to remember what an outhouse was. Then she gaped at her mom in horror.

"Seriously, Mom?" she asked. "You were going to bring me home to a place where the only bathroom was a little shack with a hole in the ground? Outdoors?"

"Exactly," Mom said, ducking her head as if in shame. "*We* were happy, but you would need more than that. We knew that our lives looked to the outside world like . . . poverty. Deprivation. What if you needed a computer for school? What if other kids made fun of you for having homemade clothes? We couldn't afford anything else."

"But that's—" Zola began, automatically ready with a typical line about how in 2193, everybody had everything they needed or wanted.

But it wasn't actually 2193.

And even in the fake version of 2193 she'd lived in, all her luxuries had depended on Puck's Futureville, a place where people really were poor. Starving, even.

It doesn't have to be this way, Zola thought stubbornly. *That's not even how the Futurevilles organizers claim they set things up.*

Mom wrapped her arm around Zola's shoulders and dropped her chin to Zola's head, as if to warn her that the rest of the story would be harder to hear.

"Your father took on more hours at work," Mom said.

Zola went silent, because Mom was going to go there. She was going to talk about Dad. About him dying.

The truth.

"And I didn't know this until later, but the woodshop where he worked, they didn't follow all the safety requirements," Mom said. "They were under such pressure to do everything fast, everyone all crowded together around electric saws. . . . Your father told the bosses someone was going to get hurt. And then . . . he was the one who got hurt." Mom's voice dropped to a whisper. "And some people say he might have been pushed. By someone who just didn't like him."

Zola felt like she'd been punched in the stomach. She'd never actually been punched ever in her life, even in a VR. But this had to be the feeling.

"If I had any choice at all, how could I raise you in a world with such terrible, malfunctioning machines?" Mom asked. "With even the possibility that people could be so evil? When I knew people *had* been evil, dealing with Clifton Village? You were two days old, and I was suddenly your only parent. After what happened to your father, all I could think about was protecting you. That's why we moved here. It seemed like the safest choice."

She gave a bitter laugh.

"Little did I know, nowhere's safe."

Zola could feel her mother's despair tugging at her, pulling her down. It was a pressure just as steady as the feel of Mom's chin against her head, Mom's arm around her shoulders.

This all makes sense . . . for Mom, Zola thought.

But Zola was a different person. She'd had a different life, different experiences, different hopes and dreams.

Some of them were even real.

Zola thought about how she'd felt the night before, surrounded by everyone making plans at Jessie's house.

"But . . . but . . . I read Jessie's letter," Zola said, pulling back from Mom. "I met Aunt Nicole and Uncle Andy. And lots of other people. *They* would have helped you raise me in, uh, modern ways. And, I guess, they would have protected me, too. They wanted to take care of us both. They still want to. They—"

"It's too late," Mom said. Her eyes swam with unshed tears. "I messed up too badly. I thought I *was* sending you to safety yesterday, but . . . you came back. All we can do is pretend everything's back to 'normal,' and we're going to do what they want. And maybe they won't punish us too harshly, maybe—"

"Mom, that is *not* the only choice," Zola said.

"You don't have my experience," Mom said, shaking her head despairingly. "From the very beginning, every time I tried to get out to see my family—as I'd been *promised* I'd be allowed to do—there was some punishment, some privilege taken away from me. And they'd threaten to send you to the other Futureville, without me. Your life would have been just like Puck's. Or maybe worse."

In spite of herself, Zola couldn't hold back a shiver of fear.

"Given that choice—that, that *blackmail*—how could I actively resist?" Mom moaned.

"You helped Puck," Zola said stubbornly. "You *did* resist."

"Only in secret," Mom said. "Only in ways that couldn't be seen by the tourists. And, I hoped, only in ways that no one but Puck knew about."

In VRs, Zola had seen people in jails and prisons—even in cages. She felt like she was talking to one of those trapped people right now.

"I told myself it didn't matter what happened to me, as long as you were okay," Mom said. "And at first, you had everything a child could possibly want. Except a father."

Zola grimaced.

"And except a mother who was truly happy and felt safe herself," Zola muttered. "And . . . except for knowing the truth about what was really going on around me. And then, well, you know. The way almost my whole life is virtual now. My whole life . . . except for arguing with you. I didn't even know how much I missed seeing other real people until I met Puck."

Mom met Zola's gaze exactly.

"I'm so sorry," she said. "I wanted everything to be better for you than it was for me. Your father wanted that, too.

When I sent you away yesterday, I was ready to be miserable the rest of my life, missing you, but . . . oh, is this selfish? It does help *me* that you're here with me again. We'll find a way to keep helping Puck and avoid getting in trouble again. We'll just have to . . . stay under the radar for a while. Hide everything real. Pretend we're obeying completely. Maybe then there won't be any punishment. Maybe then . . ."

"No," Zola said.

This felt so familiar, Zola disagreeing with her mother. On any day in the past year, she usually found about twelve different things to argue with her mother about just during breakfast. She saw now that she'd disagreed constantly with her mother—and no one else—because her mother was the only one she ever interacted with who was *real*, not some prettied-up virtual version whose every word and gesture was digitally altered to be completely bland, completely perfect.

And completely fake.

And, anyhow, a lot of Zola's disagreements with Mom had been because of things Zola hadn't understood—the way Mom was so often just pretending for the sake of the tourists, the way she was so often deeply afraid.

Somehow Zola had sensed something was wrong even before she'd known for sure.

But this disagreement wasn't like all those other times. It wasn't about Insta-Closet clothes or the food from the Insta-Fridge.

This time, what Zola was arguing about *mattered.*

"We are *not* going to pretend we're obeying completely," Zola said. "We're not going to hide. We're not going to cower in fear and have our Insta-Closets be the only place we allow ourselves to be real."

"Zola—" Mom protested.

"We're not going to do any of that," Zola said. "Because, instead, we're going to get rid of all the fear forever."

Mom shook her head. Tears rolled down her face now.

"Oh, Zola, I'm glad that you're so brave," she said. "Even after hearing the truth about your dad—and your grand-father—you're still much, much braver than me. But you don't understand. You haven't seen enough of the real world. You—"

The mirror of the Insta-Closet rattled in its frame. Mom recoiled, but Zola edged closer. Even before she caught the first glimpse of who was on the other side of the frame, she was reaching out her hand, ready to help.

The mirror slid down, revealing Puck again.

"Ready?" Zola asked breathlessly.

Puck was panting, as if he'd raced up and down stairs, run up and down the tunnel.

"It's time," he said.

44

Mom was still gasping, "No, wait—let's talk about this first! Please! You don't know what you're risking!" But Puck and Zola were already pushing their way out of the Insta-Closet, running through the house—and then shoving their way out the front door. Mom ran after them, crying, "No! Don't! Please—" Zola heard Sirilex calling after her, too. "Wait, Zola, you forgot your goggles!" But she ignored that, too.

Zola knew a split second of fear when they reached the street and they were the only ones in sight not wearing goggles. Her face felt distressingly bare.

No one will see us. No one will hear us. It won't matter what we do or say—we'll be erased from everything they do see and hear through their goggles, and with just Puck and me, we won't be able to change anything. . . .

But then the door of the house next door opened slowly, and a girl peered out.

That girl's face—like Zola's and Puck's—was bare. The girl's brown eyes were wide and frightened, but they weren't covered by any VR goggles.

Another bare-faced girl peeked out from behind the first.

And then, up and down the street, all sorts of people stepped out of their houses without goggles on their faces. There were kids—and adults—in ragged clothes like Puck had always worn; there were women and men and children in fashionable outfits that Zola could tell had been ordered fresh from an Insta-Closet that very morning. Some doors stayed stubbornly shut, but Zola tallied up the number of bare-faced people emerging into the open air.

Twenty? Thirty? That's enough, isn't it? Too many for the VR to erase us all?

One of the kids Zola saw, far up the street, was her friend Beatriz. Zola longed to run directly to her and hug her and proclaim, "We can talk for real now! Without any goggles changing what we say!"

But Puck and Mom were both tugging on Zola's arms—tugging her in opposite directions—and Zola knew she couldn't think about Beatriz right now. She didn't have time yet to work out anything about their friendship.

So, instead, Zola called out in her loudest voice, "Hello, tourists! You have to help us! Just about everything you've been told about how our Futurevilles work has been a lie!"

Mom tightened her grip on Zola's arm, pulling her back toward the house.

"That won't work unless we take the tourist goggles off," she gasped. "You and Puck go back into the house—I'll do this so I'm the only one punished . . . you and Puck will be safe. . . ."

"No, wait, Mom," Zola demanded. "This is only the first part of our plan, but there's a second part coming. . . . Now!"

She waved her arms dramatically, the cue she and Puck had arranged.

For a second, nothing happened. Then all the tourists around them began gasping or gulping or even shrieking or cursing. A teenager cried, "My goggles just shocked me! Are anybody else's goggles going crazy?" An elderly man hollered, "My goggles are malfunctioning! Everything's gone black!" Almost completely in sync, one tourist after the other began yanking the goggles from their heads and throwing them to the ground.

At the same time, the lights Zola and Mom and their neighbors had left on in their houses snapped out. As far as Zola could tell, the power grid for the entire Futurevilles had gone dead.

Everything was working out just right.

"Thank you!" Zola cried. "Now everyone can see and hear what's really happening!"

She winked at a woman in a polo shirt and khakis standing in the crowd of tourists—one of the women who'd been at Jessie Keyser's house the night before. Zola looked around for other people from Jessie's house who'd been seeded into the crowd. She knew the man in an Indiana Pacers ball cap was some sort of relative, and a woman in a bright yellow dress had been in the group her uncle Andy had called "the church grandmas" the night before. They were the only allies she could see, but she knew there were others throughout both Futurevilles—people undoubtedly telling the other tourists, "Look, we need to listen carefully now, and maybe you'll want to record all this on your phone, too?" And she knew that at least one person from the tech group last night at Jessie's house had reached the control room for all of the Futurevilles complex.

"We can tell you everything now!" Puck shouted at all the tourists. "And if you don't want to hear it from Zola or me, there are lots of others who will tell you the truth, too!"

"This . . . this . . . just might work," Mom murmured, gazing around at the crowd of Futurevilles residents starting to mix with the tourists.

But just as quickly, a squad of men and women in dark uniforms appeared around the corner. They carried no weapons—no weapons Zola could see, at least—but they all had insignia on their pockets that declared them "Futurevilles Security." They spread through the crowd of tourists, apologizing, "We're so sorry. There's been a power outage, and you'll need to exit the park immediately. Here—here's a voucher to get your money back and to return once we've repaired our system, free of charge. *And* to make sure everyone evacuates immediately, the first hundred people through the exits will automatically be entered into a drawing to win a thousand dollars. . . ."

They were ready for this, Zola thought numbly. *They were just as prepared as we were. They don't even care if they start a stampede!*

The tourists were turning to go. Most of them were turning rapidly. And running.

"There's still time!" Zola screamed, trying to encourage Puck and all the other Futurevilles residents who'd been brave enough to step outside their houses. She shoved her way back in front of the tourists and pleaded, "Listen! You have to listen!"

Then a gray-haired man in an official-looking Futurevilles jacket—a guide? A security guard?—sidled over beside Zola and whispered in her ear, "Are you trying to get your aunt Jessie killed?"

45

Zola hadn't realized it, but Mom was standing right beside her. Clearly she had heard the man's whisper, too. And she reacted before Zola did: Mom shoved the man away and cried, "Get away from my daughter! And stay away from Jessie! How dare you . . . Mr. Seward, you are the most despicable person I've ever known!"

"Mr. Seward?" Zola repeated numbly. "*This* is my grandfather?"

He was so old. He didn't *look* like the monster Mom had described. He had bushy eyebrows and little hairs sprouting from his ears. He had lines across his face.

He had sad, clouded eyes.

But Mom snarled, "He dishonors the name 'grandfather.' Arthur was right to cut off ties to him, and—"

"Hannah, Hannah, Hannah," Mr. Seward said, shaking his head in what looked like true sorrow. "You never understood. I just wanted what was best for all of us. Don't you see we've been on the same side all along?"

"Nooo," Mom moaned, staggering backward. "That's not true! Zola, don't believe him!"

Zola was too stunned to react. But Puck caught Mom's arm and began yelling at the departing tourists, "Are you watching this? Did you hear what's really going on, or are you only interested in fake scenes?"

"Puck, no," Mom murmured. "Don't . . . call attention to us. Not if he's threatening Jessie. Not if he's saying . . . We can't . . . we can't . . ."

The tourists continued to flee. But Zola saw the "tourist" in the yellow dress—one of the secret allies—hunch over her purse, whispering.

Nicole said there'd be allies around with low-tech devices called walkie-talkies, that wouldn't need a power grid or cell phone service to work, Zola remembered. *So that woman must have one of those walkie-talkie things in her purse. She's calling for reinforcements. Everything's going to be okay.*

In a VR, this would be the end. The reinforcements would be there instantly, and Zola could let things fade to black. Zola waited for the sense of exhilaration that always hit at the close of the best VRs, when she felt the most triumphant.

But this was real life, and the air around her still seemed to crackle with danger. She still had the words "Are you trying to get your aunt Jessie killed?" echoing in her ears. She was still caught between Mom and Mr. Seward, each of them glaring poisonously at the other.

She still didn't understand.

"Why?" she said aloud. She looked straight at Mr. Seward. "Why would you even care what Mom and I do or where we live? Why would you want anything bad to happen to Jessie?"

"Zola!" Mom hissed. "Don't remind him. . . ."

Oh, right, Zola thought belatedly. *Jessie rescued the kids from Clifton Village. So he might blame her for sending him to prison. And for my father rejecting him.*

Mr. Seward started pulling something from his coat pocket.

Puck stumbled away, then rushed back to tug on Zola's and Mom's arms.

"Run!" he commanded them. "Hide! If that's a weapon—"

It wasn't a weapon. Mr. Seward's hand came free from his pocket, lifting out a pair of ancient-looking goggles. They were made of rubber—or maybe some more of the awful twenty-first-century plastic.

"This is what I watch all the time in *my* VRs," said Mr. Seward. "Look."

With one trembling hand, he held the goggles out to Zola.

"Watch out!" Puck warned. "This could be a trick!"

"What could an old pair of goggles do to me?" Zola asked. "I mean, that hasn't already happened? Oh—they won't work, anyhow. Because the power grid is down."

"They run on normal batteries," Mr. Seward said.

Zola was pretty sure that by "normal" he meant the horrible old-fashioned kind that contained dangerous chemicals. But she put one side of the goggles up to her right eye, and settled the earbud into place. Mom leaned her head close, peering into the left side of the goggles.

A scene appeared before them of a boy racing into an old-fashioned store, past bolts of calico and barrels labeled "FLOUR," "SUGAR," and "SALT." It felt like, if she'd wanted to, Zola could have reached out and touched his face. The boy grinned and announced, "Pa, when I grow up, I'm going to be just like you! I'm going to run the Clifton Store with you, and I'm going to marry Hannah Keyser and we'll have so many sons—and they'll be storekeepers, too—"

Zola recoiled a bit at the "we'll have so many sons . . ." but Mom was already ripping the goggles away from her face.

"After he left Clifton Village, he wanted daughters, too!" she spat at Mr. Seward. "And if you wanted to just sit around watching old home movies all the time—old video from Clifton Village—you didn't have to involve Zola and me for that!"

"Oh, but I did," Mr. Seward said. "For the rest of it . . ."

He hit some control on the goggles, and shoved them back toward Zola and Mom.

This time the scene was familiar: Mom and Zola sitting at their kitchen table. Only, it was a younger version of

Zola—she was only seven or eight. With a joyous smile, she declared, "I love you so much, Grandpa!"

Mom and Zola both yanked the goggles away from their heads. Mom threw them to the ground, and crushed them under her heel.

"That never happened!" Mom cried.

"Motion capture," Zola said numbly. "Deepfake tools changing what we said. You've been using all the technology of our Futureville to pretend . . . to pretend . . ."

She couldn't finish the sentence. She couldn't bear to add ". . . that we love you."

"And yet, you never once apologized," Mom fumed. "You never once asked for forgiveness. You just . . . used us!" She waved her hand, indicating all of Futureville around them. "And you used all the other people here, too. . . ."

"*And* the people in my Futureville," Puck muttered.

"There's always a price," Mr. Seward said with a shrug, as if Puck didn't matter. As if nothing but his own desires mattered. "And Hannah, Zola, don't you see how it all worked out so well for the two of you? You have everything here—everything. People wait on you hand and foot, and you don't even have to see them. Or pay them. Everything you could possibly want or need comes to you immediately through the Insta-Closet, the Insta-Oven, the Insta-Fridge. Hannah, you can just play with your silly little art projects. Zola, you can bask on a tropical beach or sit on a mountain peak—or pretend to be a hero—anytime you want. Why would you ever want to leave?"

"Because none of it's real," Zola said. Her voice came out strong and true. "Because we're not here by choice. You've kept Mom trapped by fear. And I just heard you threaten to kill my aunt! I heard it with my own ears!"

"Zola, don't antagonize him," Mom whispered, clutching Zola's arm. "You don't know everything he's capable of. I always wondered . . . with Arthur's death . . ."

"You think he killed my father, too?" Zola gasped.

Her voice rang out too loudly this time. Too late, Zola remembered that the reinforcements hadn't come yet. And that this wasn't a VR where she was only pretending to be in danger. All the tourists seemed far away now. And most of the Futurevilles people seemed to have either run for the exit—or crept back into their own houses.

But Mr. Seward didn't lash out this time. He clutched his midsection as if Zola had hurt him.

"Killed him?" he repeated. "My own son? No . . . no . . . We were going to make up! This Futureville was going to be my gift to him. . . . He could have had any fantasy he wanted. Now, after he died, I might have helped spread the rumors that it could have been murder, because I needed that to convince Hannah to come here. . . ."

"That was a lie, too?" Mom wailed. "The very thing that made me bring Zola here?"

"You lie about everything," Puck growled at Mr. Seward. "That's your pattern. You're just a . . . a bully!"

That made Mr. Seward straighten up. He towered over Puck. And Mom and Zola, too.

"You little piece of garbage," he snarled at Puck. "You don't know anything about how the world really works. Or how much a place like this costs. All that we've created with the Futurevilles—things *had* to be this way. I also needed Zola and Hannah as proof for everyone else. I'd recruited my own granddaughter for this experiment—why would anyone doubt my intentions? Do you know what our sales brochures say? 'All the luxuries and safety of the twenty-second century, delivered to your family now.'"

"That's not the Futurevilles slogan," Puck corrected. He looked down, as if expecting to see the ragged Futurevilles T-shirt he'd worn the day before. But he was in newer clothes now—ones Nicole had bought so he could blend in as a tourist. He still recited bitterly, "The slogan's always been, 'Which Future Do You Choose?'"

"Of course no one would choose *your* future for themselves," Mr. Seward said dismissively. "But *this* Futureville . . ." He waved his arm expansively, indicating the tidy homes, the beautiful landscaping—everything was still so nice, even without VR enhancements. He turned back to Zola. "Even a rebellious brat like you recognized that everything's better here. The outside world terrified you—of course you came back!"

"That's not why I came back!" Zola protested.

"Doesn't matter," Mr. Seward said, shrugging. This made his suit puff out, making him look bigger and more powerful than before. "I have video of you returning. I have the perfect spin for anyone who questions it."

So that's why no one stopped Puck and me leaving, Zola thought numbly. *They knew all along. They* expected *us to return.*

"But that's not the truth!" Puck argued.

"The truth doesn't matter as much as what you can get people to believe," Mr. Seward said.

Zola shook her head, trying to clear it. It felt like there was some thread of truth in Mr. Seward's lies, if only she could find it.

"You said the word 'experiment' a few minutes ago," Zola said tentatively. She remembered the wall back at Jessie's house, the scribbled notes. "You don't tell the tourists the truth about what's happening here. You've made kids like me more and more isolated, almost like we're all in separate control groups. Or, is Puck's Futureville a control group for mine? People are disappearing, and people aren't allowed to talk to each other for real. Is it all . . . psychological experiments? Is that the point? For doctors who want to know about mental health, and—"

"Doctors? Mental health?" Mr. Seward sounded incredulous. He cast a glance over his shoulder, but no one else was in earshot. Zola and Puck's allies were staying far back, still pretending to be tourists. And it was taking way too long for anyone else to come to their rescue.

Someone is coming, aren't they? Zola wondered.

Mr. Seward's face twisted into a sneer. His veneer of a loving grandpa was gone.

"You always seemed smarter in my VRs," he mocked Zola. "You use millions of dollars' worth of experimental technology every day, and you still don't understand? Can't you see how much the technology companies need us? They pay any amount we name, to have their every whim tested on willing subjects. Under any conditions they want. And in as much isolation and secrecy as they desire."

"This is about the VRs then," Zola whispered. "Everything we see every day . . ."

"Ding ding ding!" Mr. Seward crowed, as if pretending she'd won a prize. "There's nothing the technology companies won't do for me now, to keep our arrangement. And you're so gullible, you were fooled by a few fake rent-a-cops at a Target, a wall of hacked screens with a fake newscast . . . as if anyone out there cares about the Futurevilles, except for the money they're making!"

So everything that had frightened Zola and Puck in the outside world had been fake, too. How could she ever trust her own instincts?

Or her own ears and eyes?

"But you *don't* have willing test subjects to sell to those technology companies," Mom said. Her voice wavered, but her gaze burned. "You never had permission for that. You lied to me and the other parents, and you forced us to keep our children ignorant, and—"

"And what are you going to do about it?" Mr. Seward mocked her. "You know I can just send you and Zola to the other Futureville if you give me any more trouble. Your daughter can work and starve right along with everyone else. . . ."

"No!" Mom said. "Please—I'll do whatever I have to, to prevent that. Just don't hurt Zola or Puck or Jessie or . . . or anyone else from my family. Leave them all alone. And maybe . . . maybe you can find it in your heart to just let Zola and Puck go completely? Since they know the truth now and aren't as . . . gullible? If they promise to stay silent? This place is all make-believe, anyway, now—you can sub in some other kid to pretend to be my child. . . ."

"Mom, *no*," Zola cried. She was about to say, "I'm not keeping any more secrets!" But other words slipped out first: "I want to rescue you, too!"

Frantically, she peered around again, looking for someone who could help. The people she'd counted as allies were milling about uncertainly, several paces away. The other tourists were even farther away, practically out of sight. The other Futurevilles residents had vanished completely.

What could Zola and Puck and Mom do without any help?

And then Zola saw a woman running toward them,

against the tide of the fleeing crowd. The woman threw back her head, and Zola caught a glimpse of a familiar face.

"Nicole!" Zola cried. She yanked on her mother's arm, pulling her away from the house. "Mom, this is Aunt Jessie's best friend! She's related to us now, too! She'll help!"

But Mom jerked back.

"Nicole!" Mom yelled. "They're threatening Jessie! We've got to stop rebelling! We've got to give up!"

Nicole stopped in front of Mom. Nicole's brown eyes bored into Mom's blue ones.

"You know Jessie would risk anything for you," Nicole said evenly. "You've known since you were a teenager that Jessie would willingly sacrifice herself for her family and friends."

"So you'd let your own sister *die* just because you've gotten a little tired of your perfect life?" Mr. Seward taunted.

"You're lying! You always lie!" Puck shouted at Mr. Seward. "You had someone hack into Jessie's phone and email—that's all! It doesn't mean you know anything about where she is!"

Mr. Seward smiled.

"Oh, but I have proof," he said. "Want to see where Jessie Keyser is this very minute?"

46

Mr. Seward reached into his pocket again and drew out a rectangular device—his phone.

"Oh, phones aren't working right now," Zola told Mr. Seward. "Too bad."

Mr. Seward touched the screen.

"Seems to be working fine," he said.

Zola looked desperately toward Nicole.

"We . . . we had to turn the cell service back on for the next stage of our plan . . . ," she murmured.

Zola and the others watched helplessly as Mr. Seward tapped his phone screen a few times, and then turned it toward them.

The image on the phone was of a woman with long brown hair and a gag over her mouth. She sat in an ordinary chair—no, she was *tied* to an ordinary chair, her wrists and ankles bound tightly. She struggled against the ropes, trying again and again to break free.

It was an agonizing thing to watch. How could someone try and try and try and fail every time?

"That's a live feed," Mr. Seward said, giving his oily smile again. "Jessie's right here in the Futurevilles." He lowered the phone and pointed to Zola and Mom and Puck. "And that's why the three of you are going to march back through this door and return to your usual lives." He went over and stood beside the door to Mom and Zola's house, which was open just a crack. He turned toward Nicole. "And you're going to go back out to your fellow schemers and stop them from doing anything else. *You'll* tell all the Futurevilles residents they have to come back. And you'll never come here or criticize this place ever again. Or else Jessie will pay."

Mom and Nicole seemed frozen. But Puck called out, "Your plan will never work! If Jessie's here, some tourist will see her. Or someone from my Futureville will find her. . . ."

"Oh, but you don't know the rest of the Futurevilles plan," Mr. Seward said, his greasy smile deepening. "Tomorrow we're shutting down to tourists. Everything the tourists see has been through VR goggles for years—so they'll still be able to access a view of the Futurevilles digitally. For a fee, of course. We'll just send out a collection of tourist goggles to schools that want to make field trips, with the ease of staying in their own classrooms. And the same goes for other tourists. We'll have total control of everything they experience. We'll say the bad behavior of tourists today drove us to that approach."

"That won't work, either!" Zola protested. But her heart wasn't in it. Because she'd experienced virtual school for years.

And she could see how the rebellion she'd helped orchestrate could backfire.

Mr. Seward ignored her, anyway. He shoved the door of Mom and Zola's house open, as if holding it for them as a courtesy.

"Once you step back into this house, you'll never have to leave again," he said. "We've been testing new approaches—keeping people home entirely, letting them get food and clothing delivered by drone. That way, there's not even the risk of them having contact with people from the bad Futureville. . . ."

Zola exchanged a startled glance with Puck. Zola remembered the five houses on her street he'd told her were abandoned.

Maybe they weren't empty, after all, she thought. *They were just test cases for this new approach. . . .*

And maybe people were trapped there still.

"Then what will happen to the people from my Futureville?" Puck asked forlornly.

"Oh, we'll still need some of you for general labor," Mr. Seward said, as if it really didn't matter. "Maybe some of the particularly *obedient* people will get a chance to move to the good Futureville and take part in the tech experiments themselves. The rest—who cares?"

Mr. Seward held up his phone again.

"Now, ladies, what will it be?" he asked, peering at Mom and Nicole as if their decisions mattered more than Zola's and Puck's. "Do you follow orders? Or do I give a command to have Jessie . . . oh, I guess I wouldn't actually have her killed. Not right away. I'd just make her wish she was dead."

Mom and Nicole could have been statues. But Zola cried out desperately, "That footage could be fake! You could have made up everything you said about Jessie! And about the Futurevilles! You could be lying through your teeth! Again!"

Mr. Seward barely turned his head.

"Do you really want to take that chance?" he asked. "Do you want to gamble with your aunt's life?"

He lifted his phone toward his mouth, as if he truly was about to command someone to hurt Jessie.

Zola felt powerless watching him. She felt as helpless as Jessie had seemed in the video, struggling against the ropes again and again without any success.

But Jessie didn't stop trying. . . .

Mom bowed her head and took a tiny step back toward the doorway. Zola hesitated, then moved alongside her.

But Zola didn't meekly step across the threshold into the house. Instead, at the last minute, she leaped toward Mr. Seward.

In one smooth move, she yanked the phone from his hand. And then she gave him a hard shove, propelling him backward into the house. He landed on the floor, and Zola yanked the door shut behind him.

"Keep him in there!" she screamed at Mom and Puck and Nicole. "I'm going to go rescue Jessie!"

47

Zola ran as fast as she could.

She heard someone yell behind her, "Go, Zola!" and maybe, "We'll hold the door!" She couldn't tell if it was Puck or Mom or Nicole, or all three of them at once.

She knew they would try.

She didn't actually know what she should do next.

Go house to house? Round up all the helpers and tell them what to do?

Everything she thought of seemed like it would take too long.

She half expected some Futurevilles guard to grab her right away, but apparently they'd all left with the tourists.

Or maybe . . .

She risked a glance over her shoulder, confirming her fears.

Three men in dark blue Futurevilles jackets were chasing her.

And they were gaining ground.

Zola made herself run even faster.

No time to search any houses, she thought disjointedly. *No time to find help. . . .*

This wasn't like any of the VRs she'd ever done. There, she could always see a right answer directly in front of her. Or, if she didn't see it immediately, it would glow to give her a hint. Or a "Helpful Clue Source" sign would pop up.

Or she could freeze the action, and give herself time to think.

Now all she could do was run and run and run.

She didn't bother looking back again. Blindly, she dashed toward her town's central plaza, where both the entrance and exit were located.

Maybe I could lose myself in the crowd—if there's still a crowd there. Or I could find some of the other allies. . . .

It wasn't quite a plan, but it was better than nothing.

She passed houses with their doors hanging open and houses with people peeking out fearfully. Far ahead of her, she saw one house with a guard standing out front like a sentry, and she jumped a fence and darted through a backyard to avoid him.

Finally she turned the corner into the plaza—and everything ahead of her was chaos.

All sorts of people were running and screaming. Guards were yelling into blocky objects that Zola thought might be walkie-talkies, "What are our instructions? Who's giving orders now?"

And dozens of people were holding up phones, as if they were filming everything around them. Zola veered close to a teenager who narrated as he turned in a slow circle, "This is the scene at the Futurevilles near Indianapolis, Indiana, where mayhem has broken out after the power went out. . . . I guess the future's not as perfect as it looked!"

"Can you help me?" Zola asked him. But the boy just glared at her, shook his head, and went on filming.

Zola saw one of the guards shoving toward her, through the crowd. She ducked under the boy's outstretched arm to hide behind him.

And then, while she still had her head down, she heard a familiar voice from the crowd ahead: "No, I'm not getting out of here until I know *all* my friends are safe!"

It was Beatriz. She was standing in the middle of a group of kids who all looked unfamiliar— so they were probably tourists.

"I know Zola left her house, but where is she now?" Beatriz was asking. "Can you help me find her?"

"Beatriz!" Zola screamed, running toward her. "I'm here!"

She wanted to fling herself at her friend and hug her—for real for once. She wanted to explain that they could still be friends, even though they'd only ever known one another through the VR goggles.

But there wasn't time.

"It's my aunt Jessie we need to rescue!" Zola cried. She held up Mr. Seward's phone, showing them the video of Jessie. It was still playing; Jessie was still struggling against the ropes.

"Wait a minute—how are they doing a live feed if the power's down in the entire Futurevilles?" one of the tourist boys asked.

"Let me look. . . ." One of the girls took the phone from Zola. She tapped the screen again and again. "Oh, that was set on a loop. *This* looks like it really is a livestream. Must be from some battery-operated camera."

She held up the phone again.

Now the screen showed Jessie out of the chair, tiptoeing toward a door, opening the door a crack. . . .

"I know where that is!" Zola screamed. Because now she could see a guard's back, a street scene just beyond. "Jessie's in one of the houses I just passed! We have to go help her before they catch her escaping!"

"Who's with us?" Beatriz asked.

All the kids around them raised their hands. Zola took off running again. But this time she was in the middle of a pack of ten or fifteen other kids. The crowd parted before them.

Even as she ran, Zola was making plans: "You, you, you, and you," she said, pointing. "When we get there, surround the guard and distract him. Beatriz and I will get Jessie out. You, you, and you, run on another ten or twelve houses down, to where two women and a boy are holding on to a doorknob, keeping a door shut. You take control of that house, and tell Mom and Nicole and Puck to come meet Beatriz and Jessie and me. . . ."

Zola hung back when they reached the house where Jessie was hidden. She didn't want the guard to recognize her. But the tourist kids swarmed the guard, battering him with questions: "When's the snack shop going to open again? I'm hungry!" "When will we get our money back?" "Can't the buses just drive in here to pick us up, so we don't have to walk as far?"

"Are you kidding me?" the guard snarled. He pulled off his Futurevilles jacket and threw it to the ground. "They don't pay me enough for this! I quit!"

Zola started to push her way into the house, but just then Mom and Nicole and Puck came running toward her.

"Zola! You're safe!" Mom cried. "And Jessie—?"

Ahead of her, Zola saw Beatriz hugging Jessie, even as Beatriz gave her a thumbs-up over Jessie's shoulder.

"She's safe, too!" Zola shouted. She glanced quickly at the guard, now stalking away from the tourist kids. "I mean, as long as the next part of the plan works. . . ."

Nicole dug in a pocket and held out her phone to Zola.

"Want to do the honors?" Nicole asked.

Zola shouted into the phone, so relieved to be connected once again with all the allies Nicole had recruited: "All systems go! Call the police to arrest Mr. Seward and everyone else who held people against their will! Release the video Puck and I taped last night to the national media! Call local media to get them to come right now to film everything going on here! Or—tell them they can use what people here are already filming for . . . what's it called? TikTok? YouTube? Instagram Live?"

"I don't even understand what you're talking about," Mom said. "But . . . did you just do everything Jessie did for Clifton Village, when she called her news conference?"

"Pretty much," Zola said. She looked around at the tourist kids she'd met only five minutes earlier. She thought about the allies spread out through both Futurevilles: the tech experts, the church ladies, Jessie's coworkers. The family. She reached out and squeezed Puck's hand. "I just had a lot more help."

Even as Zola, Mom, and Nicole pushed their way into the strange house, Zola could hear sirens off in the distance. Some of the tourist kids had apparently looped their phones into some live feed from the Futureville plaza, and through those phones, Zola could hear Futurevilles residents describing their ordeal: "I've been trapped here for years, and I wasn't allowed to escape. . . ."

Zola let Mom and Nicole go to Jessie first, all three women wrapping their arms around each other.

"You never gave up," Mom murmured into Jessie's hair.

"Of course not," Jessie whispered back. "You're my sister."

Through the open doorway to the side, Zola saw Mr. Seward and a bunch of other people being led away in handcuffs.

And then someone tapped Zola on her shoulder. She turned and there was Jessie, holding out her arms to Zola.

"All these years, I wanted so badly to rescue you," Jessie said. "I didn't know *you* would be the one to rescue *me*. Either way, I've been waiting twelve years for this moment!"

Zola stepped into her aunt's embrace.

"Me, too," Zola said. "Me, too. I just didn't know it!"

EPILOGUE
2 WEEKS LATER

Zola sat in her aunt Jessie's backyard, a triangle of watermelon in her hand.

It turned out, watermelon in 2023 didn't just come in perfectly shaped cubes. In its more original form, watermelon had a rind.

And seeds.

And it attracted bugs.

But somehow it still tasted more delicious than anything Zola had ever eaten from the Insta-Fridge or Insta-Oven in the kitchen back in her Futureville.

That's because Zola was eating this watermelon at a reunion picnic with all the family members she'd met over the past two weeks, as well as friends who'd escaped the Futurevilles with her.

She had *good* grandparents now to offset the awfulness of Mr. Seward: Grandpa Keyser was a gentle old man who'd offered to show Zola how to make a horseshoe in his old-fashioned smithy shop. Zola hadn't told him yet that she didn't have a clue what a horseshoe was—but he said it would bring her good luck.

Grandma Keyser, who was a retired nurse, could recite folk remedies from memory, without once having to consult anything like Sirilexagoogle. (Or what Zola had discovered was the 2020s equivalent: Siri or Alexa or Google. Zola thought they were all about the same. Who needed *three* Sirilexagoogles?)

And Zola had more than a dozen aunts and uncles now—both ones who were related by blood, and ones who were just family friends she was supposed to call "aunt" or "uncle," because hardly anyone remembered anymore that they *weren't* related.

She had even more cousins, ranging from babies to teenagers. Most of them were currently busy with a contest where they were spitting watermelon seeds at the fence. As far as Zola could tell, the winner would be the person whose seed stuck the longest.

She'd never seen anything like this in a VR. It was a completely pointless game.

But everyone was laughing *so* hard.

Zola turned, and saw that someone else was watching all the watermelon-seed-spitting just as intently as she was: Beatriz.

Beatriz had been so helpful that last day in their Futureville, but Zola hadn't seen her since. Now, she felt almost shy gazing at the other girl. It was so weird that Zola could know the exact placement of every freckle on Beatriz's face, but know so little about her otherwise.

But she wasn't going to leave our Futureville until she was sure I was safe. . . .

Zola put down her watermelon and walked over to Beatriz.

"Thank you," she said.

"Oh!" Beatriz said, jumping a little as though Zola had frightened her. "You're not mad at my family? Because we arrived in the good Futureville after yours, when we should have *known* what was going on, and what my parents were agreeing to, to get all the luxuries? And—"

"I would never think that," Zola said quickly. "I don't blame your family for anything."

But she knew some people did. She'd been watching TV and reading newspapers (They still did actually exist in the 2020s!) and all sorts of commentary online. It felt like the whole world was watching to see who would be sent to prison over what was now being called "The Futurevilles Scams," and who deserved to be compensated as a victim.

But the rest of the world wasn't standing there with Zola and Beatriz. Sirilex wasn't listening, either; neither were any security cameras or mood sensors. It was just Zola and Beatriz—two girls, standing alone. Able to say anything they wanted.

"I just wanted to say I will always think of you as a friend,"

Zola said. "Even if I never really knew you. Even if your family's moving back to Bolivia now."

Beatriz laughed.

"Zola, I've never even been to Bolivia! My family's from Nebraska!"

"Yeah, well, I've never been outside of Indiana," Zola said with a shrug. "The farthest I've ever gone from where I was born is fifty miles."

It felt crazy to admit that, since she'd walked so much of the planet—but only virtually.

"After I move back to Nebraska," Beatriz said, a familiar grin sprouting on her face, "we can text and call and play video games together online. . . ."

"And maybe send snail-mail letters back and forth?" Zola asked.

Playing video games together online would feel a little bit too much like being back in the Futurevilles. Some of her cousins had patiently tried to explain the difference—kids playing Minecraft, for example, *knew* it wasn't real. Nobody was being tricked. Or held captive.

But Zola liked knowing for sure what was real and what wasn't. She wasn't fond of *anything* digital right now.

Maybe Beatriz felt the same way, because her grin spread even wider.

"Deal," she said. "And maybe Amir and Eromi and our other friends would join us, too. . . ."

"And Puck," Zola said.

"Sure—if he wants," Beatriz said.

"He will," Zola said confidently. "Want to know a secret? My mom's trying to adopt him. I'm going to have a brother!"

"That's great," Beatriz said, as if she was truly happy for both Zola and Puck. She looked around and lowered her voice. "You know . . . my family was helping some people from the other Futureville, too."

"I'm not surprised," Zola said, beaming at her.

In all the news coverage Zola had seen and read, commentators had marveled again and again at how many people in the "perfect" Futureville had worked in secret to give food and other resources to the people who were struggling to survive in the "bad" Futureville. Some speculated that that was the only way people in the bad Futureville had managed to stay alive.

Even the Technologists who installed Zola's new Insta-Closet had secretly been working to help the other side. There'd been a whole network of helpers Zola—and Mom—had never known about.

Zola especially liked one headline she'd seen, spelling out how the people of the two Futurevilles had been able to triumph over the awful people like Mr. Seward who wanted to keep everyone trapped: "Secret Good Wins Out Over Secret Evil."

"It's okay to say everything out loud now, to let people know you helped," Zola told Beatriz.

"Well, *I* didn't," Beatriz said, as if she was ashamed. "I

didn't know anything about what was really going on. So I didn't know to help."

"But then you helped at the end," Zola said. "When I really needed you."

Somehow, having that conversation with Beatriz gave Zola the courage to go over and stand next to Puck—even though he was in the center of a group of kids from the other Futureville. They all wore new clothes now. They'd all been to the dentist for the first time in their lives; they'd gotten medical care and soap and shampoo and clean water. They didn't look anything like the wild, filthy people Zola had seen each time she'd stepped out of the tunnel into their Futureville.

But Zola couldn't forget that they'd had a very different Futurevilles experience than hers. She knew they couldn't forget, either.

"Princess!" one of the boys called as Zola approached.

Puck immediately slugged the boy in the stomach.

"Don't call her that!" he scolded. "Zola risked everything to help us—show some respect!"

"I was!" the boy protested, hitting Puck back. "I wasn't making fun of her—honest!"

Zola could not get used to seeing people hit each other. Even playfully. But Puck just grinned.

"Okay, then," he said.

"You risked everything, too, Puck," Zola said.

"Yeah, he risked skipping out on his work shift for an

entire day, and the rest of us had to cover for him," one of the other kids muttered.

"And I had to reprogram the security codes at the end of the tunnel again and again," another one agreed.

"And *I'm* the person who found him a scrap of paper, because he had the crazy idea to write a note to you in the first place," a small girl with hair like dandelion fluff said. "'Zola's only seen paper in historical VRs,' he said. 'It'll take something like paper to really get her attention.'"

The girl imitated Puck's voice the way a kid sister might— as if he annoyed her, but she loved him anyway.

"I—I didn't know," Zola said. "I never knew how many people were involved."

The girl sniffed.

"And people say ours was the bad Futureville," she muttered.

It was so confusing. Zola now knew the good Futureville had never been entirely good, and the bad Futureville had never been entirely bad. To keep all the illusions of the good Futureville, the people in charge had had to isolate everyone more and more, the longer the place existed. Some of that had been to fit the demands of the technology companies paying for experiments; some of it had been to make sure people like Mom kept obeying. And some of it was just because the world outside was changing.

The parents who'd taken their kids to the "good" Futureville—including Mom—had never been able to protect their children completely from the present.

Maybe nobody could ever truly step out of their own time period.

Or "fall" out of time.

The 2020s were a mix of good and bad, too.

"What? *No!*"

That was Mom's voice, ringing out from across the backyard. She was standing on the deck, staring at her new phone.

In an instant, Jessie was there beside her, putting her arm around Mom and pulling her back into the house.

Zola could see Jessie gesturing as she shut the sliding glass door behind them—one of those hand motions that seemed to mean "Go on with the party, everyone. I'm taking care of this."

But Zola still turned and rushed after her mother and aunt.

To her surprise, Puck came with her.

"You can stay with your friends, Puck," Zola told him. "It's okay."

"No—she's going to be my mom now, too. Remember?"

"Oh—right," Zola said.

There were going to be advantages to having a brother that Zola hadn't even thought of yet.

They climbed up to the deck and slipped in through the sliding glass door just behind Mom and Jessie. The two sisters were sitting on the couch now, both peering at the phone. Zola peeked over their shoulders to see a headline:

"Futurevilles Organizers' Alibi: We Had Arrangements to Take Care of All Residents."

"*This* is going to be their legal defense?" Mom was fuming. "That they knew the good people of my Futureville would step forward to take care of people in the other Futureville? And it's clear they knew that was happening, because they never punished us for that particular 'rebellion'? So I was a dupe all around—playing into their plans completely?"

"No, no," Jessie said soothingly, patting Mom's shoulder. "You were making the best of a bad situation. And you *were* helping people."

"And if you had played into their plans completely, we'd all still be in Futurevilles," Zola said.

Behind Mom's back, Jessie gave her a thumbs-up.

Mom flinched and shook her head at Zola.

"Only because you and Puck were brave," Mom said. "Only because I put you at risk. And Jessie, too . . ."

"But we're all safe now," Jessie said firmly. "And *you* weren't the one who kidnapped me. You weren't the one so desperate to make yourself *feel* like everyone loved you that you set up two entire fake villages to deceive everyone."

Oddly enough, Mom and Jessie actually believed that part of Mr. Seward's excuses: that he had started the Future-villes so he himself could live in a fictional VR world. They believed all his other crimes grew out of that.

"Guilt makes people do strange things," Mom murmured.

"So does forgiveness," Jessie added.

If Zola wasn't careful, Mom would start apologizing all over again.

"And, Mom—seriously, are you really going to make me do this?" Zola asked.

"Do what?" Mom asked.

"Give you credit," Zola said. "I'm almost a teenager, remember? No almost-teenager wants to say thank you to their mom. But here goes. All those VRs you made sure I watched, of people making a difference—that really did make a difference. Those VRs really did make me want to be brave."

"And overhearing Zola with those VRs, that's what made me think I could trust her," Puck added.

"And you gave me the book about Jessie's bravery two hundred years ago—I mean, two and a half decades ago," Zola corrected herself quickly. "And, Mom, I had *you* as a role model. You thought you were risking everything helping Puck. But you did it anyway. That counts for something, no matter what Mr. Seward or anyone else says about it. I was able to be brave because of you. I am so lucky that you're my mom."

"And I was able to be brave because of you," Mom whispered back. "*I'm* the lucky one."

"Oh, brother," Puck said. "Is this what it's going to be like all the time, living in a family? This mushy?"

"No," Zola said. "You will never hear me say those words again."

"Same here," Mom said. "Zola and I will be back to arguing by breakfast time tomorrow."

But her eyes were shining. They would probably tell each other how lucky they were to have each other again and again in the future. Now that they didn't have to talk constantly about Insta-Closets and Insta-Ovens—or the other glories of 2193—they'd have plenty of time to fill.

"I *am* sorry for taking you to the Futurevilles," Mom said. "And making it so you're not actually prepared for . . ." She waved her hand, indicating the cell phone she'd now dropped to the couch, the television across the room, the decidedly primitive kitchen off to the side.

"Oh, I'm prepared all right," Zola said. "I know everything depends on what happens in the 2020s."

Puck gawked at her.

"You still believe that?" he mocked. "Don't you know they just said that in our Futurevilles for the sake of the tourists?"

"I know," Zola said. "But that doesn't mean it isn't true."

Mom and Jessie both looked confused.

"Because the 2020s are the present," Zola said. "And the present is the only thing we can change. We can't change the past, we're not in the future yet—the only impact we can have is with what's happening right now."

Now Mom and Jessie both looked amused. Their eyes danced in the same way.

"Good point," Jessie said. "So what are you going to do right now?"

Zola could have given so many different answers. This wasn't a VR, where the choices were limited. If she'd wanted to please a Helpful Clue Source or get a good grade on a test, she would have said, "Work toward a good future. One we *all* want to live in."

But she'd had enough of serious talk for now.

"I'm going to go get some more watermelon," she said. "And then I'm going to go play that seed-spitting game with my cousins. I'll invite Puck and Beatriz and all the other kids, too, so everyone gets to know one another. For real. Not just playing a fake role. So everyone can be *prepared* to work together."

It wasn't solving all the world's problems—now that she knew the world really did have lots and lots of problems.

But it was a start.

ACKNOWLEDGMENTS

It is a very odd thing to write a sequel more than twenty years after the original book. When *Running Out of Time*—my very first book—came out in 1995, I had a hard time believing I really had managed to write a book and have it published. The first few times I heard someone say, "You *have* to write a sequel! We have to know what happens next!" I felt absolutely certain that what they were asking for was impossible: I couldn't see how to do it.

But readers kept asking. And they began suggesting ideas of their own—some outlandish, some hilarious, some far beyond anything I could have dreamed up. Nobody ever said, "Write a next-generation story about Jessie's niece and how she has to escape a 'different time period' village of her own." But all those unrelated ideas were like stairsteps lifting me toward some "What if . . . ?" ideas of my own. They made me keep thinking about the Keyser family and Jessie's world and what might have happened next (or twenty-seven years later). This book exists because of all those readers who had more faith in my sequel-writing ability than I did, and I owe a huge debt of gratitude to almost three decades' worth of kids, parents, teachers, librarians, and booksellers. Thank you! You all are wonderful.

I also owe a huge debt to my agent, Tracey Adams. I started writing this book in the midst of a global pandemic and—just coincidentally—the same week as the January 6, 2021, attack on the US Capitol. It was a horrifying and disorienting time, and a hard time to imagine anything optimistic about the future. Her steady, constant encouragement kept me going.

Thank you as well to my editor, Katherine Tegen, whose insights, questions, and suggestions made this a much stronger book. I also appreciate the help of everyone else at Katherine Tegen Books and HarperCollins who worked on this book: Sara Schonfeld, Kathryn Silsand, Stephanie Evans, Jennifer Moles, Mark Rifkin, Christina MacDonald, Vanessa Nuttry, Molly Fehr, Amy Ryan, Emily Mannon, and Abby Dommert. And thank you to Anne Lambelet for the lovely cover art for both this book and the new version of *Running Out of Time*.

As always when I'm working on a book, I asked friends and family members random research questions, and they were all very helpful (and didn't laugh too much at some of the ridiculous scenarios I suggested). My son, Connor, and my friends Ellen, Ken, and Bradley Kus answered questions about dress codes at engineering and tech companies, and my sister and nieces, Janet, Jenna, and Megan Terrell, helped me figure out certain references kids would or would not understand. My friend Scott Harding helped me decide on a character motivation I'd struggled with, and his son, Jonathan Harding, was quite helpful in explaining the most current and up-to-date VR goggles (the 2020s version, anyway). Thank you, all!

Also, as always, I appreciate the support of my family, especially my husband, Doug, and the support of the members of my two Columbus-area writers groups: Jody Casella, Julia DeVillers, Linda Gerber, Lisa Klein, Erin McCahan, Erin MacLellan, Jenny Patton, Edith Pattou, Nancy Roe Pimm, Natalie D. Richards, and Linda Stanek.

And last but definitely not least, I appreciate YOU, the reader of this book. Whether you are coming to this after reading *Running Out of Time*—maybe even decades ago—or if you are reading this book first, with no prior knowledge of the earlier book, I'm grateful for you spending this time with Zola. I hope as you think about the version of the future you want to work toward, you are like Zola: longing to make it a better place and time for everyone.